The Fire Within

The Fire Within

BOOK I
Elemental Knights Chronicles

Heather DiRocco

To order additional copies of this book, contact:
Xlibris Corporation
1-888-795-4274
www.Xlibris.com
Orders@Xlibris.com
83277

Contents

For those of you
who still have a twinge of a dream
within your hearts.
Never stop believing.

Acknowledgments

THE COUNTLESS OF people that I have met throughout my life, whether through the Marine Corps or along the way, you have all inspired me to perform to the best of my abilities, and have helped me with everything in this book! To Angela Jacobs, who never once ceased to aspire me to achieve my truest potential, and always helped me with elements of this book that I struggled with. To Chandra Charette who was the instigator in getting this book off of the ground and into publishing. If it weren't for your initial reading of this prologue, I never would have finished. To the Marines of 7th ESB Bulk Fuel Company, all of you believed in me, were excited for the book to be released, and even provided me with help on the names of some of my characters. To my family, my dad, my mom. And to my husband, for never faltering in your love for me, and allowing me the time that I needed to type up the manuscript! You are my biggest supporter and always have been. I love you!

PROLOGUE

THE HORSE'S BREATH rose like a cloud into the steamy air, sweat drained itself off of the horse's body, matting its hair in streaks of perspiration. A line of warriors stretched across the horizon, their horses stood prancing eagerly in place as they awaited the order to attack. Their leader, sat tall upon his magnificent stallion's back in front of them. His armor was thick and magnificent; it plaited the man's body perfectly, shielding him from any danger that might cross his path. The armor of his horse was designed in the same fashion as its owner, complete with two dueling dragons encrusted upon the shoulder guards upon both the man's armor, and the stallion's.

His eyes, barely visible from beneath the slit of his helmet, were fierce and full of life. If there were any fear within him, his eyes would not be the one to betray him.

He paced his horse in front of his army, watching them keenly. Knowing all too well that this was what they were trained to do, and that this might be the last time that he would see them again.

A sense of pride washed over him, as he knew that the next hour would define the training that he had spent the last three years instructing. His troops would fight to their deaths at any cost, even if it meant their souls.

KAAA!! The warrior looked to the sky, the falcon had returned, and it echoed its cry to the heavens. The man smiled beneath his helmet, the falcon had signaled the attack.

He closed his eyes; he knew what was at stake if they were to lose. Yet, he couldn't risk thinking too much into it. For if he did, it might restrain him from fighting with the pure ferocity that he had inspired his own men with.

Snapping his eyes back open, and looking towards his enemy, he raised his sword and yelled a war cry while charging his horse towards the opposing line of attackers.

The ground shook as thousands of soldiers ran at full throttle in a gallop upon their steeds. With weapons drawn, they watched their General as he rushed them forward through a wave of arrows.

The General's army was smart; as they deflected the arrows, while accelerating their speed and not a single man was scathed. The General cried once more as he swung out his sword, lashing out and attacking the front line of enemies in a fury of death. An echo of war cries followed as his men began their assault upon the enemy line. The battle raged on, until at last every adversary was dead.

The General, panting, skidded his horse to a stop and then turned to face his men. He removed his helmet, allowing his long black hair to flow down draping past his shoulders. He closed his eyes and breathed in, sucking in the cool night air to fill his lungs and to cool his stifling body temperature. His men had encircled him, each removing their helmets to continue the ritual.

The wind was calming; it penetrated their very souls as they reminisced of the battle. Silent prayers were said to the fallen, wounds were ignored, until at last the General opened his eyes. A smile grew upon his face, and a smile of victory was returned from every warrior. They had won. Yet knew, that he must return to his master, a greedy, evil master: a master of death.

Chapter One

Entrapment

S HE STILL DID not understand the calmness of his question, nor the coolness of his voice. Yet, she barely knew him, even so that every gesture that he made was vexing to her. She desired to know of his thoughts, to know what he truly felt. But first, she had to fill that void between them, almost like an eagle diving upon its prey with such vivacity that neither creature had time to think.

Perhaps then, she could draw closer to him undetected. But, he was a formidable opponent, so surely he was trained to sense or hear her if she were to try. But, she tried anyway; and in return he would stand silently, completely ignoring her gestures and attempts to draw closer to him.

Granted, it was painful for her to be completely ignored when she was so many countless times before, looked upon with great admiration. Perhaps, that was why she was so drawn to his dark form. He was the first man, who did not see her for a young beauty to which he could vex. Sure, she was his capture, but nevertheless, this dark, handsome man was something that Jenevy desired to have. She wanted him to hold, and to claim as her own, which, to that very day, Jenevy had never desired of anything; let alone anyone.

"We must move. Staying here much longer only increases our danger." His words had interrupted her thoughts, and yet she did not mind. She simply wanted to hear his cool words spoken again.

"Come, we must go if the Duke is to have you tonight before the cast of the moon befalls the country." The cloaked man spoke as he grabbed the gear for the horses. He began to work his way to prepare them for the ride. Before completely finishing, he grabbed the satchel from the ground, tied it to his horse, then threw over the reins from the other horse at Jenevy. He had thrown them with such force, that Jenevy was amazed that she had even caught the leather straps.

"Quickly now, there is no time for slowness. You must move faster!" He shouted at her, as he jumped onto the saddle of his horse. He began riding off into the trees, as Jenevy was trying to get her foot into the stirrups.

She was outraged! Not only had he completely ignored her, but also he hadn't even attempted to help her onto the horse! How was she supposed to know what to do? She had never ridden on a saddle like a man, and she could swear that it was because her feet wouldn't fit. Before she knew it, her horse began to move as its herd instincts kicked in. The mare began to trot to keep up with the cloaked man's horse, as Jenevy barely made it onto the horse's saddle.

The cloaked man slowed down his horse to wait for her, but only to grab her reins to tie them to the horn on his saddle, as he groaned with agitation.

"Honestly, I thought that women of your stature knew how to ride." He snapped at her rudely. The brute looked forward, and Jenevy glared at him.

A few hours were spent in silence, which proved to be nearly fatal for Jenevy. Quietness was not her forte, for it only fueled to her anger. The soundless ride gave way to her thoughts, and the more she started to think, the more she realized just how much trouble that she was in.

She was a bargaining chip, a prize, a treaty signed over to the Duke of Greenwiche for the mere price of a man's greed. The ruffian riding in front of her was merely the delivery boy. He was probably some peasant being paid handsomely for his assistance. But that only angered Jenevy more.

Who was this man, this boy, which cared only for money and not for the welfare of a woman?

Jenevy's mind began to think of what had happened that day. She had been sold, but why, and why so quickly? Jenevy's mind wandered to her father, the nerve of that man! Selling her to a Duke? For what? He had betrayed *her*; he had sold her like chattel! Simply sold her and had her taken away in the middle of the night like some prisoner! The nerve of him! When she had agreed to help her father in his time of need, she had no idea that he had intended for her to be sold!

'I hope that his payment was worth it.' Jenevy thought to herself. She was fuming with resentment she was practically livid. She crossed her arms and stared at the greenery around her. Soon, she would be in Greenwiche, where she would spend the rest of her nights as one of the Duke's 'girls'. Obeying his every whim, doing his dirty little fantasies, and then thrown away once her womb could not withstand the pressure again. That was to be her fate.

She sighed shaking her head. Her captor gave a backwards glance at her, then returned his focus back to the road. However, despite the certain tension between them, Jenevy decided that enough was enough. She was going to talk to this man.

"Why did you accept the job of a traitor?" Her statement pierced the silence like a pack of fierce wolves. The cloaked man looked back at her stunned. He didn't know whether to respond or not. She had taken the liberty to address him, which was a first, but the forcefulness in her voice was astounding. He slowed his horse down to match its pace with Jenevy's mare.

"You are not the only woman that has been sold for the purpose of personal gain, young mistress." He said coldly. Jenevy caught her breath. Perhaps this man was not as dumb as she had judged? Perhaps her conviction against him was completely false? She shook her head in denial, if he wasn't dumb, then he was stupid.

"Are you a knight?" She inquired boldly. The man almost seemed to smile from beneath his cloak.

"Perhaps, someday." He replied. Jenevy turned her body to look at him. The man stared at her she was breathtaking. Even more so than any of the other girls that he had delivered before. Tears glistened on her cheeks, but yet her eyes remained strong and full of life. She was nothing like the Duke's harlots at the castle. There was something special, almost enchanting about her. Jenevy was a maiden, innocent as the young mare that she rode upon. She seemed perfect to him. She sat elegantly upon the horse, her body straight, as any proper lady should be. Her arms, although folded protectively across her stomach, had no signs of labor or work upon them. She had long, dark black hair that twisted was regally and pinned to her head. Her eyes were green, and she had the lightest of cream color upon her skin. She was absolutely flawless in appearance. The only thing that was out of place was the disheveled frays of hair hanging loose from her coiffure, and the torn clothing that she wore as a result of the kidnapping from the night prior.

Suddenly, he felt a deep sorrow for having to deliver such a beauty to the heartless wretch of a man at Greenwiche. Jenevy was a maiden, a beauty fit for a king. Who probably grew up on fairy tales, and love stories, only now, to be given anything but a happy ending.

Slowly he stopped the two horses on the side of the road. Jenevy looked around her. That region was unfamiliar to her; the smells were changing in the air, as were the trees and the lush undergrowth that she had so loved back at Sarefully. Deep down, she could feel the fear trying to break its way out.

The man jumped from his horse, walked over to Jenevy and reached up a hand to assist her down.

"We will stop here and rest for a moment." He said as he looked cautiously around the area. Jenevy looked at his hand, then reluctantly grasped it and slid off of the horse's saddle. She then proceeded to keep a moderate distance from him, and started to pick flowers from the nearby clearing.

"I am going to take the horses down for some water. Don't try and run away." He ordered firmly, she looked up at him, saw the threat in his eyes then continued her charade. He quickly gathered up the horses' reins, and walked towards the woods. He knew that she would not run away.

Jenevy watched him leave, and once he was out of sight she removed her cloak and draped it over her arm. The sun shined its heat onto the ground, igniting the meadow with color and beauty. Jenevy strode around admiring the new country. She paused and looked down at herself.

Her beautiful dress was ripped. The skirt itself was stained red, she didn't know why. But it matched her anger at the moment so she didn't care so much. Jenevy sighed, as she listened to the wind blowing through the trees.

The sound of the stream could be heard as it lapped its water over rocks and fallen logs within its path. The cloaked man was at that stream, heeding to the poor, tired animals. Perhaps she should join him; she needed to wash her face anyway.

But just before she was about to step towards the trees, she heard movement from the other side of the road in the opposing tree line. Something was coming; something was about to emerge from the dense foliage. She strained her ears and listened to every detail echoing from the trees.

They were men, of that she was certain. No animal could possibly make as much noise as they were. Their footsteps were single and distinct. Gear rattled at every step, as sticks snapped from beneath their footing.

Jenevy stared into the thicket, until at last they appeared. They were rugged men, each equipped with a sword at their sides. Each spoke very quietly to one another. Their voices, although in a whisper, were rough and powerful. Right away she knew what they were and they were thieves, the murderers of the road.

Jenevy slowly looked around her, there were no weapons about, and there was nothing that could even be used as a weapon save for an ironic circumstance of the men having an allergic reaction to pollen! She had nothing, and added to that dilemma, there wasn't even a place to hide. But she couldn't just stand there, her colorful dress was sure to attract the attention of those men. Even with the vibrant colors of the flowers around her, her dress did not resemble any color that was visible within that meadow.

Her cloaked captor was down by the stream, if she screamed he might hear her, but so would the thieves. Even if she were to scream, would the cloaked man even come to her aid? Frantically her mind began to ramble with thoughts of what she should do, what there was to do, and then the men came. One by one they all noticed her standing alone in the meadow. They each looked around, they too noticed how completely helpless she was. An evil smile fell upon their faces.

Jenevy became suddenly full of fear; she tried to calm her nerves to at least look like she was not afraid. The last thing that she wanted to do was to panic.

"Well, well, well, what do we have here?!" One brute inquired of his fellow comrades.

"I'd say it was a *lady*. Are you lost my dear?" One said amidst a stout laugh. Jenevy's eyes darted anxiously from thief to thief. A man grabbed her from behind, holding her still as the other men frantically started to rip at her clothes. She stood feebly as she was helpless to fight back.

"Maybe I can help?" It was the cloaked man. He stood within a shadow behind the thieves. Jenevy felt an instant wave of relief roll through her.

Right away, the thief restraining Jenevy whipped out a knife and pressed it to her throat. The other thieves all withdrew their weapons and stood alongside Jenevy.

"Come any closer, and she's dead!" The man yelled, and he pushed the blade deeper into her neck. Jenevy winced as she felt it break her skin, she could feel a trickle of blood finding its way to her collarbone.

Masking his face even more by shadow, the cloaked man looked up at the thief.

"Wrong answer." The cloaked man reached up, and undid his shroud. He yanked it free from his body, letting it drop to the ground. Exquisite armor reflected off the sun, nearly blinding Jenevy. Jenevy was dumbfounded, she knew it! He was a knight! But what kind of a knight kidnaps helpless women from their chambers in the middle of the night? She didn't care, for now she could see who her captor was, and he was more handsome than she had imagined. His voice was deep, and comforting, and his face, body and stature completed her vision of him. At last she saw the man, whose voice was all she heard.

The thieves were clearly not as enthused as Jenevy. They all began rushing forward, with swords up ready to attack the knight before her. But he moved swiftly, countering every attack that they swung at him with ease. Never once did he draw his sword. He fought with his hands, and his body. Knocking his enemies weapons from their grasp.

His fighting was a display of effortlessness, and beauty, perfectly choreographed as if he had practiced every moment of every day. It was almost like a dance upon water. His movements were fluid, distinct, and obviously more intricate than the thieves fighting skills.

The knight continued his attack until only two thieves remained: the one holding Jenevy captive, and the one standing behind them. The thief spun from around Jenevy and the man who had taken her hostage, and lunged at the knight. The thief holding Jenevy tightened his grip on her neck, as he saw his comrade get brutally slain. The man slumped to the ground letting out a final breath of defeat.

The knight bent over, grabbed the sword from the dead thief's hand and turned to face them. Jenevy could feel the uneasiness of the thief holding her like a wave of heat. His grasp upon her neck was getting tighter, and the blade was driving deeper into her neck.

She could feel the blood starting to pour from her wound, rushing down, and absorbing into her dress.

"Move any closer, and swear she'll be dead!" The thief said forcefully. By the way that he was squeezing her, she knew that he was not bluffing. She began to feel consciousness slipping away from her, and her eyes fluttered as if in reply.

The knight looked at her, she felt relief as she saw the confidence in his eyes. But, very soon, she would not be able to stand, because the thief was unaware that the knife was being driven deeper into the side of her neck.

"Let her go, she is of no use to you." The knight's soothing voice echoed.

"On the contrary—" The thief paused to grab a strand of her hair, he sniffed it smiling wickedly. "—she is quite useful." His grasp got tighter, Jenevy began to choke.

"But this one is mine." The knight jumped out and struck at the thief. The thief deflected his attack, all the while keeping his hold on Jenevy. The knight turned and attacked again, the thief darted and fought every blow, while Jenevy was being thrown about like a ragdoll.

'Stop, stop! Ahhh.' She thought to herself, if only she could speak! But the man's grip was preventing all air to enter and exit her throat, let alone any words!

At last, the thief dropped her to continue his fight with the knight. Jenevy stumbled upon the ground, gasping for air. She reached up and grabbed her neck.

Bringing her hand down, she saw the blood upon her palm. It was dripping with the red liquid; the sight was making her queasy. She began to see stars swirling in her vision, a dark tunnel of black began to get smaller and smaller until there was nothing but a loud ringing in her ears. Then she fell, slumping to her side upon the ground.

The young warrior fought with his opponent, the thief seemed to be a more formidable attacker than the other thieves. But the knight was faster, and better, and he disarmed the thief and shoved him to the ground. The knight stared at the thief, and then he saw Jenevy. She was lying lifeless behind them. A new anger arose in him, shooting his adrenaline through the roof. He slammed his attacker again with such force that the ground cracked. He thrust his sword deep into the thief's flesh until he moved no more.

The knight stared at him for a moment, to make sure that the thief was truly dead. When the man did not move, the knight sheathed his sword and rushed to Jenevy.

"Jenevy!" He shouted. He knelt at her side, rolling her over into his arms. He sighed with relief, as he realized that she was alive.

"Jenevy . . ." He said slowly, as he ripped a piece of cloth from her skirt. He gently set her to the ground, and applied pressure to her wound.

With his other hand, he tied the strand of fabric gently, yet firmly, around her neck. He lifted her back up and into his arms, and stood up. He gently shook her, trying to coax her awake.

"Jenevy, come on. Wake up, wake up. Open your eyes." He stared at her face, watching her eyes for any movement. Her eyes fluttered.

"That's it, come on. I know it hurts, but you have to open your eyes!" He continued to try and wake her. But she remained still. He looked her up and down, frowning at what he saw. The thieves had done their part, beaten her, and ripped nearly everything from her. She was barely clad in any type of proper clothing. Her undergarments were visible from beneath her dress. Only the blue under layer of her dress was left, and even it was ripped and torn. He shook her gently again.

"Come on Jenevy. You need to wake up. The longer you stay like this, the closer death will come." This time, her eyes slowly fluttered open. Her pupils were dilated, and pain was clearly apparent in her eyes. A tinge of a smile twitched at the corner of her mouth. She looked pale; the color in her cheeks was drained. The knight didn't know if it was from her wound, or from the fear of what had happened itself. Then again, it could be a combination of the two. He smiled at her; he wanted to touch her face. He wanted to caress her, to show her that she did not have to be treated the way that she had been. But he knew, that the Duke was going to do much, much worser things to her. He felt an anger rise in him, his heart began to beat faster.

Never had he felt what he was feeling towards any woman. Never had he felt such fondness over one of his master's mistresses. Never before, had he fought to protect one, let alone rescue one.

He had revealed himself at his true nature: a knight. He was a knight, who had been sold to the Duke of Greenwiche, at a price that was immeasurable. It had cost him his knighthood, and he was to protect the Duke, even if he did not want to. He had been sold, just like Jenevy.

When Jenevy had awoken, she was looking into the eyes of a knight. A dark haired, indescribably handsome knight, whose eyes were of the bluest blue that she had ever seen. Even more indescribable, was that somewhere in those blue eyes, she saw something that she had never seen before. Something that she couldn't believe, he cared for her, and cared for her, in a way that she didn't understand. What scared her more was that she too felt the same way. It was almost as if they fell in love at first sight, but then again, he was just delivering her to an evil Duke. So that 'caring' that she saw, could very easily be towards his missing paycheck if she were to be killed.

The knight looked over her, checking for any more wounds. He then draped a cloak over her body, and carried her over to the horses. He looked at her as he walked to make sure that she was all right. When he whistled for the horses, he gently placed her upon the saddle of the mare, and jumped up behind her. He let her lean against him, and clicked his tongue signaling the horse to move forward, his stallion trotting eagerly behind them.

With his soothing voice, his words invaded her mind again: "My name . . . is William."

Chapter Two

SPECIAL DELIVERY

"I KNOW THAT IT is not much, but it will at least keep you warm." William said with a smile as he handed Jenevy a pair of trousers and a white tunic.

"If it will help, you can always pull back your hair to look as though you are a man. However, you will be treated as such." William finished apologetically, his eyebrows raised with a sincere look upon his face.

Jenevy nodded at him, and then waited for William to turn around, so that she could undress. So, maybe he didn't have a way with words, at least he was trying!?

Putting the tunic on was moderately easy for Jenevy, but the trousers were a different story. The challenge was that Jenevy understood how they were meant to look, but didn't know how to get it there. She raised them up to stare at them. There were two legs, which obviously she was to step into, but which way was the front.

Jenevy squinted at them in confusion; pursing her lips she shrugged and lowered them down to her waist. She stepped into each part of the fabric, and then squirmed a bit as she slid them up to her waist.

She paused in disbelief. How was she too secure them? Her undergarments were made in the same fashion as men's trousers but they were much easier; they had an elastic waistband . . .

But these trousers had so much fabric that they had to be tied. There were strings hanging from the waist line, all criss-crossed and disheveled. She stared at them in disbelief.

Jenevy tried numerous ways to keep them up, but they simply kept sliding down to her feet. She pulled them up to her waist once more only to sigh in frustration.

William turned around hesitantly when he sensed her agitation. He smiled coolly at her, as he watched her try desperately to succeed.

"Here, allow me." He offered. Jenevy looked at him with relief. Reluctantly she let go of the waistband and allowed William to fasten the strings. His hands worked quickly, but with precision as he securely tightened them snugly to her waist. He then tucked the loose ends into her waistband.

"There, perfect fit!" He said with a grin. Jenevy stared down at her clothing in disgust.

"If you're a pauper, then yes." She said rudely. William shook his head as he smiled at her.

"Now, once we tuck in the tunic—" He grabbed the loose ends of her tunic, and tucked them into her waistband. He then pulled up on the excess fabric, allowing it to sag a bit over her waistline. "There . . . . perfect." He finished. He stepped back to admire her.

"Forgive me, but you blend in rather well with the paupers of this world." He said with a grin. Jenevy rolled her eyes.

"I sincerely hope not. I'll just pretend that you didn't say that." She responded.

"Never matter. This attire is only temporary. I'm sure that the Duke will have a much better selection of wardrobe once we have arrived at the castle." He replied rudely. He turned around and headed back to his horse. Jenevy watched him, as he seemed to float rather than climb, into the saddle.

Jenevy sneered and walked over to her horse, she attempted to glide onto her saddle as well. But nearly toppled over when she tried to step into the stirrup. William rolled his eyes in impatience, and led his horse towards her.

"Here." He said offering his hand. Jenevy batted it away.

"Don't bother." She said coldly, and stepped into the stirrup again, then swung her leg over the horses back and onto the saddle.

"Besides, you can't very well assist me when I am supposed to be acting as a man." She retorted. William nodded in agreement. Then kicked the horse onto the road, and Jenevy led her horse to follow.

❖   Each and every time that the horse's hooves hit the earth, it was like a song being played. Their incandescent thumps, made a harmonious beat.

First Jenevy's mare would start the beat, then William's horse would follow. They pulsated together perfectly, each on their own accord. They paused, changed step, and continued their song all in the swift motions. Never missing a beat.

The birds too seemed to coincide with their charade, followed by the trees and the animal noises. Even the water, and it's lapping song upon the rocks, added its rhythm to their song.

Jenevy's mood seemed to perk up once hearing the noises of the forest; she was actually enjoying the ride. Even the smell of lush ripe flowers added to her euphoria.

Jenevy was even more delighted with the fact that she was not riding sidesaddle. She had never ridden a horse like a man before, but she definitely couldn't object to it now. No longer was she meant to look or seem refined.

Slouching was allowed, as was sitting comfortably. She leaned back a bit, holding firmly to the reins, and closed her eyes. She could feel the cool, crisp wind hitting her skin. Goosebumps began to shiver their way along her arms, all the way down to her legs.

She could smell the fresh, crisp water of a stream in the distance. She could practically feel the coolness of the air, sweeping away as the sun's rays shone down upon them.

Before she knew it, Jenevy began to hum, adding a new melody to the serenade. William looked over at Jenevy, puzzled as to why she was humming. She was completely relaxed, smiling as the wind whipped her hair across her face. She began to sway, almost as if in a trance.

Smoothly her humming turned into a song, and she sang it with the beat of the horse's hooves.

"La dee dah hum. La dee dah hum.
From across the wilderness, my home lies in a place. Where all the people dance, with soft wings and face, they are a dying race. Full of love and grace. But the people here all live in fear. Of a tiny-winged fairy race. Oh how the people would love them, like the angels in heaven. But no, they run away, for fear of a place they cannot stay. But . . . . Their . . . minds . . . would . . . . soon . . . . betray. Oh how the simple ways, disappear with age. Oh how the longer days, grow shorter in every way. The world's wills soon ripen, grow old and end. We will all be there, to down without care. But what if we never loved? What if we never loved? You cannot live without love, you cannot breath without love. It's the one precious thing sent from above.
So . . . La da dee da dah dee dum. La da dee da dah dee dum. La da dee da dah dee dum."

Jenevy's rich voice filled the air, as she sang the song over and over again. William remained silent, intrigued by her song.

William was touched by her words; it sparked a feeling inside of him that he had not felt in a very, very long time.

He, at times, wanted to ask her where she had learned the song from, but was fearful that once interrupted she would not start again.

So he relented, and kept his mouth shut and patiently waited for her to stop.

She finished the chorus to the song, and stayed still. She smiled sweetly as she swayed upon the horse's saddle. She reopened her eyes, and it was as if she realized where she was, because she instantly sat up straight, looked forward and the same expression of hatred fell upon her face. William looked over at her, and smiled.

"That was beautiful!" He said to her with awe. Jenevy looked at him, nodded at his compliment, then returned her eyes to the front. William sighed and looked down the road; a few large holes lay ahead. He quietly guided his horse around them.

"William . . ." Jenevy said in a whisper. William looked over at her.

"Yes milady." He replied. She swallowed and breathed deeply as if contemplating a serious answer to a question.

"What . . . what will happen to me once we get there?" She stammered, as she asked him cautiously of the thing that she was most afraid of. William frowned; he remembered what had happened to the girls who came to his master's castle. He heard the screams, the laughs, and the noises.

He knew what happened once the girls ripened, and were taken away. And he knew that Jenevy would more than likely endure that same fate. Yet, he could not bring himself the courage to tell her what he saw.

"I'm not sure." He lied. Jenevy's back tensed, as if she knew. He saw a trickle of a tear roll its way down her cheek.

"I think I know. I also know, that I am not the first that you have delivered to your master. Nor will I be the last." Her words struck him like needles on a cloth.

How was he to tell her that she would be forced to do his masters every whim? Or that, if she refused, would be beaten because of it? What was he to say to calm her troubled mind?

When *he* had first been enslaved by the Duke of Greenwiche, he had told himself, long ago, that he would not get attached to any of the women that delivered, and he was not about to start now.

But something about Jenevy, struck him down in a way that made him want to dash out away from the fortress taking her with him and never to return again. But something else held him back, something in his mind was preventing that from happening, and he didn't know what.

Was it honor? Honor to fulfill his duties of the Duke? But what kind of honor was it, to destroy the lives of innocent people, only because he was ordered to?

What kind of code, had he fallen into following? William shook his head, as if trying to shake the thoughts from his mind. What was wrong with him?

"I . . . am not afraid of this man. I am just here to make sure that my father, in all of his disreputable arrogance, never has to fear poverty again." Jenevy interrupted his thoughts. William remained solemn after her remarks. She spoke with true nobility and royalty. Truly, she was someone of noble blood, and she was about to lose everything.

But the worst part of it all was that William would have to watch.

Jenevy could not believe her eyes. Her new home stood before her. It was vast, tall, dark, and mysterious. The entire castle was covered in vines that stretched their limbs up and down the outside walls, as if enclosing the interior into a prison. Jenevy shuddered at the thought of what might be going on inside the evil citadel.

"Perhaps, the inside is brighter and more cheerful?" She asked hopefully. William looked at her; she was smiling almost as if her forcing a smile would brighten her spirits. Jenevy eagerly urged her horse forward, and William followed her from behind.

'Happy and cheerful? In this castle? The dark lord's castle is anything but happy. Dark and full of death would be more appropriate.' William thought to himself. William began to picture the inside of the Duke's castle. People lurked around as if in a trance, some were in a daze, almost as if they were imagining themselves walking through a grander hallway.

The rooms inside were larger than peasant homes, each furnished with elaborate and expensive furniture. The master's maidens had even larger rooms. They slumbered within their rooms, upon foreign silk, and the softest cushions. They were given everything that their hearts desired. Clothing, jewelry, money, animals, no matter the price. But, in return, they were never allowed to leave the castle or it's grounds. Not that they could anyway. For the castle was surrounded by the strongest and tallest wall that any castle had ever had.

Guards lay at every corner within the castle, and the outer wall itself was heavily guarded. Each soldier armed to the max, and given orders to shoot anything that moved unless it knew the password.

The trapped mistresses were never allowed to talk to their families again, thus the maidens were driven mad. They became depressed and full of despair all the way until their untimely deaths. Plus, with the Dark Lord using them for his sick pleasures, many of his 'pets' found different ways to castrate their bodies. In hopes that the Duke would leave them alone, and that the pain would drown out their sorrow.

William had had to watch this unfold again, and again. He had to climb up to the highest balcony to cut down a hanging maiden. He had to clean up the blood spewing upon the floor, when a maiden had decided to jump to her death. Then he would have to go and fetch his master a new playmate, and wait to see when that one would collapse.

Sure, he felt bad for the women, he always did. But most chose that lifestyle anyway. They wanted wealth, and riches, and would do anything to get it. But sometimes wealth isn't everything.

Only a few of the women were actually sold into the slavery of the Duke. Ones who's hearts were fair and good. They were just and honest, even after being sold for the greed of their families.

But, only one had every volunteered to be sold to William's master. Only one woman had agreed to be sold, in order to save her family, in order to save her father and his greed for wealth. One who had given up everything, if it only meant that her father would be safe, and happy. A selfless service for a hateful family, and yet it was all that she had to give. And that woman was Jenevy.

"Halt! Who goes here?" Came the barking order from a tower guard.

"Tis I, keeper of the guard, and friend to the king." William's voice echoed off of the walls of the guard tower.

"William? Is that you?" Came the guards reply, as he shielded his eyes from the sun to stare down at them. "Well, it is Sir William! Why didn't you just say so? Besides, you don't need *our* permission to enter here! You could have just used the secret entrance!" The guard yelled back at him. William rolled his eyes in disapproval.

"Yes, I could have, but Master would have not been too pleased if his new maiden to were to know about that escape!" William barked up at the guard. The gate guard looked down at Jenevy, and a wicked smile spread across his face.

"So, he's got a new one eh? I wonder how long *this* one will last for?!" The guard started laughing evilly into the air. The guard disappeared from view, and then the rusty gate began to rise up. Its large, iron bars creaking as it opened.

Jenevy looked over at William, he glanced over at her. She looked puzzled, and stared at him for answers. William shook his head sadly, and then urged their horses forward. Once they passed through the gate, it slammed shut behind them. Jenevy jumped in reaction, the sound seemed to snap her into reality. Her eyes filled with fear, and she began to shake all over.

Jenevy looked around her, the entire place held a heavy feeling of death. It sank upon her like a cold, dense fog. The trees looked too dark, and sickly. The underbrush was dying, and all lush beauty that should have been there, was fading away. Life itself was being sucked out of that place like a plague. Suddenly, Jenevy didn't feel quite so brave, she felt as if she had just walked into one of her worst childish nightmares.

"There's something . . . . that you're not telling me, isn't there?" She whimpered from behind William. Her voice was cold, flat, and full of despair. William looked back at her, her face was white, dull and her beauty had been drained.

"Something, horrible has happened here hasn't it? I feel as if thousands of people are telling me to run away, to get out while I still can. And those people, who are warning me, are dead . . . . aren't they?" She paused. "They were people, women just like me . . . . weren't they? Only . . . . they never got out, did they?"

William didn't know how to respond, he stared at her blankly. Jenevy continued.

"Those are spirits aren't they? Only, they're trapped here, trapped within those gates forever . . . . " She took a deep breath, and held it as the castle steps came into view.

The doors were large and luminous; they were just as deadly as the world around her. Jenevy stopped her horse, slid from the saddle and caught herself upon the ground. She stood up tall, and looked back at William. William quickly jumped down, and grabbed the reins of both horses. Jenevy looked up at the doors, and walked up the large steps. She felt as if she were about to walk through the very gates of hell itself. Before she reached the threshold of the castle, she stopped to look back at William.

The face that William saw, he never forgot even in his sleep. For Jenevy's face was completely drained of all beauty, all hope, and all life. It was dull, and lifeless, there was no love, no happiness, not even fear upon her face.

There was nothing. She said five last words to William before she walked inside. The look of nothing upon her face, combined with the lifeless words that she spoke, would haunt William for years to come:

"And now, it's my turn."

Chapter Three

DUTY

OVER THE NEXT few days, William began to hear more and more of Jenevy. She was being stubborn to the boss, ignoring his calls, not coming when beckoned, nor attending meals with the rest of the maidens.

When spoken to, she was either silent, or responded with the most vulgar phrases that she knew. Which surprisingly, was many. She also had not yet met the master in bed.

This came to William as a surprise. At first he had to smile, knowing all too well that Jenevy definitely could do such acts. But at the same time, could not believe it. Usually this type of behavior would have had the maiden executed.

William had assumed that the other guards were exaggerating. But then one night, he overheard his master talking of Jenevy, and how she in intrigued him in such a way that he was willing to let her acts be ignored. The Duke sought her out, like a honeybee would a flower.

Her beauty was exceedingly more stunning than all of the other girls combined. Yet, she had the courage and the strength of a lioness guarding her cubs. She had a bite and a powerful one at that. One that got her noticed far passed her beauty.

From that day, William would simply smile when he heard of the stories that the guards told about her. He liked knowing that she was still alive and pugnacious.

William continued to shove the hay from the stalls of the horses, reminiscing of the past, when he heard the guards yelling. William looked out of the barn door to see what the commotion was about.

Upon the castle's walls, the guards had their bows drawn, and were pointing within the courtyard and someone was yelling up at them.

"Go ahead! Shoot me! I cannot be his slave any longer!" It was one of the Lord's girls. William looked at her disheveled figure. Her dress was torn, and ripped at practically every angle. Her hair was loose and stringy, and her face was scratched, bruised and bleeding. Apparently, she had leapt through a window to get outside, and she was doing anything in her power to escape.

William slammed his shovel into the ground and walked out from within the barn. He stared at the girl, as she raised her arms to the sky to await her fate.

"Release your fury! Unleash hell! For you will all soon join me there!" She screamed in tears.

There was a loud snap, as the twinges of hundreds of bow strings were fired, launching the arrows into the damsel's body. Her body went rigid and she slumped to her knees.

"May God forgive me . . ." She said solemnly and fell over dead. William waited for the guards to return to their posts before he approached her. He could hear the guards laughing, and cracking jokes about the dead woman as they disappeared from sight.

Once the courtyard was empty, William emerged out onto the stone pavement. She lay still upon that dark, unforgiving ground. William walked towards her, and looked down at her lifeless body. Kneeling down next to her, he slowly examined her face.

Beneath the sweat, blood, and aged skin her beauty remained. Despite all that she had done, all she had gone through, he remembered exactly how she had looked before he had brought her to that forsaken place.

She was the daughter of a bankrupt duke. Beauty had been her common trait, but to her, she felt that her words were of something more. Of course, none of that mattered now, she was like the others, once the guilt had set in, and once realizing that she could not return home, had killed herself.

William sighed, and slowly reached a hand down to close her eyes. He grabbed the stems of the arrows protruding from body, and removed them one by one. He laid her gently down upon the ground, and stood up. He walked back towards the barn, grabbed a large woolen sack, and then yanking the shovel back out of the ground, he returned to her side. He gently wrapped her body up in the sack, and then lifted her into his arms.

She would be placed in a shallow grave, in a decrepit graveyard, next to her other fallen sisters. She would remain in that graveyard without a name placard, without her family to mourn her, and without anyone to know of her fate.But this was how it was to be; this was how the Duke wanted it. And William's duty, that he was sworn to do, was to bring and to remove all of the Dark Lord's maidens.

The guards watched as William carried the woman away, his dark shadow retreating into the shade of the castle. Some laughed, some remained quiet, but most, simply did not care.

And somewhere high up, looking down from his balcony stood the Duke. He sneered at the ground below. With a whip of his cape he ducked inside his room, and slammed the window shut.

❖ Jenevy sighed, breathing deeply. The stagnant air within her room filled her lungs practically choking off her air supply with its odor. Jenevy frowned at the smell.

She sat at her bureau looking into its clouded mirror. She slowly brushed her hair, admiring the silkiness it still maintained. Her room was large and elegant. A window out looked the beauty of the magical mountains nestled far from view. Often, she would go to her window, stand on her balcony, and imagine herself free to roam those mountains. That imagery alone would help her to sleep at night.

Her four-poster bed was enormous and extremely comfortable. Covered with silks from across the world, and massive pillows with equally exquisite silk and laying upon its comforter was a beautiful dress and garments. The dress too carried the mark of foreign creation.

Her bureau held exotic, intoxicating fragrances and perfumes, countless items of beauty, and beautiful jewelry. Even the floors of her room, were covered with the skins of every known creature, all lain before her as a queen. The walls held pictures of design and color. Most were probably worth more than the contents of the room themselves.

But none of this mattered to Jenevy. They were all just trinkets designed for her interlude with the Duke, and she wanted nothing to do with them. The Duke had been trying everything in his power to lure her to his bed. But she, being the eluding one, had feigned his attempts and kept him waiting.

She continued to brush her long hair. Once she had combed through a section of hair, she would pin it elegantly atop her head. She continued to do this over, and over, until every bit of her long, luminous black hair lay in a poised spiral molded atop her head.

She sat there for a moment, turning her head to admire her hair. Then stood up, set down the brush and walked over to her bed. Instead of putting on the dress of fastidious beauty, she again put on her tattered and ripped dress from whence she arrived in. It was the only thing that she still had left to remind her of home, and if she were to ever not wear it, it would surely get thrown out.

Jenevy finished dressing, and then walked over to the large windows and she turned the creaking handle slowly, until she heard the latch click out of place. Grasping the cold metal, she yanked the window open.

A breeze of fresh, mountain air flourished in upon her like a wave of cool water. She closed her eyes, and absorbed the misty air. She tried to remember her home, but slowly the picture was fading bit by bit, and even her drawings were failing to awaken even the smallest of memories.

She opened her eyes once more, and looked out at the vast mountains. Somewhere, out there, laid her hope. Someday, she would find it, even if it took her an eternity to do so, she would. She vowed then and there, that nothing was to keep her from her freedom. She didn't care if it meant losing her home, because in the end, she knew that her father would never care for her safety.

Jenevy felt a twinge of sorrow building in her chest; it sprang up and shot tears to her eyes. Jenevy rushed over to the balcony railing, and fell over onto them, allowing her tears to pour freely onto her cheeks. She stayed there for a moment, sobbing as she reflected her past.

Why had she even agreed to be sold to the Duke? What was the purpose? So what if her father was to be rich for the rest of his existence? The fact that he knew what selling her to the Duke would entail flat out irritated her!

Why had she let herself be sold? Was her love for her father that immense that she would risk everything? Jenevy raised her head.

"Yes, my father's happiness is worth all of my existence. No matter the price." She said aloud.

Jenevy closed her eyes, as the wind swept through her hair, releasing the pins that had held it in place. She smiled, as she remembered a time, when she was young and the wind had done that same thing to her.

She was riding her horse galloping through the countryside and nothing mattered then. There wasn't a care in the world as she strode through that empty abyss of pure nothingness. She was content then, nothing was expected of her, and she would give anything to return to that time and place.

"Mistress?" A voice interrupted her thoughts.

Jenevy turned around, and quickly wiped the tears from her face; a maid stood at her door.

"The master would like a word with you." The maid instructed. Jenevy nodded, stood up, readjusted her posture and then walked over to the door. The maid quickly rushed over to the window, shut them and locked them in place. She then proceeded out of the room and followed Jenevy into the hallway. She closed Jenevy's door as they exited her room.

They walked quietly down the corridor. It's gothic décor sent chills down Jenevy's spine at every step. The maid quickened her step to walk in front of Jenevy, and then led her towards the stairs. Jenevy glided down those stairs, her feet moved quickly down the steps as the rest of her body remained rigidly straight, as years of refinement lessons had taught her to do so. The maid turned down a hallway on the floor below, and guided them to the entrance of the library. The maid opened the doors, and rushed Jenevy inside.

"Here is Lady Jenevy my master." The maid said with a bow. A dark figure lurked in the shadows.

"Very well, return to your duties." The man said. The maid nodded and rushed out of the room, making sure to close the doors as she left. The dark figure walked forward, and emerged from the shadows.

"I see you did not find the dress that I gave you to your standards milady?" He said with a smirk. "And apparently the jewelry was not to your liking as well?" He added. The man looked at her intuitively, she remained quiet. He frowned and continued.

"Do you read Lady Jenevy?" He inquired. Jenevy did not respond. The Dark Lord looked at her with glowering eyes.

"I'm sure that a woman of your stature must read." He said as he picked up a book and opened its cover. He scanned the pages as if the story perplexed him.

"You refuse my gifts, ignore my callings, and deny my invitations to dinner. I am beginning to think that you don't like your stay in my castle." He searched her face.

"Have you not been treated well? Given food or clothing? Or a place to sleep?" Yet, despite everything, I still find you standing here before me." He paused. "Why is it that the only time you desire to see me, is when you feel like it?" He asked of her. Jenevy stood silently.

"Well?!" He asked louder. She remained still. With a whip of his hand, he smacked her delicate cheek as hard as he could. She flew to the ground with a thud.

"Perhaps, I am being too nice." He said agitatedly. Jenevy slowly looked up at him, wiping the blood from her lip. She pushed herself back up to her feet and glared at him.

"No matter what you do, I will never be yours." She answered with a forceful tone. The Duke smiled at her.

"We shall see about that!" He threatened. He heard a knock at the door and turned to see the same maid rush inside. She bowed instinctively before him.

"What is it now?" He annoyingly asked her.

"Sir William has brought Miss Briana as you requested milord." She said quickly.

The Duke looked back at Jenevy, a wicked smile spread across his face, as he greedily rubbed his hands together.

"Excellent. Well, Lady Jenevy, we are not finished my pet, simply postponed.

We will continue this conversation momentarily . . . ." He swung around, and then added.

"And this time, you *will* say yes."

The Duke rushed out of the door, slamming it behind him. Jenevy closed her eyes with a sigh of relief, and rubbed her sore cheek.

"Milady, he will kill you if you do not give in to his demands." The maid said warningly. Jenevy nodded.

"I know Christine, but until then, I will not lose my honor to that poor excuse of a man." She said confidently.

"But, is it really worth dying for?" The maid asked worriedly.

"Christine, my honor is worth a thousand deaths. I don't expect you to understand, but someday you will." Jenevy explained. The maid nodded in reply, smiling faintly. The maid silently opened the door.

"Do you need anything milady?" She asked before leaving. Jenevy smiled over to her.

"No, just take a break before he summons you again." She answered. The maid bowed and walked out of the room, Jenevy glanced up at the bookshelves. Walking over to the closest shelf, she gazed her eyes over the titles, guiding her fingers across the spines.

She gripped the shelf instinctively, as she felt her body start to shake violently. She had promised herself when she had first arrived at that prison, to not break down into tears in front of the Duke. She had never broken that vow to herself, and she did not want to break it then.

She closed her eyes, waiting for the convulsions of fear and sorrow to subside. She would wait until she was within the safety of her room, to unleash her tears.

Once her composure returned, she reopened her eyes and looked at the books once more. Pulling one from off the shelf, she clutched it to her chest.

Silently, she left that room and walked up the foreboding stairs and into the safety of her chambers. Once the door was closed, she leaned back against the door, and gripped the book tighter.

She sank to her knees as the tears rolled freely down her cheek; she then let her grief consume her, as she cried in long spasms of anguish, until every last tear soaked her dress. She sniffled, and stared at the floor. She felt sorry for the girl Brianna, wherever she was, knowing all too well, what was about to happen to her. She secretly prayed that the slaves of the Duke would be comforted, and would not forget who they truly were.

Quietly she stood back up and walked over to her bed. She toppled over, slumping onto its sheets, and stared lifelessly into the darkness.

❖ Moonlight was shining through the windows of William's room. He took of his cloak and tunic, and then walked into his washroom. Hanging up his clothes on a hook on the wall, he walked over to his tub basin.

The bath's hot water steamed up into the room, and William eagerly invited the heat to his skin. Undressing fully, William stepped into the basin, and sank down into the hot water. The heat pooled over his muscles, relaxing him to his core. He sighed, closed his eyes and tried to forget the memories of that day.

He had brought another girl to his master; this one was from a poor family, the woman had reluctantly had agreed to come to the castle just to make her feel wealthy. She was another greedy woman, adding to a long list of greed that quenched the Duke's lust.

William had seen Jenevy that day, only briefly, but what he saw remained in his thoughts despite his best attempts to clear his mind. She was in the library with his master, and when Christine had opened the door, he had seen her standing against the far wall.

She was still wearing her old garments that she had worn when William had first laid eyes upon her, and despite the months that she had been at the castle, she had refused to change her attire. Any other woman would have eagerly dressed in the silks and linen that were given to her, but not Jenevy.

She looked sad, depressed, but still strong and beautiful as they day he had met her. But her cheek was red and swollen, which meant only one thing: she had again, refused the Duke.

Deep down, William hoped that his master would not kill her for her refusal of that day. That somewhere, she was still alive and safe within the fortress walls. William didn't know how much longer the Duke would put up with her insolence, but he felt that it wouldn't be for much more. So far, she had lasted the longest out of all of the women that William had delivered. Even the insubordinate guards of the castle couldn't stop talking about her existence.

William reached down to grab the soap from the floor, and scrubbed his body of the filth from that day. Tomorrow, he had a new maiden to trap and bring, who would replace Mary Beth, whom he had buried that evening after her encounter with the guards' arrows. This time, the maiden that was being sought, was not a volunteer, but had been sold to the Duke again out of pure greed by a penniless father. William pitied the father who had sold his child for wealth and fortune.

William finished bathing, and stepped up out of the water. Drying his body, he silently dressed into his clean clothes. He walked out of the washroom, and began to gather up his attire, and belongings that would accompany him on the trip for the next day.

After blowing out the candle on his nightstand, he laid down onto his shallow bed. After pulling the covers to his chin, he looked at the ceiling above and let his thoughts take control.

He hated having to bring so many innocent women to his master. He hated even more having to see their lifeless bodies in his mind night after night. But, he had learned to channel his emotions to try and ignore the sins that he was forced to commit.

But still, every night, the countless numbers of faces haunted his memories, and it was getting harder, and harder, to forget them.

William sighed at the realization of what the next day was, it was Sunday, and Sundays were never good for William.

William arose early that next morning, and he went through the same motions that he did day after day. He got dressed, adorned his armor, grabbed his gear and walked to the stable where he would then grabb his saddle, and strap it to his horse. William slouched as he unhooked his sword, and then attached it to the saddle, and pulled his horse outside. Once outside, he climbed onto his horse's back and kicked him forward.

"Out to get another one are we?" Shouted one of the guards from the gate. William nodded.

"Yes, now open the gates!" William demanded.

The guards shrugged and did as they were told.

"Good luck buddy, see you tomorrow!" The guard shouted, and he watched William walk through the gate.

William pulled out his map, routed a course, and then proceeded towards the city where he was to retrieve the girl.

His journey took most of the day, but at last he reached the small farmhouse where the girl lived. It was a small home, barely standing even with the support from the tall, wooden beams. Crusted mud lay all around the entrance to the house, and dead blades of grass and hay littered the area.

William guided his horse over the ruts in the road, and parked him at the edge of the house. Sliding from the saddle, he threw the reins onto a barely standing pole, and William approached the farmhouse door, and knocked briskly upon the wood.

He waited, listening for footsteps within. After a few moments, he knocked again.

The door slowly opened, and through the crack of the entrance, a tiny voice sounded.

"Who are you?" It barked at him. William opened his mouth to answer, but was interrupted by a man behind him.

"Where's the money?!" The man ordered. William slowly turned around.

"Where's the money?!" The man shouted again. William frowned.

"You know the rules." William replied coldly. The door opened behind him and two men came out with swords drawn. William peered over his shoulder to glance at them, and then raised his arms to signal that he was unarmed.

The man in front of William spoke again, this time pointing his sword at William's neck.

"Now, I'll ask again. Where's . . . . the money?!"

"You *know* the rules!" William repeated hotly. The man in front of William stepped closer, and pressed his blade against William's neck.

"That's not what I asked!" The man noted. William sighed; he hated it when people didn't follow the rules.

"Now, give us what we want, or suffer the consequences!" A man barked from behind William. William shook his head slowly.

"You don't want to do this." William threatened. The men laughed at him.

"Actually. Yes, we do!" One of ruffians replied amidst a malevolent laugh.

William heard the men's swords thrust forward making a hiss within the air. Instantly, William spun away from the sword upon his neck, twisted around to see the sword coming at him, and grabbed the man's hand that was holding the hilt of it, causing it to drop down towards the ground. The man froze.

William, while still holding the man's armed hand, took that moment to strike. He kicked up at the other man, slamming his foot into the man's face. Then elbowed the other man in the neck, which caused him to release his sword.

William's hand clasped the sword's hilt, and spun it up towards the sky, and aimed it at the man that was in front of him. The man, whom William had kicked, was instantly to his feet. He swung his sword up and then back down at William's head. But William rose up his free arm, and caught the sword on his forearm with a clank.

The man looked at William in confusion. William twisted his wrist, and with a sickening crunch the blade fell to pieces. The spiked gauntlet upon William's arm shone through his now ripped cloak. William glared at the man, threatening him to try again.

"He's got on armor!" The man shrieked. The men backed off, as William removed his cloak dropping it to the ground. His metallic armor glistened in the moonlight.

William twisted his wrist, snapping the foldable spikes back to lying flat upon his arm. He raised the man's sword that he had disarmed, up and ready for the next attack.

"Now, I fear, it is you whom will suffer the consequences." William stated ferociously. The men glanced at one another, but raised their swords in response nevertheless. William stood tall, awaiting the next move.

The men lunged forward; William deflected their attacks, pushing their swords to the side. He slammed his forearm onto their blades again, and snapped his gauntlet's razor-spikes back out, and shattered the swords into pieces at impact.

Twirling around, William grabbed one man's arm, and yanked him down onto his blade and sliced the blade onto the man's chest. The man fell to the ground in pain. William flipped forward, in midair twisted over an attack, and grabbed a hold of the other man's throat in mid flight.

Using the momentum from his acrobatic flip, he slammed his foot onto the man's chest, fell to the ground, and sent the man flying over him. Rolling back to his feet, William tossed the sword at the last standing man. The strength of William's throw sent the man flying into the farmhouse's wall, and William watched as the sword speared into the man's stomach pinning him to the wall.

The man that William had sent flying with his foot, lay writhing upon the ground. With a look of anger upon his face, William walked towards him. William withdrew his hidden longblade, and pointed it directly at the man.

The man's eyes filled with fear, and he stared up at William in defeat.

"I am in *no* mood to play your games!" William shouted ragingly. "I gave you a warning, and a warning that you did not heed! And now, I am forced to carry out what my master wants of me. Give me the girl now!!" William screamed at the man.

The man lay quivering beneath his stare, and he gulped in desperation. He nodded quickly.

"Yes . . . yess . . . . But where is my—" William stepped closer cutting him off.

"Now!" William ordered.

"But . . . . There is no . . . g . . .g . . .g . . .irl!" The man stammered. William let out a yell in anger. He lunged forward, grabbed the man's scalp and yanked him into the air. William pressed his blade hard enough so that he could see blood on the man's neck. The man shrieked in pain.

"Do not make me kill you like I did your friends!" William warned.

"But there is no girl!" The man sobbed again. William leaned in closer.

"Last chance! Give me the girl, or meet your maker!" William ordered warningly. The man began to shake in William's grasp.

"Please . . .please! Don't kill me! There . . . there is a girl. She's in the barn!! But she's not mine to give!" The man bellowed.

"What?!" William yelled.

"I mean she is, but she's married to my son!" He cried. "We just wanted the money!"

William scowled and dropped the man to the ground with a thud. The man coughed and grabbed his neck. William paced in front of him.

"What—" The man coughed. "What are you going to do?!" He asked in fear. William froze.

"To continue with what you agreed to do." He responded, and walked over to the barn.

"*No*! You can't!" The man shrieked, and attempted to get up. William twirled back around, and pointed his sword at the man's face. The man froze.

"You made a deal!!" He screamed at the man. "You tried to break the rules, and in that you broke the deal. You failed to produce the girl and now I must finish what I was sent here to do! You try and stop me, and I *will* kill you." William roared threateningly. The man sank away from William. William lowered his sword and turned back around.

"No!" The man shrieked. He looked around him, as William got further away. The man saw a dagger sticking out of one of the dead men's boot. He slid over to it, grabbed it and sent it flying through the air at William.

But to the man's horror, William, with lightening fast reflexes, had spun around and deflected the dagger from striking him with his arm. The dagger clanked off of William's gauntlet, where it fell and bounced off of the ground. William stared angrily at the man.

"That . . . was a mistake." William muttered. The man tried to crawl backwards away from William.

"I was going to let you live. I was going to break my word to my master by allowing a traitor to stay alive. But, now, you leave me no choice. Enjoy the afterlife."

As his heavy armored boots struck the ground, William charged at the man, running with loud thumps. The man screamed in fear and slumped to the ground.

William skidded to a stop, turned around and rushed towards the barn. He slid open the doors, and saw a girl cowering in a corner. William walked over to her, and grabbed her by the arm, pulling her to her feet.

"Why! Why did you kill him?!" She shrieked. William ignored her, and threw her over his shoulder. He walked outside, heading towards his horse. He slumped her onto the saddle, and then climbed up behind her. He grabbed the reins, and kicked the horse turning it towards the man on the ground. The girl was crying as they approached the man.

"Here is your money old man." William said as he dropped a bag of gold in front of the man. The man slowly awakened, and rubbed his head. He looked at the bag of money and then at William.

"You should have backed down when I told you. And she *might* have stayed here." William said rudely, then kicked his horse and rode off into the night. The man cried clutching the purse of money to his chest, and rubbing the lump on his head.

❖ A nightmare had awoken Jenevy, sending her sitting straight up onto her bed.

Sweat was in beads all over her body, and Jenevy was shaking. She sighed and stood up to step out onto the balcony, hoping that it would refresh her spirits.

She smiled, as she stepped onto her balcony landing and gazed up at the stars. She was right, the air really did calm her from her troubled night of sleep. The stars were bright that night, and the moon was full. She watched the moonlight as it shone down upon the mountains. They were just as beautiful at night as they were in the day. She followed the moon's rays all the way to the ground below.

Even the moonlight didn't help with the dreary, evil look of the castle grounds. She continued to look at the grounds below, and then froze in place. Something was moving, creeping through the shadows.

Jenevy leaned over on the railing of her balcony, and tried to make out the shape of the creature. It looked massive, even from her fifth-storied terrace. It moved quietly, as it snuck along the wall. It was tall, very large, and very formidable. She was sure that it was a man. But then again, had she ever known of a man to be that large?

She strained her eyes to look closer; the *'man'* crept silently towards the bottom of Jenevy's room. She wondered if it were going to just walk by on the edge of the wall below, so she rushed over to the opposite side of her balcony, and looked down. There was nothing. He seemed to have disappeared.

Jenevy shuddered as a chill crept up her spine. Perhaps the dark shadows were just playing tricks on her? But her gut was saying otherwise and Jenevy tried to swallow down her fear.

"He definitely should not be here." She said to herself. Folding her arms she quickly rushed inside, and made sure to lock her window doors. As an afterthought, she closed the curtains as well.

Jenevy rushed to her bureau away from the window, as a loud clank echoed outside. She jumped back in fear, and knocked the perfumes off of her dresser.

She listened intently to the noise, as she heard scraping, and the sound of rubbing wood. Almost as if . . . .

"Someone is coming." Jenevy said aloud. Frantically she ran to the door of her room, and turned the knob. It wouldn't budge.

"Locked!" She screamed. She spun back around, as a loud thud hit her window.

Jenevy looked around her room; she saw her long golden hairpin on the floor next to her bureau, and rushed over to it. She grabbed it from off of the floor, and held it to her.

Jenevy could feel her heart pounding in her chest. Her ears rang and echoed her heavily beating heart. She stared at the window, looking at the figure on the other side of her drapes.

Then, it disappeared, and the noise stopped. Instantly, the entire room was still. A deadly silence echoed through her room and it was too quiet for comfort.

Apprehension arose stronger in her body; as she stood there, stationary, waiting for something to happen: and then it did.

The glass from her window shattered, sending the shards flying through the room. Jenevy shrieked and fell to her knees, as she covered her face.

She heard a thud; and looked up to see a large foot stepping in from her broken balcony window. Jenevy's eyes slowly crept up the leg of the intruder and screamed.

It was not a man at all! But a large, menacing troll! It towered over her like a huge beast. It had an axe held securely over one shoulder, and a hammer dragging on the ground. It glared at Jenevy.

"Ummm . . . ." Jenevy grunted. She suddenly felt very insignificant armed with only a hairpin. The troll turned its head to examine her, its eyes were lifeless, and drool dripped from its jaws. Large fangs held the source of a smelly saliva.

Jenevy slowly stood to her feet, and the troll crept towards her. Jenevy backed herself towards her lcoked door, and pressed flat up against the wall beside it. She extended her arm out and reached for the handle, trying to open the door was out of the question, she forgot it was locked!

The troll drew closer and closer, as Jenevy grimaced as its stinky breath invaded her nostrils, it smelled like a mixture between decaying carcasses, and rotten vegetables. The smell was nauseating her, practically suffocating her. She wanted to run, but there was nowhere *to* run. What was she to do, jump out of the window?

No! She had to stand her ground! Every book that she had ever read from the Dark Lord's library, said that a troll is easily provoked when its prey tries to run.

So, Jenevy remained still, even though every fiber in her being urged her not to. The troll sniffed the air, smelling at her as it sneezed, it then stepped back.

"You. Are one of the Duke's slaves?" It inquired. Jenevy's eyes widened, she didn't know that trolls could talk! It glared at her, awaiting her reply. She nodded slowly.

"Then, take me to him." The troll ordered. Jenevy jumped as the troll twisted her around and shoved her towards the door. Jenevy groaned as she hit the door with a thud. She could practically see stars due to the force that the troll used when he slammed her forward.

"As much as I would like to oblige, I can't. The door is locked." She said matter-of-factly. The troll sneered, then pushed her to the side. With a grunt, the troll kicked it, and the door flew from its hinges and slammed into the hallway. The troll grabbed Jenevy and shoved her out into the corridor as well.

"Now take me!" It instructed. Jenevy nodded and ran down the hallway, and the troll thumped behind her. Jenevy had never been to the Dark Lord's room, nor did she want to go there then. For surely some punishment would await her for delivery of the troll.

But, seeing how either way some sort of pain awaited, she at least hoped that the creature would bring some sort of bad news to the Duke, something to dampen his day, or even perhaps his week. With those thoughts in her mind, Jenevy smiled and kept walking.

The troll behind her, thumped louder the faster it got, as it dragged its large hammer at its feet.

Jenevy walked swiftly, trying to maintain a speed faster than the troll's. Jenevy looked around the corridors, hoping that someone would be walking nearby. The hallways were beginning to grow unfamiliar to her.

She was never allowed to explore the castle, and since she had never even made it out except for to go to the library, she knew that it was only a matter of time before the troll realized that she was lost.

She started to think about where the Duke would dwindle. A very deep and mysterious man, he kept to himself except when his slaves were summoned. He ventured out only long enough to fetch a maiden or to terrorize his workers. She didn't know if he ever walked outside and the only time that he seemed to escape to the lower levels was if she was in the library.

Jenevy, decided that he must live on a higher level, away from everyone, but high enough to watch his minions in their foolish escape attempts. Besides, he loved torture, so long walks to his room allowed for plenty of fear to fill every maiden's heart, as she would walk to entice his sick fantasies. Jenevy turned to a staircase, walking quickly up the stairs. The troll followed closely behind.

"Where is your master?" It questioned. Jenevy stopped and pointed up the stairs.

"Just up there!" She said panting. The troll nodded, and they continued forward. Jenevy saw the next landing to the floor above, and rushed towards it staring out into the hallway.

Once her eyes had adjusted, she knew that her theory was correct. For instead of dull, mahogany doors outlining the walls, that level had only one door: a huge, dark, red pine door. All over this door, were intricately carved designs of evil demons and sorcery. The hallway was dimly lit, and a blood colored carpet lay at her feet. Jenevy stopped and awaited the troll.

"He is in there." She said excitedly, while pointing down the hallway. The troll gleamed its disgusting teeth, and trudged forward. Jenevy watched his huge hand push open the door and Jenevy quickly ran back down the stairs before the Duke would see her.

She paused, once out of sight and away from the troll to breathe deeply. She could hear the Duke quarreling with the troll above. Jenevy continued forward and rushed down the stairs, and then down the hallway to her room. Her door lay twisted and in shambles against the wall across from her room, and its hinges were hanging weakly from the doorway.

Before Jenevy could walk inside, she heard the troll roar. She froze and stared at the ceiling. She heard the thumping steps of the troll as it ran down the hallway; she watched the ceiling, and she followed the noises with her eyes.

She heard the troll, as it bounded down the stairs. Should she run? Her door was obviously unlocked, but where would she go? She wasn't allowed to roam the mansion, and she would certainly get shot if she ventured outside. Besides, it was dark out, and not knowing the castle grounds would mean that she would certainly get lost.

She heard a door slam above, and someone came running after the troll. Jenevy stood motionless in the hallway, as the troll crept closer. The troll whirled around the corner, and it ran towards Jenevy.

Jenevy held her breath and closed her eyes, waiting to feel some sort of pain. But the troll ran right past her, and leapt from the window. Jenevy opened her eyes, and watched its body disappear from view. Then the man chasing the troll emerged.

"You!!!" It was the Duke. He raced forward and grabbed Jenevy by the throat, and Jenevy instinctively grabbed his wrist. She clawed at them, as she felt her air being cut off.

"Do you have any idea of what you've done?!" He screamed, as his grip tightened. Jenevy scratched at his wrists but he only lifted her up higher, just to slam her against the wall.

"You will pay for this!" He shrieked. Jenevy stared at him; his face was bleeding from a gash above his right eye, and his cloak was shredded, with pieces of it dangled on the floor.

"Good. I hope . . . that it has brought you . . . to your end!" Jenevy forced the words out, as she was wheezing from her air being cut off. The Duke sneered and then dropped her. Jenevy slumped down coughing.

The Duke was pressing his hand to the gash on his forehead, as Jenevy pushed herself back up to her feet. The Duke glared at her.

"He has not brought mine, but yours!" He shrieked, and he grabbed her arm and dragged her down the hallway. Jenevy had no choice but to follow him.

CHAPTER FOUR

CAGED

H E YANKED HER up one staircase after another. At first she thought that he was taking her to his chambers, but sighed with relief when they climbed even higher.

The Duke pulled her faster and faster until she practically tripped up them and then he stopped, as the stairs ended and a dark door lay ahead of them. The Duke dragged her towards it, and then using a key on his neck, he unlocked the door, and kicked it open. Another staircase lay ahead of them; except for it was made of stone, and spiraled in shallow curves, in steep inclines.

The Duke threw her against the wall, grabbed a candlestick, and then raced up the stairs dragging her behind him. Jenevy fell halfway up the stairs, but the duke didn't stop to allow her to stand. He instead, yanked her up them and she felt the stone steps bumping against her chin with such force that she was practically in tears by the time they reached the top.

The Duke let go of her for a moment, only to open the door with the key on his neck once more. Jenevy looked at the door as it swung open revealing the room inside.

There was a walkway that went past several other small rooms. The rooms were all barred, resembling a prison more than anything else. Each room had a barred window that looked out into the sky, bringing its inhabitants a false sense of hope.

The Duke pushed towards one of the prison cells, opened the door, and then threw her in so hard that she was sent flying into the back wall. Her head slammed onto the stone, causing her to fall over in pain.

"I hope that you enjoy it here. For these walls will be the last that you will ever see!" The Duke yelled at her as he slammed the door shut behind him, and locked it. Jenevy looked up at the door, while she felt the warm liquid of blood seeping out of her forehead and down her cheek.

For the first time since she had arrived in that castle, she began to feel alarmed. It was a feeling of there being no way of escape, and no way for her to ever survive.

Wincing, she pushed herself to her feet and looked around her cell, she screamed in horror at what she saw. Corpses lay all around her, and sizable maggots feasted upon the rotting flesh. Ripping apart any fragment of tissue that was still present, rats were tearing away the intrepid bodies, which created a brooding ground for the maggots.

Jenevy covered her mouth in repulsion as a sickening smell invaded her mind. Every corpse in there was a woman, a woman, who just like Jenevy, had refused that cursed man. The lucky ones were brought to the dungeons below, to die quickly. But not the ones that lay before her. Those women were sent up there to starve, thirst, and to die slowly.

Jenevy shoved herself against the wall, convulsing into tears. She closed her eyes, and tried to think of someplace better than where she was.

The breeze from the world outside rushed in through the window and chilled her skin. She reopened her eyes, and violently through her body against the window.

She turned around and gripped the bars with both of her hands. She let out the most terrifying scream that anyone had ever heard, it was loud, and long so that all could hear her.

❖   William awoke to the sound of someone screaming. He rushed out into the hallway and looked around frantically.

There were other guards standing in the hallway as well, all awoken by the same horrific scream that had plagued their dreams.

"Return to your rooms immediately!" It was the Duke. William turned to go back inside his quarters, but the Duke stopped him.

"Not you William. Get fully dressed and meet me in the Library." The Duke ordered and he stormed away. William nodded and rushed back into his room.

William raced down the stairs moments later, still dressing as he was moving, he rushed into the library as he was finishing the tying his tunic.

"A troll attacked me." The Duke stated as he paced in the circular room. William paused and looked at the Duke in confusion.

"When?" He asked dumbfounded.

"Just a few moments ago." The Duke replied.

"In the castle?" William asked mystified.

"Yes! In my chambers, while I was preoccupied!" The Duke shouted, glaring at William. William frowned and looked out one of the windows.

"How did it get in?" He asked out loud, puzzled.

"One of the girls brought him right to me!" The Duke responded in outrage. William stared at him, not sure how to react.

"You are to find him, follow that repulsive creature and do whatever means necessary to stop him! If it is ever to reach the outer kingdoms, we are all doomed!" The Duke shouted in anger. William nodded.

"Find the troll, kill it, and bring back what it has stolen from me!" The Duke instructed.

"Yes milord." William said in addition to his bow at the Duke's side.

"Now leave!" The Duke ordered and turned back around. William retreated to his room, and began to pack up his belongings once again.

At least this time, his task would be a bit more challenging and enjoyable! William loved tracked and loved fights with trolls even more!

❖ Jenevy wasn't feeling too good, the smell of the room was sickening and nauseating her, and she hadn't slept the whole night because of it. Instead, she sat sitting against the wall shaking at the horror that lay before her.

The sun crept slowly into the sky, sending rays of light through her barred window. It lit up the room, and Jenevy's eyes widened in disbelief.

There were many more bodies in there than she had realized. Most of them, were recently dead, but a few had been there for a while and they smelled the worst.

"They must have been here for months." She said aloud. Jenevy stood up, and stepped gently over them and approached the door. She looked out the bars, and glanced around.

"Is anyone out there?" She said quietly, there was no reply. Jenevy sighed, and dropped her head letting it clank onto the bars. She sighed again and closed her eyes.

Opening them slowly she stared at the floor, Jenevy squinted as she saw something shining from beneath the door. Jenevy cocked her head to the side and bent over to examine it.

It glinted in the sunlight, she attempted to touch it with her finger, but shrieked when it moved and yanked her hand back. In her error, she had moved it farther under the door, and even farther from reach. Jenevy grunted as she slid her arm back through the bars and tried to reach it.

"Come on!" She whispered impatiently. She grumbled when she realized that it was just out of reach. Jenevy hit the bar in anger and she looked around her, trying to find something that she could use to reach it.

A bone lay upon the floor, Jenevy frowned in disgust and gently picked up the bone. Sliding it through the bars, she scraped it across the shining object and dragged it towards her. Jenevy dropped the bone and grabbed the object excitedly.

"It's a key!" She shrieked. Jenevy jumped to her feet, and looked at the keyhole on her prison door. She licked her lips and put the key into the lock.

"Please . . . please . . . please . . . ." CLICK! The door opened and Jenevy instantly pushed open the door with a creak. She walked out of the room and looked at the hallway around her.

There were three other chambers inside that area, each housing more corpses and even more rats. Jenevy shuddered in revulsion. She looked over down the other side of the hallway, and saw the door that the Duke had opened earlier. She ran over to it, and inserted the key. She tried to turn it, but nothing happened.

"Locked!" She looked at the key. What had she expected? The Duke to purposely use the same lock, for each door in case he was to drop his key? Jenevy frowned in disappointment.

Twirling around, she looked down the hallway. A look of stern curiosity crossed her face when she noticed a room in the back that she hadn't noticed before. This room was not barred, and was not made of stone. Rather, it was made of wood, with a single keyless door holding its secrets.

Jenevy walked over to it, grasped the handle and turned it slowly. Jenevy screamed as a man fell on her, and she fell to the floor as his body weight overpowered her.

She shrieked and frantically rolled him off of her. Hyperventilating, she jumped to her feet clutching her chest as her heart was deafening in her temples.

The man was dead, but hadn't been for very long. He wore a cloak, with a green and brown tunic. He had a hilt for a sword strapped to his belt, and there was a dagger protruding from his back. Jenevy winced at the sight of him.

Hesitantly, she looked into the room that he had come from, and to her surprise saw a girl staring back at her from the floor.

"Christine!" Jenevy yelped, and she ran to her side.

"What . . . what has happened to you?" Jenevy asked, as she consolingly placed a hand on the chambermaids shoulder.

Jenevy puckered her brow as she felt liquid beneath her palm, and looked at her hand. Christine was bleeding, and badly. She looked sickeningly pale, and held her side in pain.

Jenevy cautiously looked around her; the room was definitely made for a guard. It had a table, a bed, and a litter of random weapons displayed across the wall.

"Come on." Jenevy insisted as she helped Christine to her feet and led her to the bed.

"The . . . Dark Lord was displeased with me." Christine stated monotonously. Jenevy laid Christine down upon the bed, and placed a pillow under her head.

"He brought me here, a few days ago to die. That guard had seen me, and took me in here. He tried to . . . . rape me! But when I refused and fought back, he used his dagger and stabbed me over and over . . . ." She cutoff to cry against Jenevy's shoulder.

Jenevy's face dropped in sorrow, and she hugged her friend. Jenevy looked back at the lifeless man in the hallway.

"So, you killed him." Jenevy said slowly. Christine nodded. Jenevy could only imagine what the guard must have done to the other women that were brought up there. But that thought only made Jenevy angrier.

"Jenevy!" Christine grabbed her hand. "You have to get out of here!" She yelped.

"But how? The door is locked!" Jenevy said skeptically. Christine winced as she raised a hand to point over at the desk.

"There is a key, over there." She said slowly. Jenevy looked over her shoulder and saw a key sitting on the desk.

"But . . . what of the other doors? What if I should run into the Dark Lord, or the other guards? How am I to escape?" Jenevy said in uncertainty. Christine smiled.

"I'll tell you . . . . "

Moments later, Jenevy finished dressing herself in the guard's attire. She draped the cloak over her body, and smiled down at Christine, the maid lay peacefully on the bed.

"I wish that I could have saved you too." Jenevy whispered in an apology. Then closed her eyes, to regain her composure. Reopening her eyes, she turned and raced out of the dark tower.

CHAPTER FIVE

A CHARTLESS PATH

WILLIAM'S KEEN EYES looked at the ground below, he saw the tracks from the troll and they were still filled with liquid. Jumping from his horse, he knelt beside the deep footprints to examine them. They were still warm, which meant that he was catching up to the creature.

William climbed back onto the horse's saddle and watched the ground, leading his horse to follow the tracks. The grass continued to break all of the way into the forest where the troll had walked. William pulled the reins of his horse, as he kept a solid, thin line on the side of the trail that he was following.

"Come on troll, where are you going?" William asked aloud. The footprints went farther into the woods, and the steps were growing farther and farther apart.

William trudged along as the forest foliage began to get thicker and thicker. The troll had apparently grown frustrated with the trees, for its trail led through the forest like a tunnel. It had crushed and pushed the trees out of its way, sending them flying in splinters around its path.

William smiled as he looked down the newly formed path through the trees. At least now, William wouldn't have to get off of his horse in order to track the trolls path.

William traveled through the carved tunnel for hours, until at last he made it to a clearing. The footprints turned sharply to William's left, and formed a new tunnel through the trees.

William's horse turned and walked alongside the footprints, making sure to not disturb the tracks. William pushed hanging branches that blocked his way, and kept his horse moving.

"The troll must have been very angry." William noted to himself, as he watched the footprints of the troll lengthen in distance even farther. Trees were getting sliced and literally thrown in every direction.

William slid off his saddle once more, and pressed his hand to a footprint. William stared down the tunnel, noting the footprints carved in mud.

"He was running." William looked around warily. "But from what?" He pondered. A bit farther down the path, the troll had tripped and blood lay splattered on the dense underbrush.

William rushed forward to the site, and noticed a different set of tracks imprinted into the ground.

"He was being followed." William observed that the footprints following the troll, were much smaller and more distinct. " . . . and they were on horseback." William added. William stood back up to his feet and noticed sporadic arrows were littering the trees. Whatever had been following the troll, was trying to kill it.

"So the troll was being chased." William said guardedly as he climbed back onto his horse. He looked around him, taking note of every object that might be out of place.

He pranced his horse in circles, looking cautiously throughout the trees. William then kicked his horse back onto the trail of the troll, and kept notice of the horse's ears. If the horse heard anything, which was usually before William anyway, then he was going to be ready.

William kicked his heels into the horse's flanks, the horse reared back, squealed, and then took off after the running troll and its mysterious attacker. Mud was sent flying up behind them as the horse's hooves dug into the dirt like a drill.

Whatever was chasing that troll, might very well be seeking the same thing that William was, and William was not about to let that happen.

❖ "STOP!!" Jenevy screeched to a halt, sliding on the slick marble floor at the command.

"When did William leave this morning?" It was the Duke. Jenevy's eyes widened.

"Uhh." She said as she diverted his eyes, and tried to disguise her voice.

"Well?" The Duke asked impatiently.

"Um . . .Early this morning milord." She lied. The Duke groaned.

"Very well." He said and he took off down the hallway. Jenevy watched him leave, and then let out a sigh of relief.

'Great. Of all the people to run into.' She thought to herself frustrated. Jenevy breathed in a deep breath of air to calm her, and then walked into the library. She was relieved to find it empty.

"Now. Christine said . . . . the second bookshelf." Jenevy instructed herself as she looked around the room. She approached one of the shelves.

" . . . Next to a statue of the angel with the broken wing . . ." Jenevy scanned the shelves. " . . .none of these even have statues!" She said in disbelief. She frowned crossing her arms. Jenevy stared at the books, practically glaring at them secretly hoping that they would give her some answers.

That was when a book caught her eye. Jenevy stood up straight in excitement and rushed over to it. It read: The Statue of the Angel with the Broken Wing.

"Oh! It's a book!" She said eagerly. Jenevy slid the book from the shelf, and looked behind it. A small handle lay against the wall, Jenevy curled her fingers around it, lifted it, and then pushed it back into the wall.

Jenevy jumped in surprise. She was expecting the shelf to move, not the floor! She whirled around and watched as the table in the center of the room, twisted and swirled down into the floor. It created a flight of spiral stairs leading into the darkness below. Jenevy smiled in excitement.

Replacing the book upon its shelf, she walked over to the edge of the stairs.

"Well . . . here goes!" She said as she stepped onto the stairs and started down into the darkness. The farther down she walked, the steeper the stairs got. Water was collecting on the stone, making her journey more perilous.

As Jenevy walked down, that it became darker and darker at every step. She felt as if she were walking down the steps to hell itself.

Then at last, light began to emerge from the bottom. Squinting, Jenevy realized that it was a torch hung upon the wall, which signaled the end of the stairs. Approaching the torch, she gripped it and pulled down.

The grinding of stone echoed above as the stairs retreated back to the surface. Jenevy closed her eyes as the entrance above shut, sending wind flying all around her like a vortex.

Reopening her eyes, she continued down the tunnel that lay before her. A few torches dimly lit her path, and the air was growing stale and aged. A wave of uneasiness washed over her like a strong current of water. Jenevy shuddered in response.

She thought back to Christine's instructions.

" . . .Once you walk down those stairs, you will be within the realm of the abandoned maidens of the Dark Lord. That domain is unknown to anyone living in the castle except for those who had been sent there to perish. Make sure that you keep your mind focused upon what you are seeking, and *never* let your eyes wander except to the path in front of you . . . ." Christine's voice echoed in Jenevy's head as if she were standing right next to her.

HEATHER DIROCCO

The ghosts of the past were trapped there, trapped to an eternity of torture to both the living and the dead, and those spirits were going to try anything to keep her imprisoned there with them. Jenevy looked down at the floor below her, and her boots caught her eye.

"Oh no . . ." She said aloud. "Me looking like a guard is not going to make this crossing any easier." She said nervously as she stared at the guard's clothing that she was wearing.

Jenevy trudged forward as fear set down upon her at every step. She saw a stone door ahead of her, its iron handle gleaming against the firelight. Quickening her steps, she rushed to the door and gripped the handle.

"Well, here goes!" She said as she turned the handle, and pushed open the door with a creak. She grunted, as the stone door required more of her strength to open then she realized.

As soon as she stepped into the room, a wave of energy hit her like a rock. Jenevy stumbled, falling backwards against the door and it slammed shut. Shaking her head from the pain, she regained focus and stared in disbelief.

Faces flashed in front of her. They were blue, hazy and frozen with fear. They seemed to be floating all around her. Jenevy stepped forward, and literally had to push through them. But with every step that she took, the beings would pull her back twice as hard. Jenevy froze.

"The souls of the dead." She mused. She watched them as they silently floated around her. She had an idea.

"Listen! I am not here to harm you!" She shouted. But they seemed to be ignoring her, and kept pulling at her, trying to suck her towards the center of the room. Jenevy strained to stand still. Reaching a hand up, she yanked down the hood of her cloak and revealed her face.

"If anything, I am just like you!" She shouted even louder. But they still kept up the attack.

"Listen! I am trapped here too! I too, am one of the Dark Lord's maidens! Imprisoned to do his every whim! But not anymore!" She bellowed. The spirits stopped, and a voice echoed from amongst them.

"We have heard this before, by women only wanting to escape." They sung together. Jenevy frowned.

"But weren't you doing the same thing once too?" She asked in confusion.

"Perhaps . . . ." The voice rang.

"Then . . . I don't understand." Jenevy stated skeptically.

"What makes you think, that we want you to escape?! When we are forever imprisoned here?" The voices grew louder, and angrier. Jenevy looked around her, watching as the spirits floated over her arms, and restrained her wrists in the air. Next they grabbed at her feet, and then very violently spun her around. They began to pull her aggressively towards the eerie center of the room once again.

Jenevy tried with all of her might to stop, but nothing was working.

"Wait, wait!" She pleaded, while she tried anything that she could do to escape. A thought emerged in her mind.

"What . . ." She paused, choosing her words carefully. " . . . What if I freed you?" She inquired. The spirits froze, and Jenevy stopped moving. It worked. They swirled out in front of her.

"If you truly do want to release us, then the truth in your words would overpower your fear. And it doesn't" The voices said mystically.

"Well of course I am afraid!" Jenevy shrieked. "I was locked in the high tower because I sent a troll to the Duke. It nearly killed him! So he locked me up there to die, in hopes that I would learn my lesson." She said whimsically.

"What . . . does that have to do with us?!" They shrieked ferociously. Jenevy jumped back.

"Because the only way *to* escape is by coming down here!" She wailed.

"Isn't that convenient." They latched hold of her again, and pulled even harder. Jenevy felt as if her limbs were about to rip off, Jenevy screamed in pain.

"Wait . . .wait!" She panted. "If I were to kill the Duke, would that free you!" She shouted. They stopped again, and Jenevy looked around her.

"Yes." They boomed.

"Then help me!" Jenevy pleaded. The souls released her, and they all appeared in front of her.

"How? How can we help you!?" They bellowed in unison, and looked at her for answers, but Jenevy had no idea.

"I cannot do this alone, at least not now." Jenevy solemnly stated. The souls peered at her. "But . . . with your help maybe I can." She added. The spirits glanced at one another, and then faded into the darkness.

"Wait! Wait!" Jenevy yelled, reaching out to them. The room was dark and completely still. Jenevy was at a loss for words. What now?

"We will help you."

Jenevy spun around. A woman stood before her. She was tall and elegant and a bit older than Jenevy. She was very slender and wore the most unique clothing that Jenevy had ever seen. It resembled a luxurious ball gown, but seemed somehow different, almost . . . . older, as if it had belonged to something of the past. The woman, unlike the other spirits, looked real, Jenevy felt that she could reach out and touch the woman.

"Forgive them. They only do as I say." The woman said. Jenevy froze; it was as if she were paralyzed.

"I am lady Olivia. Wife of the Duke."

Jenevy's jaw dropped.

"Yes. You heard me correctly. I was the first of his many, many victims." Olivia stated. Jenevy looked away in confusion.

"So . . . you are going to help me to kill your husband?" Jenevy asked confounded.

"Yes."

"Why? I mean, well wow! How long have you been down here brooding?" Jenevy questioned. Olivia laughed.

"Over three-hundred years." Olivia said melancholy.

"What?! But how?!" Jenevy asked bewildered.

"Because of the trinket that a certain troll stole from him the other night. That same troll, which you let in." Olivia said with a smile. Jenevy looked at Olivia with a look of surprise.

"The troll? A trinket? Obviously there are greater powers in play here, and I might not stand a chance against this man!" Jenevy shouted in disbelief. Olivia frowned.

"Jenevy, with the powers that we are all going to give you, very little will stand in your way." Jenevy stared wide eyed at her.

"Power?"

"Yes. Each soul has some sort of power and energy, if you will, that allows them to move things. Just as they did to you when they yanked you from your freedom."

"Ok. You've got a point." Jenevy said in amazement.

"But be careful. Even with this power, the Duke is still much stronger."

"Then . . . how am I supposed to . . . . ?" Jenevy drawled off. Olivia smiled.

"Listen carefully Lady Jenevy. Once you have our powers, you must leave here and try to harness those powers. You will need to learn their ways, and learn to fight with them. Do you understand?" Olivia asked with a stern expression upon her face.

"Yes. But that will take months, even years to do! Lady Olivia, I used to be a countess, a . . . . a . . . Noble! I am not used to fighting, to . . . to . . . well anything! Everything outside of these walls is foreign to me!" Jenevy shrieked hopelessly, covering her face with her hands.

"Perhaps. But you did stand up to the Duke right?"

Jenevy looked up at Olivia.

"Yes." Jenevy said bemused.

"And you did maintain your dignity for this long correct?"

"Yes." Jenevy said again.

"And you did lead a mountain troll into the very chambers of the man who would kill you for it correct?" Olivia added with a smile.

"YES!!" Jenevy said excitedly. Olivia approached her.

"And aren't you the same one who escaped from the tower, snuck down here and stood up to us?" Jenevy's eyes widened.

"Yes!!!" She exclaimed.

"Then . . . where's the problem?" Olivia stated with a grin. Jenevy's smile faded.

"The problem is: who will train me who knows how to harness these powers? And the training might take a very long time to accomplish. I might not be able to kill the Duke for a very, very long time!" Jenevy said disappointedly. Olivia paced in front of her.

"Well. First of all, you will find someone to train you, and secondly, we've been trapped here for hundreds of years. What's a few more?" Olivia said with a smile. "Besides . . . we trust you."

Jenevy smiled in return, a feeling of relief fell upon her.

"Now . . . hold still!" Olivia instructed, and then she disappeared. Jenevy glanced around her in dismay. Within an instant, a beam of light shot out of the center of the room, and it twirled until a cyclone of light lay in front of her. The vortex flew over to her, and encircled her body.

Jenevy watched as every color both known and unknown to man swirled in the air. She reached a hand out to touch it, but it simply made a wave over her fingers to rejoin its brothers. Jenevy peered at the lights, wondering what was about to happen.

With a rush, they all slammed into Jenevy, disappearing within her body. Jenevy flew to the ground. She landed with a thud, staring into the darkness. Everything was still, and then Jenevy screamed. The beams of color radiated out of her, rushing down her entire body in waves of enormous pain. Jenevy writhed in turmoil upon the floor as she felt the power surge through her.

Her body went into convulsions as spasms shook her all over. And with one final shockwave, she was knocked unconscious. She heard a voice echoing throughout her mind as the blackness invaded her vision.

> *'When you awake, you will be outside of these walls. Be without fear*
> *Lady Jenevy, for you have come to this castle for a reason. And this power*
> *will help you to do it . . . . '*

❖   William stopped short, his horse reared in disapproval at the sudden jerk to its bit. William leapt onto the ground and raced forward.

"Oh no." He said aloud. A large creature lay dead in front of him. It was severely wounded, and reeking internal fluids seeped from it, pooling onto the ground. A large hammer stuck out from its massive chest, piercing away the soft tissue and underlying bone. Broken pieces of wood protruded out from the creature's massive lesions. William knelt down next to the creature examining its exterior. It was the troll.

Scanning the troll's body, William looked for any type of object that might seem out of the ordinary. Moving the troll's clothing back and forth he examined every part of the creature's body. Nothing looked unorthodox.

William sighed in disapproval.

"Nothing." He muttered to himself. William looked around the clearing; he stood up and began to walk around. He searched under ever blade of grass, every rock, and any other object that moved. Then sighed in defeat.

"Something beat me to it." William said, as he walked back over to the troll. He yanked an arrow from the dead troll's leg. He looked at the tip, examining it for its origin. He sighed again and threw the arrow onto the ground.

William bent over and gazed at the ground. Within moments he found what he was searching for, and whisked over to a set of tracks leading away from the clearing.

The assailant was on horseback, and had a companion with him. The tracks led into a gallop back through the path that William had just come from. The assailants were seemed to be heading back towards the Duke's castle.

William whistled for his horse, and jumped back up onto the saddle. He spun the horse around, and kicked its flanks hard. The horse ninnied and ran off following the recently traveled trail.

There was a city, not too far from there, one that William had passed while he was following the repulsive troll, and he would bet anything that the two attackers lay resting within that very town.

❖ Jenevy's eyes flickered open, the sun had set and at last she could see the stars. Jenevy didn't know how long it had been since she was able to stare out at the stars, but it seemed like it were ages ago.

Jenevy blinked. She had this feeling of confusion and desertion. How had she gotten there? What had happened? And where was she? She slowly sat up and looked around her.

She saw a large stone wall behind her, one that resembled that of the Duke's own castle walls. Was she outside the castle? Jenevy rubbed her head in confusion. She had to be outside the wall, because the nature around her seemed more alive than it did within the borders of the Duke's walls.

Jenevy looked down at her clothes and was stunned as to what she saw. She was no longer wearing the attire of the guard's that she had stolen, but had on some sort of armor. It glistened in the moonlight, and was cool to the touch. Jenevy smiled when she saw that two demonic stallions were engraved upon the metal on her chest. Both steeds seemed malicious and strong in appearance, yet noble and trusting at the same time.

Slowly, Jenevy stepped to her feet, amazed at how light the armor was. It looked sturdy and strong, but to her she felt nothing but the clothes upon her back. A cape was attached to her back, right beneath where the breastplate attached to her back plating.

The cape was of a deep scarlet red, with a silver moon encircled in a blazing blue flame. Jenevy smiled in amazement as to how similar in appearance her armor was to that of William's. They both reeked of pure nobility.

Jenevy frowned as her quick movement of standing had caused her to feel lightheaded. She instantly fell to the ground once more. She closed her eyes, and tried to keep the world from spinning within her mind.

Upon re-opening her eyes, she noticed a cloak that lay at her feet. Squinting in puzzlement, she leaned over and grabbed it. Staring at it longer, made her realize why it was there. She had to cover herself up. Just as William did, it was a way of disguising oneself from being noticed, and from being recognized. And with Jenevy's armor, she didn't really have a choice.

Getting to her feet once more, she lifted up the cloak and draped it over her body. Lifting up her arms, she reached back and made sure that she raised the hood over her head.

Glancing sideways, she peered outward from beneath her hood and stepped away from the castle. She was half tempted to return and to kill the Duke right then and there! But, then again, now that she had the abilities to do so, it would be a waste to not learn how to actually *use* them.

Sighing, she realized that she had no idea of where to go. How was she supposed to harness the powers that the spirits had so trustingly betrothed her with? Jenevy was unsure of what cities to even go to. She didn't even know which territory the Duke's castle was a part of.

Jenevy thought of William, he might be able to help her! He certainly knew how to fight! She smiled and turned around.

'What am I doing?!' She thought to herself, stopping in her tracks. *'I can't go back there!'* Jenevy stared up at the sinister wall in front of the castle. She could see the silhouettes of the guards as they patrolled their posts. She sighed and walked back in the other direction.

She knew that the trapped souls of the castle were depending on her; even if it would take her years to accomplish, they would wait. But, she felt as if it would take years before she even found anyone to begin training for that pivotal moment!

Silently she prayed for a way to know of what she was supposed to be doing. She carefully watched her footing, making sure that nothing would attract her attention. But her thinking too much, caused her to crack a twig beneath her foot.

She closed her eyes in displeasure at her mistake. She frowned and angrily cursed to herself. She waited a moment or two, listening for anything that might signal that she had been heard. Thankfully, nothing stirred due to her oversight, and she stepped forward once more.

'If only I could fly!' She said to herself. The woods were getting darker and darker at every step. Despite the moonlight, the branchy fingers of the trees seemed to be reaching up and choking out whatever splinter of light that shone through.

Jenevy looked away and tried to focus on something else. The last thing that she needed was to feel scared. Especially when the most dangerous of guards might be listening.

Thinking to herself, she tried to visualize a plan on how to accomplish her assigned mission. First and foremost, she had to figure out what exactly those spirits had bestowed upon her. Secondly, she had to discover how she could harness that power and to use it in battle. Thirdly, and most importantly, she had to learn to fight.

She had read many books of knights and sorcerers with power in her many readings at the Duke's library. They would shoot lightning bolts from their hands, and fire would distinguish their enemies that they themselves had ignited from practically nothing. But then again, most of those books were all stories that had no way of proving their legitimacy or not.

But as Jenevy thought about it more, she realized that parts of the stories *had* to be true. How else would the stories have been created? Also, there would be no *real* mages, sorcerers or witches lying dormant in the neighboring cities of her village that held those fabled powers.

In fact, most mages used some sort of rhyme to explode the powers of their own potions. Perhaps a simple rhyme could bring out her newly acquired powers?

Jenevy laughed at the thought, but then again, it wouldn't hurt to try.

Looking cautiously around her, she paused for a moment to think of a spell. She had read of one in a book at the castle, and it seemed quaint for the moment.

"The woods are dark, there is no light. Quickly make this world seem—" She stopped short. "Wait, I don't want anyone to see me. Hmmm." She looked around her deep in thought.

"Got it! These woods are dark, there is no light. Let me be the only one who sees it bright." She shouted. She closed her eyes, raised her hands and waited. She stood there, silently amongst the night creatures expecting to feel some sort of shock or tremble from her words. But nothing happened. She slowly opened her eyes in dismay.

Jenevy's eyes widened at what she saw, the entire world around her was lit up. The trees, the ground, even the sky. Only the sky still had the moon and stars out. Jenevy looked around her and smiled.

HEATHER DIROCCO

"I always wondered what it was like to be a wolf running through the night!" She exclaimed.

Jenevy was excited about her newly adapted talent. So she quickly thought to herself of another rhyme.

"Conceal me from hidden eyes, give me flight to the skies!" Jenevy said, but nothing happened and she stayed upon the ground. Jenevy frowned and looked around confused. She looked down at her feet thinking that maybe she had said something wrong.

"Upon my back give me wings, to glide me away from things." Jenevy rose her arms and waited. Nothing. She dropped her hands in disappointment, gave up, and continued walking.

"Ahhh!" She screamed and fell to her knees. Her back was wrenching with pain. It felt as if a knife were slicing right through her flesh. She instantly clutched her shoulder, hoping that the pressure would subside the pain, but it only made it worse.

Reaching back even further, she felt in horror as her armor began to mold away. Her flesh tore and ripped from beneath her grip, and the bones on her back rippled from beneath her muscle.

Jenevy cried out in pain as her shoulder blades remolded and arched, sending two large bones protruding out of her skin on both sides. With a sickening crunch, the bones extended out snapping and bending as her muscle stretched out of her body expanding onto the bones. Her skin seemed to melt from right underneath her hand, and formed over the bones and tissue, protruding from her back.

Biting her lip, Jenevy could feel her back readjusting to support the two new limbs, as they stretched out even longer. Within moments, she gained feeling with the two extremities as if they had been attached to her since her birth.

Giving out a sigh of relief, Jenevy relaxed as the pain slowly drained out of her. Her body could sense that there were two new appendages upon her back, and without thinking Jenevy lowered her right arm down, and brought her wing around to her face.

She touched it delicately, afraid that it would be cold. But, in fact, was completely the opposite; it was warm and rubbery. It felt like leather, and was very black in appearance.

Her skin was stretched so thin that Jenevy found it amazing that it didn't tear when she bent her wings. The bones upon her back, stretched out like fingers. Each having a massive amount of webbed, leathery skin attaching it to the next.

The last time that Jenevy had ever seen anything similar to her wings, was in a book that she had read on dragons. Jenevy guffawed at her new realization. She flapped her wings a bit, letting the air billow up, and slowly raise her off of the ground. When she would stop flapping, she would sink back down. There was a gleam of mischief dancing in her eye, as she smiled and jumped off of the ground. Fluttering her wings, she sped into the sky.

The thrill of adrenaline descended upon Jenevy in an instant, and she couldn't get enough. She wanted to fly faster, harder and stronger. Jenevy bounded and leapt upon the air. Gliding left and then right, she would dive down the ground only to ascend back up and soar into the atmosphere. She couldn't describe the sensations that she was feeling, but she never wanted them to go away.

Once she had had enough, she slowed down, and looked at the ground below her. A thought struck her mind, and she recited another spell as she flew through the wind.

"This power that I hold, give me the knowledge of its control." Information and facts soared into Jenevy's mind instantaneously. It rushed through her so quickly, that she stuttered in midflight and practically fell to the ground. Somehow, she was able to stop herself just before crashing, and landed on her feet.

HEATHER DIROCCO

That was when the bulk of the power's knowledge descended upon her, sending her head back, and her eyes rolling to white.

Jenevy's body began to shake and shake until her body could not withstand the seizures anymore. She slammed onto the ground like a wooden plank falling from a wagon. Moments later, everything stopped and Jenevy lay upon the ground covered in sweat. She slowly opened her eyes, and sat back up.

"The power, is easy to control . . ." She said as a blue sphere of energy materialized out of her palm. She stared at it.

"But every spell that I say, will be permanent." She said slowly, and stood to her feet. She watched the fire ball dance within her hand, as it floated in midair just inches about her palm. She slowly changed its color from blue to black. Squeezing her hand around the sphere she tightened her grip into a fist, and the flame disappeared, leaving only a few shards fading into the darkness.

"But I still need someone to train me. To show me how to use my powers by instinct. And I need someone to train me . . . . to fight."

❖ William yanked on the reins, causing his horse to skid to a stop. His horse pranced in place and William rotated his body to look further on down the road, a village lay ahead. Frowning, he pulled his hood up over his head, and made sure that his armor lay concealed from sight.

William snapped the reins and urged the horse forward again. William had a bad feeling about the village, and usually his bad feelings resulted in death.

The horse made its way down the hill and trotted up to the gates of the small town. Apparently William wasn't the only nervous one, for his horse's flanks were twitching in uneasiness as well.

"Can I help you sir?" The gate guard posed.

"Perhaps. My horse seems to have lost a shoe, is there a blacksmith in this village?" William asked, choosing his words carefully. The guard sneered and looked William up and down skeptically.

"A blacksmith? I suppose we do. Do ye uh . . . got any money on ya?" The guard's taste for vocabulary made William cringe.

"Enough for the blacksmith." William stated quickly.

"Alright, well ye best hurry up eh? We don't like no suh strangers!" The guard retorted. William nodded and watched the gate rise up in front of him. He rushed inside the village.

'Don't have to tell me twice' He thought to himself. Glancing around at the town he realized that it was a poor district. The few stores that it did have were barely standing. The homes themselves were basic straw and mud dwellings, even the animals were as sick looking as their surroundings. William quivered in distaste, apparently the Duke had a farther reign than William had originally considered.

William frowned when he saw the brothel, it stood tall, sturdy and looked more homely than the actual homes of the city. It was a sure-tale sign that the Duke had his foot fully set into that town.

Jumping from his horse, William grabbed the reins and walked up to a man sitting outside of one of the disheveled buildings.

"Pardon me sir." William said to the old man. The man glanced up at him, jumped up and starting to walk away.

"I ain't done nothing wrong! Leave me alone!" The man said as he disappeared around the side of the building. William frowned, and continued walking. The villagers were scared, they all sank behind tall windowsills, and short tables. William looked at himself and realized that compared to everyone in that city, he looked to be a powerful and rich man.

William quickened his step. He had to find the man who had killed the troll quickly, before the villagers died from sheer fright!

Then he heard it, men were talking in the alley. They were trying to talk quietly, and they assumed that no one would hear them. But with William's highly trained keen hearing, he made out every word.

"What is it?" One man whispered.

"I don't know Lance!"

"Well it has to be something important if Sir John wanted it so bad!" Lance spoke.

'Sir John?' William thought to himself. That man was a knight, and a very noble and well-known knight at that. William had heard of him before William had ever attained his own knighthood. And William had made it his personal goal to aspire to the greatness that Sir John had. Sir John was a very revered and very powerful knight in all of the Knighthood teachings. Sir John's status in the knight realm was strikingly similar to royalty amongst peasants, and William had been the first knight that had ever gotten as close to being as great as Sir John.

William was sure that Sir John would not have forgotten who William was. How could he? William thought of how he could possibly persuade Sir John to hand over the stolen trinket of the troll, but maybe William's own face would be enough?

"Maybe we should keep it?" Lance asked his companion excitedly.

"Shhhh! Are you mad! No one breaks a bind with John! We will give this to him come morning. For now, let us return and enjoy ourselves." The other man said quietly.

'Morning? Had John even gotten there yet?'

William smirked at himself as he realized that even if Sir John weren't in the city, then the two boys would be an easy target to steal from.

"On second thought . . ." William said aloud as he jumped onto his horse. "Pardon me!" William shouted as he rushed the horse over to them. The men jumped and stared at William.

"Who goes there?!" The man asked. William kept on moving forward, while slowly loosening his cloak.

"Would you mind telling me where Sir John is?" William asked confidently. The other man frowned and stepped forward aggressively.

"Who wants to know?" The man barked rudely.

"Please. I don't mean any trouble . . ." William said while lifting up his arms.

"—and I will pay you for your time." He finished.

The man continued forward and reached for his sword.

"Hold on. That is not necessary." William said frowning. He could feel the anger rising in him. The man didn't stop, William sighed, and reached for his own sword.

But as he did so, his cloak swayed back and a glint of his armor peaked out from beneath.

The other man, whom William assumed was Lance, had a look of surprise on his face. And he jumped forward and grabbed his friend's arm. The man stopped and glared at Lance.

Lance shook his head and then pointed at William. The man turned and he too saw the glint of metal from beneath William's cloak. They both dropped to their knees.

"I'm sorry milord." They said in unison.

"Please, forgive my friend." Lance pleaded. "We are not used to seeing knights in these parts." He whimpered. William smiled. It was just as he had thought. They were squires to Sir John, hence the sudden anger and defensiveness that the first man had gotten when William mentioned Sir John's name.

And just like any knight's squire, they were instantly bound to kneel in respect towards any knight whom crossed their path. William dismounted and rushed over to them. He knelt down in front of them and looked at them suppliantly.

"Now please. It is imperative that I speak with John, immediately!" William ordered. The first man jumped to his feet.

"Please. If you will, follow me." He said, and then grabbed Lance and headed towards the village's sole Inn. William walked and kept up pace with them as he sneered secretly in victory at his game.

The Inn was literally around the corner and it was small; it had few rooms, but was somehow was kept warm and homely in appearance.

"Please, this way." Lance said, as he directed William towards a long hallway, where stairs lay at the end. William took them two at a time and he waited for the squires once he reached the landing. Lance brushed by him, knocked on the door and waited for a reply.

When nothing returned the call of his bangs, Lance stepped closer towards the door.

"Sir John." he paused. "A knight wishes to speak with you." Lance finished. The ear piercing sound of wood scraping across the floor echoed into William's ears. He cringed as he stood impatiently beside Lance.

The door creaked open, allowing a small splinter of light to hit the floorboards. William looked at the man that peered out at him.

"Send him in." The man said, as he traced his eyes skeptically through the hallway. William nodded, and walked inside.

The two squires rushed in behind him, and quietly shut the door, securing the hatch to the doorframe.

The room was dark, and it took a bit for William's eyes to adjust. Once they did, he saw John sitting by a small table. His armor lay neatly next to his bed and a small meal lay untouched at his feet.

Manuscripts and documents lay stretched out in front of John, covering every inch of the small table. John's face held no expression as he glared at William. William could practically feel John's eyes burning a hole right through him. Shuddering from uneasiness between them, William untied his cloak and slid it from his body and draped it over his arm.

A hint of a smile twitched at William's mouth, as he saw John's expression change from suspicion to surprise. John sat back down into his chair with a huge grin.

"Leave us!" He ordered his squires; they nodded and rushed from the room. John stared at William, and once he heard the familiar click of the door shutting, he began his inquiry.

"Sir William." He said as he sighed in disbelief. "Well I haven't seen you in years! Not since our last encounter that is . . . . " He added mischievously.

"Yes, it has been a while." William mused. John leaned forward.

"So, what brings you to my neighborhood?" John inquired as he lowered his voice. William shrugged.

"I was about to ask you the same question." William barked. John shifted uncomfortably in his chair. William had hit a note. No one knew of William's knighthood title being stripped from him, and he intended on keeping it that way. For it had gotten him out of many tight situations before. In fact the only reason that he was able to pull of his fake status, was by the armor that the Duke still allowed him to wear. Only knights could be distinguished among the norm. They were always attired in armor whenever they left the vicinity of their respective homelands.

"Yes well. We can't always be places that we want to be." John stated.

"True."

"But you still have not told me as to why you are here." John hissed.

"Same reason that you are Sir John." William decided that he had said enough, and closed his mouth. He was about to learn everything that he needed to know, John had always fallen for the typical lie of 'I already know'.

"So I take it that you have heard of the Moonstar pendant?" John inquired. William nodded.

"The fact that its holder is invincible to death does not frighten you?" Another nod. But William's Knighthood schooling had trained him well in not showing your surprise, but Sir John was trained in the same manner as William, so they both could have been toying with one another.

"Well, unfortunately I don't have it." John added coldly and turned back to his documents. William smiled, and walked up behind him.

"I never thought that you did." Came William's reply, and he slowly walked away. John whirled around.

"And why is that?"

"Why would you do your own dirty work? Surely a knight of *your* stature has two squires for a reason." William said as he smiled wickedly. John stared at William's back.

"Me having squires, have *nothing* to do with this." John said angrily.

William spun around and stared at Sir John.

"Then you, being the knight that you are, *have* the pendent yourself." John glared at him. "—And you are seriously willing to lie to me, to keep it? Who sent you John?!"

John slowly rose to his feet and came within inches of William's face. His breath stank of barbequed meet and bitter wine. William's nose twitched as his sensitive senses activated.

"I do not lie."

William raised an eyebrow. John continued.

"If you are assuming that my squires have the pendant, than you are horribly mistaken. Nothing that they do escapes my knowledge."

"Ah! And that is where you are wrong!" William said, placing a finger on John's nose like a mother punishing her disobedient child.

"For you see. Your squires *did*, in fact, have it." William said as he paced within the room.

"*Did?*" John said sternly.

"Yes, until it was traded in the marketplace. Hence why I am here right now, in this very room." John shifted his weight back and forth nervously on each foot.

William continued his charade, feeding off of John's uneasiness. William was about to beat the strongest knight . . . . *again*.

"So, if you desire the pendant that both of us are so *desperately* trying to find. I would suggest that you track down the pallet merchant that just left this city." William paused. "Before I do." William said with a wicked grin. John looked defiantly at him.

"You wouldn't possibly being trying to defeat me are you?" John asked rudely, with raised eyebrows.

"Why? Wasn't it enough of an embarrassment last time?" William said with another evil smile, John frowned. "In the mean time, I really must be going. My journey continues south."

"South?"

"Yes. There are rumors of a dead troll." William watched as John's eyes lit up with laughter. William knew why the older knight was so cheerful. And William realized who had killed that troll.

Reeling back around, William placed his cloak back onto his shoulders and headed towards the door.

"Sir William."

"Yes Sir John."

"Why not stop the merchant yourself? Why are you helping me, by telling me where the pendant is?"

William stopped in his tracks.

"Because once, long ago, I almost destroyed your reputation." William wished that it was true, him helping Sir John, but he couldn't risk losing the pendant. And Sir John would have been a great ally to have, but it wasn't going to happen then. Yet again the Duke had ruined another important matter.

William walked out slamming the door behind him. He practically knocked over Lance as he did so.

"S—ss—sorry milord!" The squire stuttered. William smiled and patted the boy's back.

"Quite alright lad." He replied, and headed fast down the stairs. His horse stood sleeping, tied to its post.

"Come on boy! We're done here!" He said as he nudged the stallion awake. William climbed onto the saddle, wheeled the horse around, and kicked it into a gallop.

Once they had passed under the gates, and were a distance from the town, William pulled out the pendant. He raised it to eyelevel and stared at it.

It really was quite exquisite. It had what looked like a giant diamond in the center, which William assumed was the so-called 'Moonstar'.

"So *this* is why my master is never injured, sick and has so much knowledge. This has kept him alive." William said in awe.

"The only fragment left of the Moonstar gem, in all its glory, has been held by the Duke of Greenwiche this entire time." William said dumbfounded. The 'Moonstar' stone was the only fragment still left from the ancient gem relic known as the Moon-Spark. A stone that was said to have held so much power, that the ancient ancestors of mankind had destroyed it in order to prevent man from destroying themselves.

In his knighthood training, William laughed when he had first learned of the stones destruction, so much for *preventing* mankind's annihilation. If only the ancestors could see them now.

Nevertheless, William raised the chain over his neck and stuffed it inside of his breastplate. It seemed to fit perfectly against the medal.

William felt a sudden wave of energy and strength wash over him. It was intoxicating. The medallion was very, very powerful; and the last person it should belong to was the Duke of Greenwiche.

Chapter Six

HARNESSING THE POWER

JENEVY SOARED THROUGH the sky, as she stared at the ground far below. Her night vision was amazing as it provided her the illumination and clarity that she needed. It also had magnifying properties to it; she was able to focus on far away objects with just the squint of her eyes. As helpful as that may sound, it was also a nuisance. For even the slightest bit of peering would trigger it at terrible times.

Jenevy stared at creatures that slept peacefully upon the forest floor. But the animals that did not sleep were hunting, and the creatures that they hunted were dying. Often displaying gruesome sights that any human being wouldn't instantly wish to become a vegetarian and to vow off meat for eternity.

She had no idea of what she was looking for, but she knew that she could not stop until she had found it. She had to press on, she had find someone, anyone that would understand her powers and how to use them.

But finding someone like that, one whom could also keep the secrecy of her training would be the true test of her findings. Being inconspicuous, she would have to find a trainer, get his allegiance and ultimately gain his trust.

Not only would he have to be skilled in the forms of power and magic, but of fighting and combat as well. She was going to have to find, in her eyes, the ultimate warrior. But where would one look for such a being?

'A mage' Jenevy chimed to herself. Now she knew that to look for, but where to find one?

"A mage of all trades I desire, lead me to what I require!" Her words rang out against the sky; the power within them chimed in sickening tones.

A beam of light lit up upon the ground below, signaling the direction that she had to follow.

Jenevy flapped her wings following the light towards a small village. Then pulling in her wings, she plummeted towards the ground.

The sun was steadily rising, and Jenevy desperately needed a low profile if she were to keep up the hunt.

A barn lay at the outskirts of the town, its broken doors barely hung from its hinges. Jenevy dove towards it and landed softly upon the ground near its opening. Surely no one would see her there, and even if they did they would have hard having to explain what they had witnessed.

Folding in her wings, she pressed them flat against her back. From the front she looked practically normal, until one were to walk to her backside and see her wings.

Jenevy strained to look behind her shoulder and stared at her wings.

"Well, this won't do." She said aloud. Sneaking around the corner of the barn, she approached one of the windows. Peering through it, she made sure that it was empty. Nothing moved inside.

Jenevy ran back to the doors and rushed into the disheveled barn. It was dark, cold and damp. The smell of mildew lingered in the air. The rafters held multitudes of cobwebs hanging from its limbs. And tiny insects urged one another forwards as they scrambled for food.

Rotting hay lay in heaps in the back, complete with a few random rodents scuttling through it. Jenevy frowned in disgust. Even if it was comparably better than her previous shelters, she still hated rodents.

Jenevy's cloak had missing during her flight, and she had to find something adequate enough to not only cover her enormously folded wings, but to disguise her armor and features as well.

Once she had examined the entire barn for a cloak, feeling exceptionally defeated, she retreated back towards the entrance. Jenevy frowned in annoyance, and placed her hands upon her hips.

"Wait a minute!" She exclaimed. She thought of a cloak, concentrated on the design of the intricate robe, and then snapped her fingers. A black shroud materialized out of nowhere and landed upon her arm.

Jenevy gasped in amusement. She had found a new way to get what she wanted from her newly acquired powers. She was also pretty impressed at her witty thinking.

'Maybe this power isn't too bad after all!" She mused. Swinging the cloak over her shoulders, she fastened it around her neck. Bringing the excess fabric around from her back, she made sure that it hung loosely in front of her. It concealed her armor and wings perfectly; even when she moved.

Raising the hood, she slowly strolled out of the barn. Using her vision, she zoomed her eyesight into the heart of the village. She scanned the area, whomever she was supposed to find would be encircled in light.

Her first reconnaissance presented nothing, so she reluctantly entered the village. The town was tiny, and no amount of money would fix the broken down buildings that lay in shambles against the streets.

Even the street, couldn't even be considered a street. It was so overgrown with nature, that Jenevy's metallic boots were getting tangled within vines at every other step. Jenevy groaned in agitation.

Surveying everything that she passed, she soon realized that nothing was encircled in light. Perhaps she had missed her target? Or worse, what if her powers had not ignited her mark? How was she supposed to find this supposed *'mage'* that her powers were so sure was there?

Down a small alley way, a small boy lay sitting up against the broken bricked wall of a building. Jenevy approached him slowly, she hoped that he would not frighten easily.

HEATHER DIROCCO

"Boy." She said quietly. He looked up at her. "Do you know of a mage in this town?" She said carefully. Somehow, she felt that a mage might not be too welcome among these people. Her senses were exhibiting signs to her of evil and dissolution.

The boy silently nodded at her. Jenevy smiled down at him.

"Would you mind telling me where he is?" She asked delicately. The boy stared at her for a moment, but Jenevy knew that a child of his age would have a short attention span. That and the combination of his age, would make him forget every having met her.

"Over that way! At the Inn!" he shrieked, and then ran off. Jenevy frowned as she watched him disappear behind another building.

"Thanks." She said under her breath. She turned in the direction that the boy had pointed, and saw a two-storied building lying on the edge of town. Doors outlined the outside walls of the building, equipped with their own balconies on the second floor.

Jenevy walked towards it, and saw a sign hanging sideways off of the front.

"Tortured Mind Inn? What kind of a town is this!?" She whispered to herself. That was when Jenevy started to notice the townsfolk. They too had a dreary, creepy resentment about them. A presence that would make any evil seeking man want to run away in fear.

The whole town gave Jenevy the chills, and she wanted nothing more than to leave that place. She quickened her step and rushed towards the Inn. Once inside, the Inn Keeper lifted his stare to gaze upon her.

"May I help you stranger?" He asked curiously. Jenevy looked at him.

"Yes, maybe you can. I heard word that there was a mage dwelling within your Inn. I would like a word with him if you please." She said politely. The Inn Keeper stared at her with doubt on his face. Only blinking once to spit onto the floor.

Jenevy grimaced in disgust. Thanking the hooded shadow that covered her face that her expression had been concealed. The man was going to need some force used upon him in order to get information.

"I'm going to ask one more time old man. Tell me where the mage is, or I'll rip this whole place apart and find him myself!" She bellowed menacingly.

The Inn Keeper frowned.

"This is *my* Inn. Anyone that comes in or out of here, I know about. So your stinkin mage aint come in these parts!" Jenevy winced at the Inn Keepers use of vocabulary.

Giving up, she headed back towards the door. A weird feeling washed over her as she walked past the few people sitting downstairs. Someone was watching her.

Jenevy walked outside and rushed down an alley. But the feeling remained. She turned down another alley, and then tiptoed into a darkened doorway.

But nothing walked past her. Again she walked down the alley, and then stopped instantaneously in her tracks. She twirled around with folded arms.

A man nearly collided with her. Jenevy stared fiercely at him.

"Who are you!" She ordered.

"My . . .my name is Jeremy!" he shrieked.

"Why were you following me?!"

"You asked for a mage at the Inn. I know where one is!"

"How can I trust you?" Jenevy asked ruthlessly. Jeremy swallowed.

"I guess you can either kill or trust me! Nothing that I say now will convince you to trust me!" Jeremy cried. Jenevy glared evilly at him, deciphering the meaning behind his words. Quicker than lightening she whipped out a dagger, yanked Jeremy backwards into her arm, and pointed the dagger at his groin. She whispered briskly into his ear.

"If you try anything, I swear to you that you your fate will be something worse than death."

Jeremy quickly nodded in fear. Jenevy released him and shoved him forward, practically slamming him to the ground. Jeremy looked back at her, rubbed his neck and pointed down the alley.

"Please . . . . follow me." Jeremy stepped forward and walked quickly into the shadows. Jenevy re-sheathed her dagger and followed cautiously behind him.

Walking up to a doorway on the side of a small building, Jeremy grabbed the handle and stared back at her.

"He is in here." Jeremy pushed open the door and stepped inside. Jenevy nodded, and placed her hand firmly onto the hilt of her sword, she too stepped into the foreboding darkness of the building.

Before her eyes could even adjust to the dim lighting, the door had slammed behind her. Wheeling around she saw a frail man pressed up against the door and was staring threateningly at her.

"Who is this?!" He screamed. Jeremy rushed over with arms raised.

"Master, master! Tis alright! It is just someone that is looking for you!" He cried.

"And you let them in?! What is the matter with you?!" The man shrieked in alarm.

"Master! They do not wish to harm you! All that they need is your help!" Jeremy tried to say calmly. The mage glared at Jeremy, and then looked over at Jenevy. He surveyed her image, noting the weapons adorned to her side.

"I will be the one to judge that!" The man bellowed, and then shoved Jeremy to the side. The man feebly walked over to a table. The table was scattered with books, drawings, and other devices that Jenevy had no explanation for.

"Tell me stranger. Why are you seeking me out?" The mage asked as he began to organize the contents of the table. Jenevy stepped closer, staying well within the shadows.

"Your guidance." She said firmly.

"Guidance? Of what?" The mage inquired.

"Magic." Jenevy's voice echoed. The mage looked at her.

"I already have a squire. I will not take on another." He said irritated.

"I am not here to be your squire, but your student."

"Tis the same thing. What do you wish to know of? Potions? Spells? Plants?"

Jenevy frowned, then stepped a bit closer.

"Perhaps it would be best if I just showed you." She slowly stepped into the light, she brought out her hand from under her cloak and raised her palm up.

"To show him what knowledge I inquire, produce for me a ball of fire." The mage raised an eyebrow at her. The veins in Jenevy's arm began to ignite with color, radiating down to her palm. Instantly her hand started to glow, and to the mage's astonishment and amazement, a bright blue ball of fire seemed to sparked up out of her hand where it levitated there until she made it disappear.

Jenevy closed her palm into a fist, and the flame disappeared into millions of embers. The mage's face filled with shock, and his books, within his arms, fell to the floor with a clank.

"Impossible!" He whispered.

"No. It is very much real. And like I said, I need your help." Jenevy said again. She stared at the mage.

"You . . . you don't need my help!" The mage stammered.

"Why?" Jenevy asked in disbelief.

"Because . . . you already know magic!" The mage said in shock. Jenevy shook her head.

"No. I have power within me, a power that was given to me for one purpose. I have the knowledge of my power's capabilities, but I lack the will to control it. I don't know how to control it from within, or to let it flow freely and by sole instinct."

The mage nodded his head, and sat down on a chair. Jeremy stood back in wonder.

"Allow me to explain."

After a few hours, Jenevy had finished explaining to the mage everything about her. From her being sold, to her at the castle, her escape, then to how she had gotten the forces of darkness from the trapped spirits.

"So, you have the knowledge of you power? But that's it?" Jeremy asked puzzled.

"I can't believe that a man like that is allowed to live! I have heard of the Duke of Greenwiche, but only as the owner of the lands. Not as the evil fiend that you have just described." The mage whispered.

"But Jenevy, if you know how to use your powers, than how can we help?" Jeremy asked puzzled.

"Because, I *have* to use it instantly! Not by casting spells or chanting rhymes! I need my power to flow just by impulse."

"Jenevy that will take months. Even years to accomplish." The mage stated. Jenevy nodded.

"I know. But it's what I have to do. Besides, to the Dark Lord I am already dead!"

"You know. She does have a point master." Jeremy looked at the mage. The mage nodded, as he paced the room.

"Alright. I'll do it. But I only have one question. You said that your *spells* are permanent correct?"

Jenevy nodded.

"And only your spells?"

She nodded again.

"What spells have you cast then? To know of this?" The mage asked. Jenevy sighed and closed her eyes. She stood up, placed her helmet onto her head and walked over to the shadows. Turning around she dropped her cloak and her wings shot out, spreading to their enormous length. Jenevy looked up at the men, her eyes were glowing their deep, crimson red. The men jumped.

"Tis demonic work!" Whispered Jeremy. Jenevy with her ornamented armor, magnificent wings, and fiery red eyes, portrayed the silhouette of a demon in the darkness. Her wing span was more than seven feet wide, and her eyes shone out like blood. The helmet upon her head had two, long spikes that stretched out behind her, casting a shadow of two small horns upon her head. Jenevy's hair twisted and twirled out to her side as enormous amounts of intense energy radiated out from her. She stared at them.

"Amazing. Do you understand what you are?!" The mage asked excitedly. Jenevy stepped back into the light, once the sun's rays hit her eyes they faded back to normal. She shook her head at the mage.

"You are the Knight of Darkness! The Knight foretold many years ago by my forefathers! A legend: 'In the darkness a demon will emerge, with power of light and dark. In this Knight, the dawn of a new era will begin. And all those who oppose it, will be destroyed from this earth'. You are the Devil's Knight!"

Jenevy looked at the mage like he was crazy.

"The Devil's Knight? I am not from the depths of hell, nor do I work for him."

"It is not that you are from him, it's more like you have the powers of him. The souls, whose powers you now control, have become evil. They have given you the power of death. But with you not being evil, you also bring light."

Jenevy folded her wings back down, and stared at her hands; she ignited a fire sphere and stared at it.

"So, I am the Devil's Knight? Hmmm. Maybe I might be able to strike fear into the Duke after all?"

"And with how you look at night? You just might give him a heart attack!

The mage said with a wicked smile. Jenevy made the fire brighter, then shot it out against the wall. It exploded into a million embers, evaporating into the bricks.

"Let's get started!" She said with a smile.

Chapter Seven

THE LAST TIME

WILLIAM'S RETURN TO the castle was a hard one. His gut had never before twisted and turned as much as it did on that day. The Duke of Greenwiche was a *very* powerful man, and that was without the use of his Moonstar Pendant. William knew that by returning the pendant to the Duke, that his evil realm would be even stronger, and would grow even more. But, due to William's sacred honor of abiding to the orders of whomever he was to serve, he reluctantly had to return the necklace to his master.

Bringing his horse through the secret entrance, William gradually led his steed towards the barn. Once inside, he dismounted and threw the reins over a post. Patting the horse's shoulder he exited the dismal barn and walked towards the castle. He had barely made it inside when he heard his master yelling for him.

"William! Get in here now!" William groaned and rushed towards the library.

"I take it that you were successful?" The Duke barked. William nodded.

"Yes milord."

"Then give it to me!"

William looked down at his armor, the pendant lay hidden beneath almost as if it belonged there. William pulled the pendant up over his head, stared at it for a moment and then flung it over to the Duke.

"Yes! My precious stone!" The Duke's eyes filled with greed and he clutched the stone to his chest. "You did kill the troll?" The Duke asked without raising his eyes. William frowned as he watched the Duke raise the pendant up and over his head, sliding it down over his neck.

"Yes." William lied.

"Good." The Duke whipped around and walked away.

"Oh, and William. You are to retrieve another girl for me in the morning. The papers are on your bed." The Duke's voice echoed from the hallway as he disappeared out of sight.

William rolled his eyes in wonderment as to how the Duke never got tired of his charade. William walked out of the library and towards his room. He silently prayed that John would send another thief to that prison, and destroy the Duke once and for all.

The next morning, William woke up early and headed out to get his delivery for the week. William knew that a new girl meant another girl had perished.

'Jenevy, you better still be alive.' He thought to himself.

William slumped forward onto his horse's saddle, and headed East to a town locally known as Mistybrook. It was a large town only in comparison to the other smaller towns. But all in all, it was still very small. The only thing that Mistybrook provided more than the other cities was more shopkeepers, and more women. Mistybrook was known for its brothels, and the Duke never forgot that.

The woman that William was to retrieve was the younger daughter of a peasant. This was of no surprise to William; he usually stole the daughters from peasants. But the unfortunate part of the girl's fate, was that she was given up only because her father could not pay his taxes.

So, instead of being killed, the father eagerly shoved his daughter as a payment. William hated the men who were so willing to deliver their own kin to the whims of a sniveling man just to save their sorry hides. He himself would have rather chosen death, than to force his daughter to a life of misery. William prayed that if he were to ever have children that it would never come down to that.

William unrolled the small scroll that had the written instructions on the girl's whereabouts and delivery. Hopefully, she was not another one that was to be kidnapped while her father slept. Luckily, the instructions simply stated that William was to take the woman as soon as he arrived, and to leave without payment.

Mistybrook was a short distance from Greenwiche, so William would be arriving there before midday.

William rerolled the scroll, and urged his horse into a gallop. He passed through the gate of Greenwiche, and the other guards cheered him on as he ran into the woods.

The village was owned by the Duke, which meant that no one would give William any trouble once he entered its gates. Since Mistybrook was within the vicinity of the Duke's reign, that meant that William did not have to restrain a girl for days at a time. It would be a simple snatch and deliver.

When William arrived at Mistybrook, the girl he grabbed had no idea of what was happening. William got her onto his horse and then climbed behind her and rode off, instantly the girl was crying.

William ignored her just like he did all of the others and raced back to Greenwiche. The girl cried the entire time, until the creaking of the gates opening, faltered her tears.

William rushed his horse through Greenwiche's gates, and trotted his horse to the steps of the castle. He slid from the saddle, and reached up a hand to assist the maiden down. She folded her arms and ignored them.

"Madam, either you come down from there with my assistance, or I will force you down without it." She sneered and looked away from him. William shrugged.

"Suit yourself." He grabbed her arm and yanked her to the ground. She fell to her side upon the ground and looked up at him in shock.

"I warned you." He said sternly. The maiden stood to her feet and brushed off her skirt. William grabbed her arm and pulled her inside.

"William?" It was the Duke. "Ah! Who is this remarkable creature?" The Duke asked. William pulled his head back in aghast at the stench of liquor. The Duke was drunk on brandy, which meant a lot of pain was about to befall the maiden that would share the Duke's bed that night. Which William knew would be the one that he had just brought inside.

"Master, this is the maiden from the Gallagher home." William said, introducing the maiden. The Dark Lord sneered and walked up to her. He smelled her hair and smiled. The girl was shaking at every touch that the Duke inflicted. The Duke reached a hand to her waist, and then slid it down to between her legs. The girl smacked his hand away, and the Duke reacted by smacking her to the floor. The girl cried in alarm. The Duke smiled again.

"Ah! A virgin! This is going to be a great night!" He said smacking his lips. The Duke watched her as she stood back up, and he stepped towards her. He grabbed at her breasts. The girl shrieked, and he smacked her hard across the cheek. She shut up instantly.

"You will learn your place young lady." He yelled. She bit her lip, as the Duke continued to grope her. William stood there, waiting desperately for the Duke to dismiss him. He had had to watch his master go through the whole thing before, and he was not eager to do it again.

But the Duke was drunk, and just like last time, William was going to have to watch. Sound-lashings, three days of no food with confinement and extra work was not worth William's unapproved dismissal.

The maiden was trembling violently as the Duke's eyes filled with lust. He began to tear away at her clothes, at the girl shrieked and tried to run. The Duke grabbed her and wheeled her to the floor where he was instantly on top of her. William frowned as he saw the Duke's hand reach down in between the girl's legs. William looked away and tried to drown out the noises that were about to happen. But he couldn't. The Duke was raping the young girl, and she screamed in agony. Her blood curdling screams filled William's head to the point of insanity. William's blood began to boil in anger, and he too began to shake, he teetered back and forth in his stance. When William could take it no more he decided that he was going to stop the Duke from his evil masquerade.

But William was too late, the girl lay dead upon the floor and the Duke was wiping his hands clean of her blood. William clenched his teeth, and squeezed his hands into fists.

The Duke drunkenly stumbled away, laughing wickedly into the hallway. William watched him leave, and walked over to the dead girl. The Duke had smashed her head into the floor, and a look of terror was forever frozen into her face.

William picked her up and carried her out of the castle and towards the graves. The girl had died in less than an hour from when William had picked her up, the shortest death out of all of the Duke's prior maidens.

William yelled in anger as he stepped outside.

"John! If you don't kill this man, then I will do it myself!"

❖ "No, no, NO! It must come from your heart! Don't think, just DO!"

Jenevy nodded in understandment and then lunged into the air. She aimed her hand at the forest and then her fusing powers shot out of her palm. A lightning bolt seared from her hand, splitting the tree in two.

"That's it! Remarkable! In two years and you are fighting like you have done this your entire life!" The mage shouted animatedly.

Jenevy smiled as she floated down onto the stump of the sizzling tree. She squatted and looked over at the mage.

"I think . . . that you are ready!" The mage said with a warm smile.

"But, how can you be sure?" Jenevy asked worriedly. The mage looked at her like a father who stares at his child who had just taken their first step.

"Jenevy. I have taught you all that I know. It is up to you to use it in real life situations." The mage said calmly.

"But, what if I cannot defeat the Duke?" Jenevy asked sadly. The mage looked to the trees.

"That is why you must practice on your own. It is all up to you how your story will play out. And when you do finally confront the Duke, you will know if you are ready or not." The mage said as he looked back at her. He rose up a hand towards her. Jenevy dropped down to the ground with a thud and stepped over to him.

"Take care of yourself Lady Jenevy. The best advice that I can give you is to not criticize your strengths. You know your capabilities, don't think, just act." He said with a smile. Jenevy gripped his wrist with her hand, and the mage pulled her to him. They embraced one another for a moment, and then stepped back.

Jenevy smiled back at him, and wrapped her cloak over her body.

"Here! Don't forget this!" Jeremy tossed a book over at Jenevy. She caught it without even looking. She brought the book down and stared at its cover.

"It's of spells. The permanent ones!" Jeremy said with a grin. Jenevy looked up at him and smiled.

"Thank you!" She said as she walked over to him and gave him a hug.

"Good luck Lady Jenevy, and may God be with you."

Jenevy nodded and walked into the dark foliage of the forest.

"I'm sure that I'm the last person God wants to be with." Jenevy muttered.

❖ William shoveled the hay onto the wagon, he hated that part of his work where he had to clean out the rank flooring of the barn like some servant. Wiping the sweat from his brow he shoveled the last bit of festering animal bedding onto the buggy.

"Sir William. Need any help?" It was the stable boy.

"Do you really have to ask?" William said irritably. The stable boy shrugged his shoulders, grabbed a bale of hay and then brought it inside.

William wiped his hands off on his leg and then looked up at the castle. He hadn't heard of Jenevy at all. He didn't know if she were still denying his Master, or if she were even still alive. Which was really starting to worry him, it had been too long to have not of heard of anything.

"Oh! Did you hear?" The stable boy asked excitedly interrupting William's thoughts. William looked back at him.

"About what?"

"The Master will be leaving for a few weeks!"

"What? When?"

"Tomorrow. A messenger arrived this morning with the news!"

"Are you certain?" William asked. The boy grinned at him.

"I didn't learn eavesdropping from the best, just so that I didn't have to use it!"

William smiled and shook his head.

"I think you and I need to stop talking to one another." William announced sarcastically. The boy laughed.

"Sir William." A guard entered the barn. William looked over his shoulder at the man.

"The Duke needs to see you."

William nodded and brushed off his pants. The guard returned back to the castle. William looked over at the stable boy.

"Keep working. I should be back momentarily."

"Should huh?" The boy asked skeptically. William rolled his eyes at him. The stable boy laughed and continued to unload the bales of hay.

William ran out and rushed up the steps to the castle. A guard opened the door for him as he approached. William nodded in gratitude and stepped inside.

Once William's eyes adjusted to the dimly lit castle's main hallway, he stepped forward to find his Master.

William walked down the hallway, his footsteps echoing off of the walls. Secretly hoping that he would catch a glimpse of Jenevy, William paused every now and then to glance into the different rooms.

"Damn it Clarence. If you choose to be this indignant than I just might choose to have you hanged!" William frowned as the Duke's boorish voice interrupted William's search.

"Yes milord." Came the reply of Clarence the butler. William sneered and walked towards the voice that he so hated to hear.

Reaching the doorway of the grand ballroom, William was caught off-guard by Clarence smacking into him.

"Oof!" The skinny butler exclaimed. William quickly moved out of the fast moving butlers way.

"Sorry Clarence." William apologized. Clarence nodded at him.

"Tis no bother Sir William. But you best hurry on in there. Master is in one of his foul moods today." The butler stated and he rushed towards the kitchen.

William watched him leave then proceeded into the ballroom. He felt as if he were walking towards his doom.

Kneeling onto one knee, William announced himself to the sinister Lord.

"Ah! Sir William! At last you appear!" The Duke declared. William's eyes slowly looked up at the Duke.

"Yes milord."

"Well then, I am sure that you have heard of my traveling that I am about to embark upon?"

"Indeed yes I have milord."

"And I am also sure that you returning my most precious possession went unnoticed?"

"Milord?" William asked as he squinted in confusion.

"Yes well. I will be traveling to the Eastern edge of the kingdom. The King has requested my presence and I need you to go with me to guard me from the dangerous foes of the land.

"It will be a long journey, a few weeks in total. You remember it don't you? We travelled it before?" William nodded. "Excellent. So, I will be reinstating your Knighthood. Being as it may, you do have a few years of catching up to do. But, nevertheless the king and I are in agreement."

William's jaw dropped. He was dumbfounded. He never imagined that he was to ever regain his knighthood. Even though he was always treated as a knight, even allowed to retain his hard earned armor and weapons, he was never actually the 'knight' that he had worked to hard to achieve. He had felt horrible not being a knight, but by regaining his title by achieving an act for his Master, was nothing worth bragging about either.

"You may take on a squire if you wish. Might I suggest the stable boy that you are so fond of? Be it as it may, your duties will still remain the same." The Duke sneered and walked past William. He turned around and added.

"But remember that I was the one who stripped away your title before. And I will do it again if you force me to." And the Duke left the room.

William slowly stood to his feet. With a smile, he turned to take his leave as well.

"One thing in exchange for another. Be a knight, but escort an Evil Duke to an Evil King at the same time. Some luck I am having."

Chapter Eight

A New Beginning

J ENEVY LOVED THE smell of the forest, especially when the sun first rises to greet the dew. She was very fond of the birds' morning chirps and songs as they ate their breakfast of hiding crickets, insects, and sweet nectar.

Jenevy walked slowly upon the mossy earth, taking in the pure beauty around her. She would definitely miss the simple things that brought warmth to her cheeks.

It had been about a month or so since she had left the guidance of the mage and his student. They had both turned into very dear friends to her, and she had hoped that they would meet again.

Slowly the smells of the forest were replaced with the smell of stale hay, and burning wood. The sour stench of mold lingered within the scents of a human dwelling. A village had to be near; only humans were obtuse enough to invade the sweet aroma of nature with the unnatural.

But as Jenevy strolled forward, a clearing arose signaling a dwelling just as she had assumed, but it was not as she had anticipated.

"Or perhaps a castle?" She said to herself. A huge castle was erected in front of her, and it was much larger than the Duke of Greenwiche's. It too had a large, encircling wall that protected the castle grounds, and a dainty village with small homes lay outside of it, all squished together like a pile of seasoned hay.

A dirt road led through the village, where it rounded its way up and around to the gates of the castle. Jenevy could sense magic from within the castle, but it was a very dark, and evil magic and the decrypted and disheveled village were getting the worst of that magic.

Jenevy squinted her eyes so that her vision would zoom into the streets of the town. Once focused, her stomach began to quench in disgust, the villagers were very frightened people, who were walking strangely along the streets. They looked as if they were dying, or about to die, most of the villagers were hungry and dirty. Tall armored guards roamed the streets as well, and they were constantly pushing and poking at the townsfolk in laughter.

Jenevy frowned and looked around, she zoomed into the gates of the castle. Only two men stood watch, and whenever a villager strolled by they would throw rocks at them and then laugh as the scared people ran in fear.

A large wooden sign was slammed into the ground near the gates. It read: LéFiévre Castle.

"Elvin for snake." Jenevy remarked. "How befitting." She sneered. Jenevy sank back into the shadows of the forest, closed her eyes and clenched her fists. A swirl of magic encircled her; it twisted from around her feet and twirled upwards towards her head. When the magic passed over a part of her body, that component would transform.

Once the magic swirled over her, and vaporized over her head, she had changed into one of the villagers that she had just seen, being a perfectly mirrored reflection of that villager. They could have easily passed as twins. Using a temprorary invisibility spell, her wings were concealed from the common eye.

Jenevy walked back out of the shadows and focused her vision again. Almost instantly she surged forward through the air, and appeared within the part of the village that she had been staring at. She smiled with content at the stage of her powers.

She stepped forward and pretended as if she had been there the entire time, and hunched over as if in constant humility. First and foremost, she had to find the town's mage. She sensed that there was one near, and if she wasn't mistaken he too was in hiding.

Completing her ensemble of a frightened villager, Jenevy walked through the streets, bowed her head, and shook her body with fear. She honed in on her instincts and approached a small building.

The building was made of straw and clay, and it was barely standing. She pushed open the door and stepped inside. Jenevy jumped back against the door, slamming it shut. The room smelled of death. It was musky, and the muggy air was enveloped with dust to the point of suffocation.

Jenevy winced and covered her mouth with her sleeve. She was in a home, or rather a poor excuse of a home. The one-roomed structure was barely lit, and its walls looked worse than the outside. Food was rotting on the small wooden table, and the one and only bed was a piece of buck cloth with a mound of hay for a pillow.

A barely used feather pen and paper lay next to it, along with a melted candle. Touching the wick with her finger, she lit it aflame with a spark. She grabbed the quill pen and small book. Opening its pages, she saw a language inside that shocked her and she almost dropped the book in response.

"Beolithan!" She said excitedly. A few select individuals only knew of the ancient language of the Shempshay Dragons, and even fewer actually knew of its existence. Even with how powerful Jenevy's magic was, it would take all of her strength just to learn a character of that demonic language.

The writing was in shapes, designs, pictures, and not in simple hieroglyphics or alphabets like the rest of the world's languages. Dragons were a very ancient species, and their first ancestors used flame to write their stories, etching it permanently into the stone as they would write.

So, to any other person looking upon that book, they would see it as an artist's sketchbook and not for what it really was. Jenevy was suddenly very happy that she was allowed to read from the books in the Duke's library after all, or she too would not have recognized that book for what it truly was.

"That explains the hardly used quill. The mage had to use magic in order to write this journal. "But . . . . where is the mage?" She asked aloud.

Jenevy set the book and pen back down next to the candle and looking around the small room, she searched for the mage. She sensed that he had been there, but couldn't discover when he was there last. Snapping her eyes shut, she ignited her magic and then re-opened them. Glowing red, her magic showed her shadows of people hued with scarlet, it displayed what had happened with the mage.

He had been there; she could see him as he walked through the door. He set down food upon the small table and proceeded to sit down upon his bed where he began to write within his book. Right as he began to conjure up his magic, the door shattered open. Men rushed inside and they lunged at him. The mage jumped to his feet in alarm, as the men restrained him. Another man came through the doorway and this man had an evil presence about him. The man had powers that blocked out his image from Jenevy's mind. The man used the same magic to bind the mage, a dark magic, one that physically hurt the mage, and restrained him with pain and terror. The dark shadows of men disappeared out of the hut and Jenevy's vision returned to normal. She looked back at the book, and picked it up.

"He wrote something in here. Something he did not want anyone to read. I need to know what is in this book!" She said as she too faded into the shadows.

The journey to the mountains of Fenloré was a tedious and perilous task.

Usually an image of the place in her mind would instantly transport her to the vicinity of her vision. But since the Fenloré Mountains were rarely documented, let alone pictured, she had to find them the hard way.

By following stories, folklore, and urban legends of the legendary homestead, she had to piece together the pieces in order to determine the right route. For the mountains of Fenloré held a mystery long in the making, they were once the lair of the dragons, but not just any dragons, but the mystical, royal dragons of Shempshay.

Those dragons were the oldest, the wisest, and the strongest of any known serpents and were known by any living creature upon the planet.

Legends spoke of an old species of dragons so large, that trees looked like twigs in comparison. These ancient creatures were so powerful, that the sun's heat couldn't compare to the heat of one nostril. But, like all legends, accreditation was hard to prove on any account.

It was even said that the Shempshay dragons carried the supernatural powers over everything and anything natural. They were able to influence even the smallest of elements, and to forge it into a supernatural source.

So whether the legends were true or not, something deadly and powerful had inhibited these stories into creation, and Jenevy was going to take every precaution in deciphering them.

Jenevy remembered from many of her readings, that the original ancestral dragons were intelligent, soft-mannered, and even kind. They were the so called creators of the Beolithan language, and had actually helped mankind become the creatures of intelligence that they are. But man, as easily corrupted as they are, turned evil. With that evil, came about a great hunting of the ancient dragons. The dragons were almost completely destroyed, but the ones that had survived had reverted back into a creature, that had evolved into a beast of pure instincts for the sole point of preservation.

So any hint of whether the Shempshay dragons were even still alive, was clouded by the current presence of the demonic dragons of the present.

Jenevy slowly brought in her wings, folding them so that she could dive to the side and towards the ground. A small village had caught her eye, and an even stronger element compelled her senses.

'Magic.' She said to herself. She landed upon the ground with a soft thump, and camouflaged her huge wings. She crouched down, and tried to hone in on her senses.

Once she figured out the general direction of the hue of supernatural, she stood up and walked towards it.

A short sentry noticed her as she approached and he stood up tall and readjusted his spear so that it aimed straight at her heart. She smirked at him.

'Like that will do much.' She thought in amusement.

But the guard seemed determined in his movements and shoved out his spear in a more threatening manner. Apparently the village was not at all too thrilled of visitors.

"Halt! State your purpose!" The young sentry ordered. Jenevy faltered for a moment.

"Easy guard, I am not one to fear." She replied cautiously. The boy tightened his grip and ordered again.

"Nevertheless, no one comes here without a purpose. So state it, or be on your way."

Jenevy rolled her eyes.

"Or what?"

The guard was taken aback, and he looked at her uneasily.

"Or . . . or I shall have to kill you!" The boy stammered. Jenevy laughed, apparently this young guard was not used to people challenging his commands.

'Not likely.' Jenevy thought to herself. She shifted her weight onto one leg.

"I am here to seek aid from a mage." She lied. But to her dismay, the sentry didn't falter.

"We *have* no mage." The guard barked. Jenevy frowned. *That* she knew. The magic that she had sensed was far darker than any mage should be. The mage's energy felt surprisingly close in resemblance to her own powers, but much weaker. She had to come up with another idea and quick. She didn't want to have to kill the young soldier, who apparently looked forced into his position anyway.

"Alright. Can you direct me to where there might be one? I am in need of magical expertise." She asked slowly. The sentry dropped his spear a little, BINGO!

"On what?" He asked curiously.

"I have had a spell cast upon me. A curse really. And I am afraid that only a mage can help me. But I haven't been able to find one."

"A curse? What kind of curse?" The boy asked. He squinted his eyes as if trying to see her better. Jenevy's eyes widened.

'Maybe I should have thought this one through.' She quickly tried to think of a good curse, but given the circumstances, she didn't want the dark forces within that village to a get a hold of her powers, especially a dark, evil curse. Instead, she decided to bargain with a simpler, easier curse.

"Well, unfortunately, it only happens under a full moon. But a creature lurks within me." She said with a dark tone to her voice. At least *part* of that was true. Something really *did* lurk inside of her.

That did it; a spark of interest plagued the boy's face. His spear retreated up to his side.

"We might have someone who can help." He said in a tone that made Jenevy's spine tingle. She lowered her eyebrows and squinted at him.

"Alright? But how much will this cost me?" She asked him.

"Oh, don't worry. I am sure that any payment that they require is one that you can afford." An evil grin spread across the boy's face. He turned to his side and pulled a rope.

Instantly the ground beneath her dropped, revealing a trapped door that led to a dark room below. Jenevy groaned.

'This is going to hurt.' And she let herself fall. Now more than ever, her powers had to remain hidden. So she fell, and hard. She landed with a bang upon a surface harder than stone. She groaned with pain as the wind was knocked out of her. She looked up at the trap door, wishing that she had planned that better. The guard let out a quick snort, then slammed the door shut. The dark area echoed all around her, as the blackness recoiled out its fingers into the abyss.

Jenevy pushed herself to her feet and stared around her. Luckily her night vision was still in full array, and the area glowed like day. She had fallen into a room, a cell really. It was barely large enough to hold three people and large, rusty, iron bars barred her exit. A hallway lay on the other side of the bars, leading down to complete blackness. There wasn't a single ounce of light anywhere within that prison.

"What kind of place is this?!" She muttered aloud. Almost as if in reply, a loud vicious roar filled the room. It rattled the bars and almost knocked Jenevy to the floor.

Jenevy froze. Every fiber in her body vibrated. She could feel her head throbbing, as her body turned hot. Her blood was practically boiling as her temples throbbed in anger. Something in her had snapped, a low growl purred its way from her throat. With eyes glowing red, a huge wave of energy surged through her and shot out, splintering the bars into toothpicks.

Dust spun up in small cyclones as her wings spread out, floating her up off of the ground. She flew into the corridor, yanking the stones and bricks from the walls with her as she zoomed past. As she slammed through a wall, she entered the room where the roar had originated. The sight that she saw awoke something inside of her that she could never explain.

The room was huge, even larger than any ballroom of any castle that she had ever seen. It was stocked with every weapon, tool and blade imaginable and chains hung like tentacles from the ceiling, interlacing like fingers and falling down towards an even larger table. But what was on that table was the source of her transformation: in all its beauty and glory lay a Shempshay dragon. It's blackened scales, illuminated by fire, and its size was just as Jenevy imagined.

The room was barely large enough to hold its magnificent body, and the chains that were wrapped around it, were cutting into its flesh. Pools of blood lay beneath the dragon, and the liquid sizzled like acid upon the stone.

She didn't know how she knew that the dragon laying before her was indeed a Shempshay dragon, but her gut had ignited her powers to a level that she had never before reached. And something about that massive dragon lying before her, looked different than any other dragon that she had ever seen.

Jenevy's anger rose, she looked down at the dragon's eyes, they were weakly held open. Emotions of pain and agony whirled within the depths of its eyes. But even deeper lay the wisdom that they held. The dragon blinked, and then it noticed Jenevy. Its head raised and a look of caution mixed with curiosity swept over it.

Jenevy's jaw clenched. How could someone hold this beautiful animal in captivity? To torture it? Why would anyone want to . . . .

Jenevy stopped. She looked around and realized that she was not alone. At least half a dozen people were surrounding the dragon, all cloaked and armed with some kind of a weapon. They all stared at her, but why wouldn't they? After the entrance that she just made, she would have looked at herself!

But she couldn't have helped that, when she had heard the howl that the dragon had made, something ignited within her. Every fiber within her being had surged to life, sending her in a mad frenzy towards the source of the sound. And once she had looked at the dragon, she knew why.

A dark cloaked man appeared from the shadows, he stood tall and unafraid at her appearance. Jenevy stared at him, a memory sparked within her, she remembered his stature from the vision that she had had within the mage's hut.

That dark man had clouded her vision when she was in the mage's hut, concealing his identity to anyone who would cast a spell. He was the source of the dark magic that she had felt in the small bordering village of the LéFiévre Castle. And he was the source that she had sensed when she had come to speak with the small guard who had led her down into that dungeon. That man was a very powerful, and a very evil man, and he had the last Shempshay dragon chained like a prisoner!

A growl came from her throat, almost on its own accord. The man eyed her, and then looked at the dragon.

"And I thought that we had the last fascinating specimen on the planet." He said with a laugh. "I guess he had more tricks up his sleeve!" He finished while pulling the chains deeper into the dragon's flesh. The dragon let out a whimper of pain. Jenevy could feel her anger rising.

"Do you speak?" The man asked. Jenevy dropped down to the ground and stood there panting. She didn't want to speak for fear an incantation would escape her lips.

"Where's the mage?" She demanded, forcing herself to speak.

"Ah . . . . so it does!" He said whimsically. Jenevy frowned; she wanted to rip the very limbs off of that man.

"Where is the MAGE?!" She hissed. The man jumped.

"Ah him. Unfortunately he did not live long after he told us of where to find this beast." The man stated as he pulled the chains even tighter, the dragon groaned in immense pain, and that was all that Jenevy needed to send her overboard.

Jenevy snarled and flew into the air. Clapping her hands towards the people below, a huge shockwave knocked them to their knees. Encircling them with flame, she rose higher and higher and with a whip of her hand, the chains snapped and fell to the floor releasing the dragon.

In an instant, the beast rose to its feet and lunged into air. Jenevy blasted away the ceiling, and shrubbery from the forest above showering the men with debris. Both her and the dragon shot out into the sky.

Jenevy stopped in midflight and looked down. She dove towards the ground and slammed to a stop upon her knee, the ground cracked in protest.

She rose to her feet and walked towards the area where she had first met the sentry. To her delight he was still at his post, but he was distracted by the fiasco of the dragon being released.

Jenevy snarled and approached him with a threatening walk. She unhooked her helmet from her belt, and slammed the metal headdress on with a clank. The darkness of the night made her eyes glow their dark, blood red. The boy turned back around just in time to see Jenevy drop her cloak. Her armor created the sickly look of a demon silhouetted onto the darkening sky, and she spread her colossal wings completing her ensemble.

The boy's face grew dark with fear, and he began to frantically step backwards.

"The Devil's . . . . Kn . . . Kni . . .Knight!!!!" He screamed. He scampered backwards as Jenevy withdrew her sword, and she slammed it into him without a second thought. With a crunch, she twisted it and pulled it free, smiling as she heard the familiar sound of his spine snapping.

Whirling around, she sheathed her sword and stretched out her arms in front of her. Black flames of energy surged from her body, and shot out in flames of destruction into the city. Jenevy shot out her powers like a plague, exploding the small town with every blast that she shot out.

Slamming a fist into the ground, she sent surges of energy shock waving through the ground. Earthquakes shook into the taverns below, and the village fell into the catalysts of rooms, tunneled underneath as the supporting beams shattered.

Black lightning seared from the sky, leveling out whatever was left of the evil city. Jumping into the sky, Jenevy flew away smiling as she heard the screams of the dying echoing from below her.

Her eyes stayed their deep, evil red in the darkness, until she squinted and strained her eyes. They shone an even brighter, almost translucent red and the black flames within the city matched the color.

Snapping her eyes as wide as they would go, the flames shot into the ground and the city exploded behind her. A ball of blinding light surrounded the city as Jenevy's flame destroyed everything that would give testament to the evil that went on within that forsaken town.

Jenevy smiled with malice and her eyes returned back to their normal hue of red. Without a glance back, she darted into the sky disappearing into the darkness of the clouds as the village crumbled into pieces behind her.

Chapter Nine

The Journey

WILLIAM'S HORSE WAS growing tired; he could tell by the annoying snorts that the beast made every time that they passed water or some delectable plant.

"Easy boy. I'm tired too, it will only be a little bit longer." He said while patting the poor creatures neck. The horse ninnied its thanks, and William sighed. The truth was that William had no idea of when they *were* going to stop.

Looking behind him, he stared at the Duke's wagon. There was no movement, no sounds, and no signal of easing up on their trip. No doubt the Duke was probably sound asleep and far more comfortable than William was in his saddle. William knew that it would be an even greater feat to convince the Duke to stop, then to mêlée any creature of the night.

The Duke was on the ware ever since his encounter with the troll, and no city walls were going to appeal for his comfort of a fortnight. Which also meant that sleeping under the stars was certainly out of the question.

The King's castle was still a long way away, and they had already been traveling for two fortnights without even a stop for food.

William readjusted his body in the saddle, causing his armor to move and clank, he groaned as he felt the stiffness in his body. Pulling on the horse's reins, he slowed the horse to a steady walk beside the wagon.

"Master. We must stop our voyage. The horse's are barely able to walk, and I myself will be unfit for your protection without a rest." William stated boldly. He rolled his aching shoulders, and then waited for a reply.

The curtain on the window within the carriage shifted back slightly. Half hidden by shadow, the Duke's face emerged. William felt a bit pleased that his Master was indeed afraid; it showed weakness upon the once powerful Lord.

"Very well." His voice sounded shaky. "Do as you must. But I will not leave this carriage. So you will find somewhere to sleep where you can still guard my passage." And the curtain was whisked shut.

William frowned. So much for sleeping!

"Edmund!" William shouted. The stable boy rushed his horse forward and to William's side.

"Yes Sir William?"

"Run ahead. Find a place for shelter that is well off of our path, and completely secluded from peering eyes."

Edmund raised an eyebrow at William. William rolled his eyes.

"The Master desires to stay within the safety of his carriage." William explained.

Edmund's face lit up in understanding, and then he nodded and kicked his horse forward. William watched him run out of sight, and then smiled to himself. The expression on Edmund's face was priceless.

"My thoughts exactly." William said aloud.

William and Edmund sat by the fire as William drew out their camp site in the dirt. He sketched out a design of how the guard posts were to be set up for the night.

"Edmund, your post will be . . ." He dragged his stick over the edge of the drawing and stabbed it into the ground. " . . . here. Make sure that you walk from this tree to that one. And keep an eye on the Duke's carriage at all times." William explained to Edmund. The boy nodded in return, then stood up and rushed over to the carriage. William grabbed another stick.

"I will be here, and Luke!" William called over to the carriage busboy. Luke glanced up at him from his position atop the small wagon.

"Could you take the third watch over here?"

Luke looked down at William's drawing, and then nodded in agreement.

"Alright, we're all set then. Edmund grab a bit to eat first!" he ordered, and Edmund stopped in his tracks to turn back around and race over to the boiling pot of food.

"Rest for a bit, both of you. I will take first watch, and then we will all be at our designated spots until dawn." William instructed as he rubbed away the sketch from the dirt.

"Sir William?" Edmund called. William looked up at him.

"We only have a few hours till dusk, you sure that you don't want me on first watch so that you can sleep?"

"No Edmund, I've done longer watches with less sleep."

"I am sure that you have. But let's face it; you are the only one here who is capable of thwarting off any enemies. What if you were to fall asleep?"

William laughed aloud.

"Don't worry Edmund. I have been under worse conditions. Believe me!" William reassured. "Besides, you are young and will need the strength for your training that starts tomorrow!"

Edmund grinned excitedly.

"Oh! Alright!"

Luke walked up to them just as William got up to start his watch.

"Sir William. The Duke wishes to see you." Luke said sheepishly. William nodded, patted Luke on the back, and then rushed over to the carriage.

"My master." He said with a bow.

"William. I have a bit of a request for you."

William raised his head to look at the Duke.

"Your stable boy Edmund, you have elected as your squire correct?"

"Yes milord."

"Well 'Sir' William . . ." The Duke said with a sarcastic drawl. " . . . the King has told me that you will have Edmund trained before we reach the castle. And seeing how you *won't* be living forever, you are going to need a successor. Especially, if you want the knowledge of your trade to last for an eternity." The Duke finished, making sure that he had placed emphasis on calling William by his title. But that wasn't what worried William. What had tweaked a nerve was how the Duke had noticeably made it a point to note William's fate. What did he mean by that?

"Yes milord." William cleared his throat.

"That will be all." The Duke disappeared into the shadows of his carriage yet again.

A squire? His trade? Was the Duke referring to his Knighthood, or to his role as delivery boy? William shook his head in confusion.

As William approached the glowing embers of the fire, he looked over at Edmund snoring softly from his rucksack. William frowned and stepped out of the light.

The woods seemed much darker now that the glowing fire was behind him. He could hear small animals scratching and slithering on the forest floor, and birds, particularly owls, rustled in the trees above him as they searched for prey. Every now and then a distant howl would echo through the wind, and a larger creature would return the call.

But none of those sounds bothered William, they actually soothed him, calmed him to his very soul. The night was where he belonged, as was the dark, dismal forest.

The animals of the woods were free, no chains held them, no contracts bound them, and nothing tied them to any type of a long written law. No one could sell them for money, or food or even well being. No. Those creatures were able to live their lives as God intended.

They all had something that William so desperately desired of more than anything in the world: freedom.

His Knighthood, along with his freedom, even his very soul, had been bought and sold at a price that William could never dream of repaying. Just like the women that quenched the Duke's thirst, William could be easily destroyed.

That was what William feared most, that he would be killed for a single purpose of greed. The Duke would use William to his very death, and then enslave someone else to continue his tyranny.

William chose to not think too much into what his future might hold, but after the Duke so delicately put comment on how William was not going to be living forever, he began to seriously doubt that he had much of a future left.

The next morning, William packed up the last of the supplies and secured them to the carriage.

Luke had quickly climbed up onto the seat of the buggy and was ready to whip the horses forward before William had finished.

William tightened the last strap, and then jumped to the ground. His armor clanked as the gravity yanked at it as William landed upon the earth.

Climbing into his horse's saddle, William kicked his horse forward. The crack of Luke's whip echoed in reply, and Edmund's horse nickered from the rear.

The dark woods were vastly approaching as they climbed back out onto the road. By nightfall they would be in the city of Tonelle, and after that the hard part would begin.

The Wastelands of Caliber, followed by the volcanic region of Monia, and lastly, was the territory of the ancient Shempshay dragons. And if they made it through their alive, then they would reach the kingdom of the evil

King Alexander where William was most certain that his fate would be decided.

Trudging along through the underbrush, William noticed that the trees were thickening, and the shrubbery was getting denser.

Sliding out his sword, William began to hack and slice away at the foliage in front of him creating a path for the carriage behind him. After a few segments of the shrubbery were hacked away, William realized that the vegetation was thinning, and some were even missing.

Looking around, he then noticed that even some of the trees were missing as well. The air stank of sulfur and ash, and the ground itself was becoming uncharacteristically uneven. Then . . . there was nothing.

William yanked on the reins, his horse stopped instantly. The carriage skidded to stop just inches behind William, and the sound of Edmund's horse's hooves clomped upon the ground.

"Sir William . . . . what . . . has happened?!"

"I . . . don't know." William replied breathlessly. They looked ahead, and stared at the largest crater that they had ever seen. Its depth was so far down that getting to it would be like a drop from a steep cliff. Smoke rose from the center of the massive hole, and the entire area was smoldering and crackling with very hot coals.

The Duke walked up next to William.

"My God!"

"Milord! You need to be in the carriage! Not out in the open!" Edmund cried. The Duke ignored him.

"How . . . what . . . who has done this?!" The Duke stammered angrily. William wanted to smile, wanted to jump up and down in glee. So . . . the town of Tonelle had been destroyed as well as the evil along with it? What a wonderful miracle!

It was one more thing that had been taken away from the world, and one William was glad about it. The great ally to the Duke of Greenwiche was gone, and its remains lay in ash at their feet. Now if only King Alexander were as well.

The Duke snorted with disgrace and rushed back into his carriage.

"The King will *not* be pleased!" He grunted.

"The Dark demon, the great magic, the dark mage, gone! All gone!" The Duke muttered to himself as he slammed the door shut behind him. William glanced back at the carriage curiously.

'*Demon?*' He thought to himself.

Edmund glimpsed over at William. "What now sir?"

"Well . . . . we continue to Delmonia as planned. We will simply just have to go around." William stated as he stared one last time at the crater, before kicking his horse ahead. Edmund looked down towards the bottom of the cavity and let out a long whistle.

"Come on Edmund." William said as he cantered his horse forward. Edmund nodded and kicked his horse to catch up to the wagon.

The crater was much larger than William had anticipated; it took them nearly a day to reach the other side. What William had thought was just shadows along the tree line, had in fact been an extension to the enormous hole.

William sighed, as he knew what the night was about to bring. Since they were so far from Delmonia, even more so now because of the vast crater, that meant that William had to go hunting.

Their supplies had been dwindled down to practically nothing, but what worried William more was the possibility that any local animals had disappeared completely after the explosion that had created the crater.

The sun was practically hiding behind the mountains, and when William decided to stop the caravan it had gotten even darker. He led his horse back to join Edmund.

"We will rest here for the night." Edmund nodded in reply.

"Here?!" The Duke shrieked from his carriage.

"Yes Master. We need food and rest. Nothing should bother us anyway, for obvious reasons." William finished as he looked over at the steaming hole beside them.

"But . . . but what if whomever or whatever has destroyed this place decides to come back?!" The Duke said shakily. William fought back the urge to break out into hysterical laughter.

"Milord. If 'someone' did this, then their job is done. They won't be back. As for the 'thing', if it were to return I would be surprised. Nothing will return to this site. It's what you would call a 'Job well done'."

"Well . . . well . . . . it might!!!" The Duke cried.

"Milord, is there something that you need to tell me? Do you know what may have caused this?" William asked skeptically. As much as William loved to see weakness in the Duke, he also hated it when the Duke feared what he himself might have caused.

The Duke frowned and sat up straight on the carriage's padded bench.

"Why of course not." He said regally.

"Very well." William smiled. "We camp here for the night."

The Duke sneered at William defiantly, and dropped the curtains over the carriage window.

Edmund had begun to unload the gear and set up a makeshift campsite. Luke was busy gathering together what little supplies were left, and frowned in distaste and what he was left to cook with.

Grabbing his bow and arrows from the top of the carriage, William snuck away into the forest to begin his hunt. He prayed that something would be alive for him to shoot and bring back, or they might starve.

Delmonia was supposed to be a two day journey from the destroyed city, but now it was to turn into a four to five day journey. And with their supplies being practically gone, that would mean that William was about to have a very hungry, cranky and murderous Duke on his hands.

And nothing about that scenario William liked, he had seen it before.

❖ Jenevy followed the Great Dragon into the mountains. In order to allow her to follow him, the dragon made sure to fly slower than his usual pace. The flight was much farther than Jenevy had flown before, but nonetheless enjoyable.

She was following a Shempshay dragon! A creature thought to exist only in folklore and legends! Even love stories! But not in real life!

The dragon slowly glided down lower into the air, and awaited Jenevy to fly at his side. She dove towards him, and spread out her wings to keep her afloat as they drifted across the hot air.

The dragon looked at her curiously, gazing and watching her with precision. She returned its stare, her own curiosity molding with his.

The dragon made a noise that sounded like a mix between a dolphin's yelp and a large lion's purr. It was whimsical, soothing, and completing remarkable.

Jenevy attempted to respond, and growled back. The dragon's eyes gleamed as if he were smiling at her. Then it dove, launching itself towards the ground. Jenevy did the same, matching her speed with that of the large reptile.

The dragon flapped his wings and shot back up towards the sky, spinning through the air. Jenevy did the same.

The dragon picked up speed, coasted towards a cliff edge, and then launched himself faster into the sky by leaping off of the cliff.

Jenevy giggled, the dragon was actually playing with her, well maybe challenging her, but it felt like a game to her! She flew at the cliff edge, pointed her feet towards it, and then with the momentum of her flight landed. With one swift movement, she was able to combine her weight with her speed to skid on the surface of the cliff long enough to jump into the sky.

She too shot into the air like a rocket and was instantly behind the dragon. The dragon glanced at her, and flapped his wings to create a current under her wingspan.

Jenevy smiled at how easy it was to fly when the dragon was slicing through the air before her. Now she understood why birds flew in patterns and in groups.

The dragon looked ahead and kept up a slow pace. Jenevy wished that she could talk to him. What stories it would tell! She could only imagine what the dragon might be able to tell her!

She then contemplated about whether the tales of the dragons were even true. The dragon would know! She *had* to find a way to communicate, be for the curiosity would kill her!

The sun had started to set over the horizon, and shards of light echoed themselves throughout the forest below. Swiftly the dragon flew onward as the mountains slowly crept into view. A wave of excitement ricocheted throughout Jenevy's veins as she realized what mountains pass lay before her.

They were the Fenloré Mountains! They were just as tall and jagged as every painting of them that she had ever seen. There were large cave openings littered along the mountain's edges.

The openings were huge; they were easily ten times taller than her. The caves were high above the ground having no possible paths to reach them. And the mountainside was a steep slope so that climbing was completely out of the question.

Large towers were molded above the mountains resembling smokestacks. The peaks looked more like a giant castle-like anthill, than a mountain pass.

"Of course!" Jenevy said excitedly. Where else would the smoke exit? Dragon's nostrils were always flared, and had smoke rising out of them. And with dragons being so large, a cavern would instantly be filled up with smoke. Not that that would bother an adult dragon, but to a baby it might.

Jenevy watched as the dragon turned slightly, and headed towards a cave at the farthest end of the mountain pass. At first Jenevy pictured the dragon entering one of caves to coil up inside next to a cavern of gold, but instead he zipped up over the top of the ridgeline and disappeared from view.

Jenevy swooped down cautiously and passed over the ridge as well. Completely stunned, she stopped and hovered in midflight.

A valley lay before her; it was larger, greener, and more secluded than any valley she had ever seen. The mountains enclosed the valley like a giant, impenetrable wall. Nothing could climb up the sheer rock cliffs to get into that place, and nothing could get out. The valley was only reachable by something or someone, who could fly.

The dragon landed upon the ground, folded in its wings, and then proceeded to stretch out like a sleepy cat. He stared up at Jenevy as she shook her mind back into focus.

Flapping her wings, she swooped down towards the ground. The dragon momentarily paused its stretching to watch her approach. She landed softly upon the ground, but didn't have time to fold in her wings.

Once she had landed, the dragon nudged her forward with its tail nearly tripping her from the sheer force of his push. That was when Jenevy noticed the valley for what it really was.

The ground was green, too green. A stream echoed somewhere nearby and small ruins lay all around her. But behind those ruins lay even larger ruins, ones that could easily fit three or four very large dragons stacked atop one another.

It took her less than a minute to realize what she was looking at. What she was staring at, was the area where humans and dragons had first lived before the *'betrayal'*. Bones littered the ground like heaps of dead leaves. There were dragon bones, mixed with human.

The ruins held, long ago corroded, slash mark lines. Dragon's had clawed at the walls of the historic buildings during the Battle of the Betrayals. Some of the ruins still had char marks on them from the dragons' hot, underbelly flames.

Jenevy didn't know whether to be excited or sad at her discovery. She had found, or rather was led, to the fabled Shempshay Temple grounds. But she had hoped that she would have seen something better than just obliterated structures and proof of annihilated species. She had always imagined that place to be more of a paradise than a graveyard.

But then again, it had been a war of such magnitude that every race of human on the world had had it documented in some sort of fashion. Whether they believed it or not, the *'betrayal'* was in everyone's history books. And wars were never known to leave behind *paradises*.

Looking around the large buildings, she noticed an even larger building shielded by the sunlight. It lay built into the mountain, and the mountain over time had slowly taken back its borough. Jenevy walked towards it, making sure that she stepped over the bones lying upon the ground with great care. The last thing that she wanted was to upset the dragon because she had destroyed the last remnants of his ancestors.

When she was close enough to the building, she peered through the tall pillars holding it erect. The entire building was one, large room: a throne room.

An actual throne lay in front of her, and it was larger than anything she had ever seen. It was big enough to sit one of the enormous creatures.

The dragon walked up from behind her, and approached the huge seat. With a sigh, he stretched himself out onto it.

Jenevy swallowed, and cleared her throat. She knew that she wanted to discover if he really could speak. But was unsure as to how to spark up a conversation. She cautiously walked closer to him and stared into his dark eyes.

"Great Dragon. Can you . . . . understand me?" She asked delicately. The dragon looked at her and very nobly nodded. Jenevy smiled at him.

"Are you, one of the Shempshay Dragons of old?" There was another nod. Jenevy was getting excited.

"Can you . . . . speak?" She asked excitedly. The dragon slowly drooped his head.

"I'll take that as a no." She said with a frown. A low grumble echoed from the dragon's stomach.

"You're not . . . going to eat me are you?" She said worriedly. The dragon's throat rumbled a low growl mixed with a chirping sound echoed from his throat. He was laughing. He shook his head in reply.

"Wise one—" She paused, how was she to ask this next question? "What . . . . happened? I mean, not so much about here, that I am sure will probably be a long story. But, how did you get to where I found you?"

The dragon dropped his head in despair. Picking himself off of the throne, he made his way towards the bubbly creek that Jenevy had heard earlier.

"Great Dragon! I did not mean to offend you—" she was cut off as the dragon gently placed his tail over her mouth. She nodded in understanding.

Pulling back his tail, he continued his saunter.

"I follow. Got it." She said as she tried to stay close to the dragon's massive strides.

The stream was getting closer; she could smell its crisp freshness and her stomach began to growl in reply. The dragon looked back at her with an arched brow. Jenevy smiled embarrassedly.

"I'm hungry." She declared. The chirpy laugh of the dragon yet again filled the air. Jenevy liked the sound; it calmed her like nothing in that world had done before.

When they reached the stream, the dragon nudged her forward to drink. She smiled as she practically fell into the water, and then knelt closer to reach her hands down. Scooping up the cool water, she sipped the crystal clear liquid. She could feel the coolness spreading down her esophagus and scooped up more water eagerly.

The dragon watched her curiously as she slurped loudly. He cocked his head to the side as a dog would upon hearing strange sounds.

The flavor was intoxicating! It was so cold, so crisp, and it had a flavor that Jenevy could not describe. Once she had had her fill, she wiped her mouth and peered over at the dragon. With his tail he nudged her to her feet, and pushed her forward again.

Instead of falling to her knees from the force of the dragon's nudge, she whipped out her wings and used the momentum to glide herself over to the opposing edge of the stream. The dragon, startled at her unexpected move, stared cautiously at her.

As she spun around to face him, she pulled in her wings and cloaked them onto her back.

"Oh these?" She asked as his tail reached towards her back. She stretched one out and allowed it to be visible to her new friend. The dragon nodded in reply.

"Long story!" She said with a sigh, and pulled the limb back in. The dragon laughed, and fell upon the ground. Looking more like a cat than a large flying lizard, he too pulled in his wings, and then curled up his legs beneath him.

Jenevy smiled and let out a small chuckle.

"Alright. I'll tell mine first!" She said amidst amusement.

Her entire story from when she was captured, to the Duke, to the troll, to her being condemned to death and then receiving her powers, followed by her fate of her wings, and the rest of her life up until she met the dragon, took a lot longer to explain than she thought!.

The dragon watched her with sincere interest as she paced in front of him. Her arms gesturing at different parts of the story matched the enthusiasm in her voice, and the darker sides of her story plagued little movement upon her as she spoke.

The dragon would respond with growls and roars during her tale. The Duke seemed to anger him as much as it did her. Jenevy would watch the dragon as she explained of how she was thrown into the tower by the evil man. The dragon would respond to the Duke's name with flared, glowing nostrils. Smoke seemed to rise out quicker from the dragon's nose when he got irate.

As Jenevy told of the mage who had helped her, and then of the other mage whose book she had found, the dragon bowed his head somberly. Apparently, that mage had been a very dear friend to the mythical beast.

Lastly, Jenevy told the dragon of William. The knight whom she hoped was still alive. A wave of sadness rushed over her as she spoke his name. The dragon seemed to sense her sorrow, and with his tail pulled her in close to his side. He tightened his grip, almost as if he were comforting her with an embrace.

The dragon was warm and was very soft. Which was unexpected to Jenevy. She had expected a hard, cold, scaly lizard. She closed her eyes enjoying the companionship of her new friend. She listened to the loud heartbeat of the dragon, and heard the air entering in and out of its lungs. What's more was that another sound was echoing from within the large lizard. It was a very soft vibration which seemed to be rumbling from within its throat.

Jenevy raised her head in surprise, the dragon was purring! The dragon looked down at her, his gentle eyes peered at her as if they deciphered an entire story within its depths, whole worlds seemed to glisten within them. He truly was a very beautiful, misunderstood creature.

"So, now it's your turn. How did those men capture you? What did they want? And what happened . . . . here? And why was I so angered upon seeing you trapped and beaten that I destroyed that village? I did not know that my power could be that strong without affecting my energy!" She finished out of breath.

The dragon nodded at her, and looked around him. Standing up, he walked away from her. When she tried to follow, he stopped her and directed her to stay. She nodded, and sat down upon the grass.

Once he was a good distance away, he turned back around to face her. Sucking in air, the dragon's chest expanded. Like a loud, hollow hiss, the air rushed out of his abdomen back into the sky. Only instead of air it was fire.

Jenevy leaned back as the dragon's flame expanded in front of her. His nostrils were glowing red, and fire embers were jumping out of them. Jenevy stared at the fire in confusion, and then her eyes grew wide in disbelief. There were images emerging from the flame, and they were moving. So the dragon's communicated through images! This new realization made Jenevy excited with expectation.

The dragon's entire story was etched into the sky, and Jenevy was eager to learn.

Long ago, the dragons did live with man. They had taught them to read, to write, to live! Just like how the historians had described, human and dragon lived harmoniously together for some time.

But one day, a man stepped forward. He had greed within his heart and had wanted more than what the dragons had to offer. He wanted riches and wealth. And when the dragons refused, he retaliated by killed the dragon's youngest offspring.

In anger, the dragon's destroyed this man but had consequently started a battle from amongst his followers, and they wanted revenge.

A war broke out between man and beast. In the end, the dragon's had won, but not without loss. By winning, they had banished the humans from their land, and swore that any who trespassed upon the dragon's valley would be instantly killed.

After many years, the humans returned, but as hunters, and they began to hunt and kill the dragons. Although the humans could not cross the mountains in order to reach the valley, they would wait until the dragons would leave to hunt and then they would trap and kill the dragons.

Over time, the dragons began to evolve into a terrible creature. Out of necessity, the dragons had become nothing more than a wild lizard that would hunt, eat, mate and sleep. They soon thereafter forgot their past, forgot their wisdom, and were only vicious creatures that lived by instinct alone.

But a few, older dragons remained the same. They were the living and last bloodline of the noble Shempshay. Namely: The king, the queen and their son.

After thousands of years the king and queen eventually died, leaving behind their only son. Of course, that human that had defied them had also had sons. And down the line of that human's descendants one of them stepped forward. He was a mage, and he had a dark power to him that seemed to feed off of the revenge hidden within his eyes.

He waited for years to find the last Shempshay dragon, and killed many wild dragons in the process. Until, at last, he got a hold of the son of the royal family of Shempshay.

He subdued the dragon, trapped it, and then tortured it. He tried to steal secrets of the dragon's powers. But to no avail. The dragon lay inside *a cavern for many months in agony as he battled his willpower of wanting to end the pain.*

When at last, hope seemed lost, and he was about to give in to the pain so that the dragon could rejoin his family, a woman appeared.

Her powers shocked the dragon! Never had he seen a human with such strength, such energy, and such destructive power. She freed the dragon, and killed everyone that had held him prisoner: including the dark mage.

The woman intrigued the dragon. She had wings in similar appearance to his. And she too, could emit fire from her soul. But what was more astonishing, was that she had saved him. And for that, he owed her his life.

The dragon stopped his fire-show and looked down at Jenevy in sadness. What a horrible life this creature must have faced! To live in love, only to have everything stripped away in a blink of an eye! She could only imagine the pain that he must have felt in having to replay his history for her. With the warmest smile that she could create, she looked at him.

"Dear dragon . . . I am so sorry." She said slowly. The dragon stared at her for a moment as if confused, and then nodded in reply. Jenevy walked towards him and placed a hand upon his neck in comfort. The dragon purred in response.

"But dragon. What of the mage? And of this book?" She asked as she pulled out the tattered, leather bound book from within her cloak. The dragon frowned, and knocked the book out of her hands.

Jenevy jumped back as the dragon ignited the journal into flames. She watched mystified, as it smoldered at her feet.

"Oh . . . ." She mused.

The dragon huffed in agitation and stood to his feet. Jenevy watched him as he walked away from her, but she still had so many questions to ask! What of her powers? She had to know why she reacted in the way she did upon seeing the dragon! And maybe he could help her to tame the control of her energy and powers as well!?

"Dragon, my power is limited. I know that it does not seem like it, especially after the destruction that I caused at your prison. But it really is!" She exclaimed as she ran to catch up to him. "There is so much more that I am capable of, I can feel it! And that mage was my last hope in learning it." Jenevy paused as she leapt over a fallen log blocking her path. She raced up to the dragon's side once more and continued. "Well, my power felt like it was bound by something, almost as if it were fighting to get out. But I could never seem to release it!" She said breathlessly.

The dragon coiled its neck around to peer at her.

"Until I met you . . . ."

The dragon stopped and stared at her.

"Something much stronger than I had imagined emerged. Something . . . . both bizarre and remarkable all at once. I was . . . . astonished that such power could exist! And yet, I still don't even know how I did it! Oh!!!!" She shrieked in frustration. The dragon, startled, jumped back from her.

"Sorry." She apologized with a sheepish grin. "This would be much easier if you could talk!"

The dragon laughed, and turned back around to face the front. Jenevy felt the thundering rumbles of his enormous footsteps as he strolled forward, she stood there as she pondered of how to communicate with the dragon.

'There has to be a way of understanding him! Think about it, his power awoke mine which means that it is somehow connected! But then again, it might have just been a coincidence . . . nevertheless . . . . I have to find a way to communicate!' Jenevy pondered for a moment more and then an idea struck her mind.

"Dragon!" She shrieked. The dragon paused to look back at her again. Fluttering her wings, she leapt forward and soared towards him.

"Listen, I have an idea. It might be a bit risky but if you don't mind I would like to perform a spell." She explained. The dragon perked his head to the side.

"But . . . ." She paused and took in a deep breath. " . . . It will be permanent."

The dragon stared at her for a moment longer, and relaxed his muscles. Jenevy reached back inside of her cloak and pulled out the book of spells that Jeremy had given her.

"It's a mind-melding spell. It will give us the ability to communicate through our minds." She said slowly. The dragon looked up to the sky as he contemplated her suggestion. Jenevy swallowed, and then licked her lips. The spell also had a dark side to it. One thing that she hated about spells was that every cure or every good thing that one would cast always had a curse to bring along with it.

"Dragon . . . we would also feel each other's pain." The dragon kept his face towards the heavens. "And we would feel one another's emotions." She finished. The dragon glanced down at her, closed his eyes and nodded.

"Dragon . . . . if I do this, the only thing that will break our minds apart . . . . will be death." She stated very slowly and delicately. Again, the dragon nodded.

'Well . . . . here goes!'

❖ William quickly wrapped the dead deer in a woven cloak before placing it onto the horse's back. With sure hands, and a tight rope, the animal lay securely behind the saddle. With a groan, William picked up his quiver and bow while he walked back towards the camp. His horse trotted alongside as William tugged at its reins.

"Alright boy, let's get out of here." He said with a grunt as he swung up onto the horse's back. It had taken him a few hours to find some game, courtesy of the crater and smoldering trees. It would be nightfall soon, and his master was not known for his patience. With a kick to its flanks, the horse neighed and surged forward into the trees.

Back at the encampment, the Duke was pacing nervously in front of the newly lit fire. Luke and Edmund watched him curiously as he mumbled to himself.

"Oh! What is taking him so long?" The Duke whined.

"Milord. He will be back soon; he is an expert bowman after all." Edmund stated. The Duke glared at him.

"You don't think that I don't know that?!" The Duke exclaimed. "But how am I to feel safe when he is not here!" he shrieked.

Edmund shrugged his shoulders bewildered.

"We are here milord." Luke stated, trying to comfort the Duke.

"Oh great! A coachmen and a stable boy, I feel safer already!" The Duke said, throwing his arms into the air. "All you are of use to me is, as slaves." He added wickedly. Edmund huffed in reply.

The sound of beating horse beats echoed through the camp, and their attention was quickly drawn towards William as he galloped into view.

"Finally!" The Duke cried in outrage. William stared at him curiously as he skidded his horse to a stop. Jumping from the saddle, he yanked the dead deer down to the ground with a thump.

"Excellent! Now cook that meal quickly so that we may be on our way before something terrible happens!" The duke ordered. William looked up at him and raised an eyebrow.

"Yes milord." William said quickly and he dragged the deer towards the fire.

"Luke! Come give me a hand with this. And Edmund . . ." The boy looked up at William in surprise. "I need you to get a spit ready and quickly." William finished while looking up at the Duke curiously. Edmund rushed over to the carriage and yanked out the long, iron rods that were going to be needed for the spitted deer.

"And Edmund, you will have to be the spit boy for the night." William added. Edmund groaned in dismay. The spit boy was his least favorite job. The last thing that he wanted, was to be spinning the carcass of a dead animal for hours on end.

Luke snickered at the boys reply as he and William fastened the deer's legs together and got it ready for securing to the spit.

Once the deer was cheerfully roasting over the fire, and William had begun to scout the area, did the Duke finally retreat to the safety of his carriage.

Edmund continued to spin the deer while keeping close watch on the roasting animal. Luke would approach every now and then to season the animal with spices and other savory juices, while in between time he prepared bread and cheese to accompany the dinner.

"This is the last of it." Luke said as he sat down next to Edmund. The boy looked over at him and sighed.

"We'll have to make due with the deer for as long as we can." Edmund replied.

William appeared from the shadows and stepped towards them. Luke jumped in fright.

"Ugh! I hate it when you do that! You couldn't give some kind of warning?!" He wailed. William smiled.

"Well, I would have figured that you'd of gotten used to it by now." William responded with a laugh. Luke glared at him.

"As always, the world is quiet. Whatever created that massive crater scared everything away for miles. It's almost surreal." William said bewildered.

"I wouldn't be here either if I had a choice." Luke acknowledged.

"I just don't understand what could have caused so much destruction." Said a puzzled William.

'Well, whatever it was. It sure spooked the master!" Edmund stated quietly. William laughed to himself.

"Sir William . . ." Luke said monotonously. William arched an eyebrow at him. "This deer is all that we will have left till we reach the next town. And our water is almost spent. Plus with the Master's washes, we might be completely gone by tomorrow eve."

William groaned.

"I didn't see any source of water while hunting or scouting. How much is there exactly?"

"Well, without any more washes, I'd say give or take, two more days worth." Luke answered. William rubbed his face and sighed.

"We'll have to make it last as long as possible. It could be a while before any water is to be found. And the King's castle is still a five day trip from here."

"I agree. But I'm not sure that Master will." Luke stated. William closed his eyes and sighed once more.

Pulling a knife from his belt, William sliced off a slab of meat and dropped it onto a plate. He stepped over Edmund and grabbed a chunk of bread and slice of cheese as he made his way towards the carriage.

"I'm going to take first watch!" He yelled back. "And remember, the Duke prefers his meat dark!"

The Caliber Wastelands smelled worse than William remembered. The road was barely visible through the swampy ground, and the Duke's carriage kept sinking into the rank mud.

"Lighten the load!" William waved at Luke to keep the carriage moving, as he yelled orders to him.

"What?!" The Duke screamed. William sighed and turned his horse back to meet up with the carriage.

"Milord. You've done this trip before, yet you still bring loads of weight onboard the wagon. The Caliber Wastelands are filled with swampy water and mud that will swallow a heavy load whole. We *must* drop all unnecessary supplies!" William instructed. The Duke was outraged.

"I will *not* do that! These are my things and we have done no such thing as abandoning belongings before!"

William could feel his temple throbbing in agitation. He breathed deeply and spoke very softly like a mother would to a naive child.

"You are correct Master. But if you remember correctly, there has always been a paved road for our path. Now there is nothing but thick, sticky mud. So unless you would rather walk, I would suggest that you drop your luggage and buy more when we arrive!" William finished loudly. The Duke slid back in his seat and stared at William. The Duke was abashed.

"You do *not* order me around Sir William! Or so help me God, your Knighthood will not be the only thing that I take!" The Duke said wickedly.

'That's twice he has referred to my death and the third time he's going to need more than God to help him.' William said to himself. William glared at the Duke.

"As you wish my master." He said with gritted teeth. He kicked his horse forward and rushed to lead the caravan once more. William waved at Luke to speed up, and the mules ninnied in response to Luke's whipping. William looked back at them and frowned.

They were going to have to move fast during this trip. Not only was the carriage at risk of sinking, but all of their usual camping areas were underwater. They literally had to make it through the Wastelands with no stopping and no rest if they were to survive.

"We eat and walk gentlemen! Pick up the pace! We don't sleep till we enter the Monia Region!" William shouted and he kicked his horse faster.

❖ "Dragon, It is up to you whether you want me to do this or not. It will make it easier for us to communicate if you're willing." Jenevy asked delicately. The dragon cocked his head to the side, as if waiting to hear more.

"Let me explain again. There is a spell, a powerful spell, which will bind us until death. We will feel one another's emotions, pain and thoughts. It's a mind-meld, and it will be permanent." She paused and waited for a reply. The dragon looked to the sky, and within moments he had jumped to his feet and was staring at her with excitement.

"So . . . . yes then?" She asked. The dragon roared with enthusiasm, it shook her very bones. She smiled.

"Alright then!" She said laughing. She looked down at her book.

"Now, this incantation looks a bit tricky. I might have to practice it a few times. Um . . . ." She paused and read further down the page. "It says that we'll need to *combine our blood until the color runs red*" Wait . . . . What?" She said bewildered. The dragon sighed and took his claw up to his chest. He scraped under one of his scales and a goblet of gold liquid dropped onto the grass. The liquid hissed for a few seconds before igniting into flame.

"Oh . . ." She said matter-of-factly. "Alright, well how are we supposed to do this? In a bowl? I'll burn up if we don't!"

The dragon swung his tail around and pointed at the picture in the book. Jenevy looked down and stared at the drawing. There were two people embracing in a pool of red, blood dripped beneath them.

"Yes, I know this. But *how* are we to combine blood?"

The dragon pointed again. Jenevy looked once more at the picture, and then sighed in understanding. The two people were drawn with having blue, wavy lines surrounding them.

"So in water? But wouldn't it boil?" She asked skeptically. The dragon laughed as he walked into the water and waited for her near the deepest part of the stream.

"Hold on." She said as she quickly read the spell again. "Alright, I got it." She set the book down and joined the dragon in the water. He waited till she was close enough before grabbing her and pulling her under the water. They sank for what seemed like an eternity, before she took out her knife and cut into her arm. The dragon did the same, and they floated beneath the surface watching the blood seeping out of their bodies. The blood at first stayed in tight lines as it streamed from their arms. But, almost as if on instinct, the two streams of blood surged together and formed a cloud around them.

Jenevy closed her eyes and began the spell.

"Hüd keedgard, bréh srekcars! Narb cilrag niet muid-ōs. Elttab dor-aera oo evoba!" And the water did boil, but not with heat: with power. Their fluids swirled together once more and formed a cyclone around them. The cyclone went from reddish-gold to a deep scarlet red. Then the water current switched directions and threw them both out of the water and onto the shore.

Jenevy groaned as she pushed herself to her feet.

"Okay . . . that one hurt." She said with a sigh as she began to dust herself off.

"Are you alright child?"

Jenevy froze. She spun around and looked at the dragon.

"By the gods! It worked!" She said excitedly. The dragon smiled.

"You did not think that it twould?"

"Well, I was a bit skeptical at first, but now that it's over I know!" She shrieked. The dragon's stomach rumbled.

"Ahh!" Jenevy screamed, keeling over. "What is that pain? I feel a hunger like I have never eaten in my entire life! Plus both my throat and my stomach feel as if they are on fire!" She cried.

"Jenevy, I have not eaten since I was captured. And the fire sensation that you are felling is from the fire that I yield within my bosom. You will get accustomed to it over time."

HEATHER DIROCCO

Jenevy groaned as she slumped over and fell to the ground clenching her stomach.

"The spell said that we would feel pain and emotions! But I wasn't expecting this! Please tell me that you are feeling something in return?!" She whispered.

"Aye I am. It is a feeling of loss. And a huge emotion of dread and revenge."

Jenevy froze.

"You can feel that?"

"Just as my fire within my breast, you too are capable of growing accustomed to emotions. You are not very different from me and your emotions are not very different than my own, but they are a bit stronger. You must think of sadness and despair in immeasurable quantities." The dragon's face was filled with sorrow. Jenevy breathed in deeply and pushed herself back to her feet.

"Forgive me dragon. I had not wanted you to view my kind with distaste. We are not all like this."

"I know. But *you* are." He said carefully. Jenevy looked at him puzzled.

"But I have a reason to be." She stated with a threatening tone. The dragon's eyes softened.

"For someone as old as I, trust me when I say that keeping a grudge in your heart not only hurts you, but anyone else whom you might know."

Jenevy's eyes began to tear in reply. He was right, and she knew it. But it was hard for her to let go of her past, especially with the weight that the lost souls had put on her.

"You will find, dearest Jenevy, that your powers will flow more purely and accurately if you let go of your past, and find something to fight for. Fight for them, those souls, and not for yourself." He said coolly. Jenevy instantly burst into tears and fell onto the dragon weeping.

Very carefully, he placed a clawed foot upon her and embraced her.

"It has been a long time since any human has leaned onto me for comfort. But you will find that I am grateful for your trust." He said as he squeezed her tighter to him.

Only when her tears stopped, and he was sure that she was spent, did he let go of her. Jenevy wiped the tears from her cheek, regained her composure with a deep breath and then stood up to face him.

Her posture was strong and powerful, and the dragon could sense her powers coursing through her veins on a whole new level of dominance.

"Thank you. I too have not felt the comforting embrace of anyone in a long, long time. Even if it is from a dragon, I do greatly appreciate it." The dragon purred in response. "Great dragon . . . . do you have a name? I feel that you do, in fact I know that you do, but I can't seem to find it."

"I did . . . . once." He said with sorrow. His eyes diverted to the mountains and he seemed to be searching them for an answer. "It has been so long since I have used it, that I don't remember." He said sadly as he concentrated harder.

"My mother's name was Cirdne, my father . . . ." He paused. " . . . . was Roterub, and they called me . . . ." Another pause.

"Feau." They both said in unison. The dragon looked over at her with a toothy grin. She smiled in return.

"Yes . . . . Feau. My parents made that name by combining the first letters of all of the earthly elements." He said pleased.

"Fire, Earth, Air and . . . . What does the U stand for?" Jenevy stated.

"It is water. But we spell it with a U instead of a W. Your kind spells it as W-A-T-E-R. But my kind spelled it as Û-u-a-t-e-r. Its pronounced the same, but it can be a bit confusing, we do spell many things a lot differently than you." The dragon finished. Jenevy nodded in understanding.

"My parents also told me that someday, I would understand why they created my name. And that one day the great Dragon Deity Flares would descend upon me and would use me to make the world at peace."

"Dragon Deity?" She asked puzzled.

"An ancient tale, he is much like your God, he created my species and my way of life. But our God was known as Flares and we always referred to him as such. The Empress of the Earth is sacrificed to him every two-hundred years for protection, and unity of our species. That is, humans and dragons." He clarified.

"It is said that the Empress is chosen before she is born, and is sacrificed when she reaches adulthood. Then the stars will align and our two worlds will be combined in peace once again."

"So, this has happened before? Our two races at war with one another?" Jenevy asked perplexed.

"Yes."

"And it has always ended the same? The Empress being sacrificed and the world is at peace only to start all over again?"

"Basically yes." Feau replied.

"But what if the Empress chooses not to be sacrificed?" Jenevy asked.

"That has never happened before. It is an honor to be chosen." Feau replied matter-of-factly.

"I'm sure that it is, but what if she does?"

Feau paused for a moment.

"Well, if the Empress decides that she wishes to live, than she must defeat the Dragon Deity in battle. And you can guess how many times that that has happened." Feau said smugly.

"Yeah, I guess you're right. But how would she do that?" She asked bewildered.

"By using the combined powers of the elemental dragons." He replied.

"Wow! The Elemental Dragons? Then what are you?"

"I am an Elemental Dragon. Shempshay dragons are able to control the elements, not as strongly as humans can, but can control them nevertheless."

"You mean that humans can control the elements better that you can?" Jenevy asked dumfounded.

"Yes Jenevy. Look at your own powers and then you decide the answer to your own question." Feau stated irritatedly. Jenevy nodded and smiled at the dragon as another thought hit her mind.

"But, how are the Elemental Dragons supposed to combine their powers if you are the last?" She asked skeptically.

"Jenevy, it is a legend, much like yours, and who could possibly know if the legend is even true?" He shook his head, looking more like a horse than a dragon. Jenevy sighed.

Her stomach gurgled again, and she groaned.

"I'm hungry. Care to join me for a hunt?" Feau asked her with enthusiasm. Jenevy's eyes lit up.

"Would I ever!" She shrieked.

❖ Four long and miserable days it took to reach the edge of the Wastelands, due to the missing road, it made their trip to the King's castle even longer. The volcanic mountains lay ahead; and they sent ripples of ash into the sky that rained down upon the ground like snow. The smell of sulfur littered the air, and the murky stench of charcoal echoed throughout the wind.

William urged his horse forward, and the tired animal tried desperately to keep up its pace. William turned to watch the caravan as they came within the sulfuric scents and watched the horses warily. Luke's mules were accustomed to the eye watering stench, but Edmund's was not.

And sure enough, once the sulfur sunk within the horse's nostrils, the horse bucked and reared like a wild mustang. William laughed a bit as he watch Edmund frantically try to regain control, and luckily for William Edmund was an expert rider.

Within moments the horse was calm and trotting forward once again. William waved at the stable boy, and Edmund replied with an agitated expression.

William turned back around in his saddle and watched hesitantly at the lava spewing volcanoes.

They had not slept in four days, and were not about to yet. There were to be no rest until they reached the borders of the Selfur Kingdom and were safely inside the city of Delmonia. William always got a kick out of King Alexander's choice of words for his empire.

The King's throne lay upon molten rock, and once neighbored fiery beasts, and it too smelled like sulfur. So how befitting it was to name his throne after the very putrid stench that neighbored his home.

William's horse jumped forward as it leapt from the swampy ground onto the ash-smitten rock of the volcanic region. The horse made a whinny of pleasure in being on level ground, but once the ash began to stick to his wet hocks he grunted in disgust. William patted his neck in encouragement.

"I know boy, but we are almost there. Keep up this pace and I promise that a bushel of carrots and a bundle of apples will be waiting in your stall once we arrive." William said, bribing his stallion. The horse whinnied its approval, practically trotting with giddy.

William smiled and then sighed when he realized that the Monia Volcanoes and the Shempshay Territory were still a few days walk. And that didn't include the three extra days that it would require to reach the steps of the Selfur Castle.

The Selfur Kingdom lay neighboring both the Monia Volcanoes and the Shempshay Mountain Territory, but with how deteriorated the ground of both territories were, it required the trip to go through both.

Once they got through the Shempshay Territory, they practically had to make a u-turn in order to reach the Selfur Kingdom. What William would give to of traveled to that kingdom during the old days; it might have been a shorter trip. But then again, it would have been a deadly trip because the Shempshay Dragon's would have still been alive.

William stopped his horse, and waited for the carriage to catch up. Once the wagon was on the hard rocky ground, William instructed Luke to stop.

"What, what? What's going on?" The Duke stammered.

"Just checking the wagon for damage milord. Then we will proceed." William replied. He jumped from his saddle and walked to the back by Edmund.

"How are we doing?" William asked.

"Besides staring at the back of a carriage for four days only to be awoken by a horse gone made by a sulfuric stench? I'm just swell! How are you doing Sir William?" Edmund said dramatically. William laughed.

"Thanks for the sarcasm. Did the carriage hit anything from what you saw?" He asked while looking underneath the wagon.

"No." Edmund stated. William nodded his head and went around to the side. He checked the wheel axles, the reaches beneath the carriage, then made his way to the front of the buggy. The mule's breast collar harnesses were still sturdy, and lastly he checked the chains that were attached to the shaft.

"How is everything?" Luke asked from atop his coachman's seat.

"There are a few nicks and scratches but nothing too serious." William replied. He patted the mules' sides and muzzles. "I know guys, we're almost there." He said as he soothed the tired animals. William's stallion snorted in jealousy.

"Hold on Fivestar. I'll be with you momentarily." William shouted. Lastly, William went back to talk to his master.

"We have a three day journey through Monia, and then a two day journey through Shempshay. Selfur Kingdom won't be reached for another three days once we have cleared the Shempshay Territory milord."

"Well, carry on then. Are we to stop soon?"

"No milord. Unfortunately our last stop was supposed to be at Tonelle to resupply for this journey. But, now we must continue in due of its absence. We might be able to stop and rest in Shempshay, but Monia would be too dangerous." William explained.

"What of water then?" The Duke inquired.

"Also, unfortunately our water is gone. We have small amounts left in our gourds and sacks. We have to make it last, due the waters of Monia being poisoned."

"We are that low?" The Duke asked concerned.

"Yes milord."

The Duke sighed and opened the carriage door. Pointing at a large barrel next to him he looked at William.

"Here, give this to the horses and save some for yourselves. I'll bathe later." Whoa, what? William looked at the Duke in surprise, was this compassion?

I thought that the Duke was void of all emotions!' William thought bewildered. He nodded nonetheless, and hoisted the barrel out and onto the ground.

"Thank you milord." He said with a smile.

"Yes well, I can't have my slaves or my transportation die now can I?" The Duke said with a huff, and slammed the door shut.

And it was gone, so much for compassion.

Chapter Ten

Embracing Your Destiny

JENEVY SOARED THROUGH the sky; the wind beneath her wings was pulling her higher and higher. She smiled as the smell of fresh rain entered her nose and cleared her mind.

Feau flew ahead, flying gracefully before her. His enormous wings made shockwaves of air that surged past her. He too seemed to be happier.

Feau stretched open his wings and the leathery folds of his skin billowed out, which slowed him down dramatically.

Jenevy did the same, and then flapped her wings to stay afloat next to him. Luckily for her, he hadn't done the same yet, or else she would have been shot straight upward in a current of air.

"Most of the animals have gone. Something has frightened them. Perhaps we should travel further ahead?" Feau muttered, and in an instant had taken flight again. Jenevy dove after him.

"Feau we have already left Shempshay Mountains and the forest! Where else could they be?" She asked him with her thoughts.

"As far as the sea if we must. I do not want to be tempted with eating you!" He replied. Jenevy half laughed sarcastically, she hoped that he was kidding.

Up ahead lay another grove of trees, and Jenevy could hear something moving. But what was it? She watched as Feau dove towards the ground like a bird of prey, the grace of the dragon was astounding. He lunged with claws extended, at a large deer grazing within a small clearing. He looked like a Lion in midflight attacking an Impala.

With a sickening crack, the dragon had descended upon the creature and was ripping it into pieces. The creature didn't stand a chance.

Jenevy dropped down, landing silently upon a tree branch, and crouched down to wait.

"You don't have to wait, go and get your own!" Feau ordered.

She nodded and leapt into the sky with such force that the branch had snapped off, slamming it onto the ground below.

Feau grinned as he watched her leave, and then choked down his newly acquired feast. Jenevy knew that one small deer was not going to be nearly enough to quench the large creatures appetite, and she didn't want to stick around to find out.

Jenevy looked to the ground and scanned it for any movement. Apparently Feau had found the only living animal within miles.

The forest below was barely living, if it could even be called that. And the volcanic region would hold little else of nutrition. She knew that the volcanoes ahead of her were within a minute's flight so she quickly raised her right wing and spun back around.

Retreating to the south, she began her search again but to no avail. Slowly she felt Feau's hunger return and the pain in her stomach returned. She grimaced and clenched her abdomen as she pushed herself further.

As the trees began to thin and darken into the outer edge of the volcanic undergrowth, she noticed movement.

A large creature loomed in the sky, fluttering its wings as it flew. Jenevy squinted her eyes and her vision zoomed in to magnify the creature.

Jenevy let out a sigh of relief, it was just a dragon.

"It must be Feau." She said aloud. The dragon turned around and looked at her. It hesitated for a moment and then its speed engaged.

A feeling of dread washed over Jenevy as it dawned on her that Feau was still behind her, she could feel his anxiety as he too realized the danger ahead of her.

The dragon in the sky was a wild, demonic dragon of nature, and it was nearly upon her.

Jenevy realized her mistake and dove for the ground. But the dragon was already on top of her, and it sent a spiral of flames in her direction.

Jenevy drew in her wings and spun to the side. She skidded to a stop on the ground as the flames shot past her, singeing her arm. She had missed the dragon's first attack, but had not missed the second.

A tremor of pain wielded itself on her back as the dragon's towering legs knocked her down. It roared as it watched her bounce from the ground and plunge into a tree.

She slumped to the ground and coughed. The force of the dragon's blow had knocked the wind out of her.

She moaned and shoved herself to her feet as the dragon landed next to her. She glared at it as it snarled and hissed at her like a viscous cat.

The dragon stood menacingly over her, its head lowered down to eye level with her and roared as loud as it could at her.

The breath of the dragon was repulsive, and it shot past her sending her hair flying back like the wind did when she flew.

She grimaced in disgust at the smell of the rotting flesh that lay ingrained into the dragon's teeth.

Jenevy shook off the nausea and brought her arms to her sides. The power within her body coursed to her hands, as they charged up with energy. Blue streaks of lightening coiled down her forearms, gathering into a ball of energy within her palms.

Black flame danced upon her body as a loud humming sound echoed louder and louder.

CRACK!! She smacked both of her hands together, shooting a wave of electric energy at the wild dragon.

The trees snapped in two, earth and rocks shattered, and large boulders flew into the sky. Jenevy stood tall, and waited for the dust to settle before she would make another move.

"May the Gods protect me . . . ." she said in disbelief. The dragon was still there. But not only that, it stood completely unscathed. Her attack hadn't even affected him, all it had done was angered him more.

The dragon snarled and shifted its weight to its hind legs, and lunged forward. Jenevy was thrown to the side, where she tumbled over the remains of broken trees.

She winced as she felt the pain of a large object protruding from her arm. A large splinter of timber had wedged itself in between the shafts of the metal of her armor.

She yanked the wood from her arm and stood up in anger. The black flame ignited upon her once more, and her eyes began to glow.

She jumped forward to retaliate but Feau pushed her back as he roared at the other dragon.

'NO! He will kill you! Your powers have no affect on him!' He shouted at her. Jenevy's eyes widened in alarm and she stepped back as the two beasts began their battle.

Blood and sweat went flying, fire shot left and right, and Jenevy dove back and forth in order to avoid their destruction.

Feau's massive body dwarfed the wild dragon, and his strength could have easily conquered it. But Feau's strength was limited in comparison to the wild one. For while Feau had his sheer size and massive strength to win the fight, the other dragon had mobility and agility to outmaneuver Feau's attacks.

Every chance that Feau would try to lay a deadening blow, the other creature would easily deflect, and leap away and then retaliate with an attack of its own.

Jenevy could feel Feau's frustration as he failed over and over again to end the fighting.

Feau roared in pain as the creature sank its teeth into Feau's shoulder. Jenevy cried in misery as her shoulder began to throb and burn in spasms of pain.

Feau swung his tail around, whipping the other dragon into a tree. Before it could even stand, Feau was upon him and slashed his claws through the skin of the beast like butter.

Jenevy watched intently as the dragon screeched in pain, and fire shot out of its throat heating up Feau and Jenevy's skin.

Feau shoved his talons into the creature's jaw, knocking it into the ground with a thud. It writhed in pain, looking more like a worm drowning in water, than a giant serpent.

Pushing it further into the ground, Feau slammed his spiked tail into the dragon again. Rocks, dirt, and leaves sprang up into the air as the dragon was slammed deeper and deeper into the soil. With one last blow, Feau knocked the dragon unconscious.

Feau waited, and then moved away from the still dragon.

"Is it dead?" Jenevy asked worriedly. Feau remained quiet as he stared at the dragon.

"Not dead, not living, but between both worlds." He finally said. Jenevy walked slowly to his side, she too stared at the unconscious beast.

In a blink of an eye, the wild dragon grabbed her, growled and leapt into the air leaving Feau trying frantically to keep up.

Jenevy felt fear twanging at the back of her mind as she realized that she was incapable of release.

Her eyes glowed red as she screamed into the sky in anger, and the dragon squeezed her tighter. Feau was close behind them, gaining speed as his giant wings pushed him faster.

The wild dragon noticed Feau's pursuit and dodged faster through the sky. With every beat of its wings, its grip grew tighter and Feau grew smaller.

Jenevy could hear Feau's thoughts, but they were becoming incoherent in her mind.

"Feau . . . . I'm not . . . . going to last much . . . . longer—" and she faded into the dark abyss of her mind.

❖ William absolutely despised the Monia Volcanic Region. Not only was it littered with the most dangerous volcanoes awaiting eruption, but it had deadly plants, deadly animals and collapsible earth leading to a pit of lava laying everywhere. Plus Monia smelled horrible.

The stench was a combination of sulfur and pure liquid ammonia. Any creature within miles would run in fear from the stench of the gas smells that the region erupted.

Plus, with the smell being practically unbearable, it also contained a solid element that kept the smell with you for weeks after leaving the area.

Fivestar seemed to agree with William as his careful footing turned into spiteful stops and he kept snorting in disgust.

William glanced over his shoulder to look at Edmund. The boy's eyes showed his fear, but his body remained rigid and calm on his horse,

Luke's face was sunken with exhaustion, and he slouched upon his seat. He didn't seem to care about Monia at all, as long as he could get some shut eye soon.

Turning back around, William surveyed the land looking for the safest route. There was no trail in sight, no safe path, and no signs to follow. William sighed as he realized that his bearings were going to have to be perfect for the entire trip if they were to survive.

A huge explosion caught his attention as a volcano spewed out its molten lava, and fiery rocks. Its neighboring brother returned its call with another eruption.

Most of the flying rocks hit the ground a good distance away, but some got uncomfortably close.

William urged the caravan faster through the land, as singed tree bark slapped to the ground in response to the horse's hoof beats.

Fivestar eagerly sped up, and Edmund trotted his horse up next to William's.

"Sir William. How many days is this journey going to take?" He asked with worry.

"A few days, maybe less if we keep up this pace." He replied. Edmund shuddered.

A roar echoed through the sky, both Edmund and his horse jumped in fright. William looked up in time to see a dragon flying over their heads. Edmund practically screamed when he saw it.

"What is that beast doing over here?" William pondered.

"Don't dragons live in places like this?!" Edmund shrieked. William shook his head.

"Not everything is as you read in books." William replied. "Quickly, we must get out of sight, he may be hunting." William ordered, and he led the group through the dense, charred foliage.

Another roar shook the ground as an even larger, more deadlier dragon flew overhead in pursuit of the smaller one. William froze.

"Or *he's* hunting." He said as he gawked at the huge creature. Edmund whimpered at his side. William looked down at Edmund in amazement.

"You know, you might have to fight one of those someday. Especially if you attain Knighthood!" William whispered. Edmund looked up at him in fear.

"And live?!" He exclaimed. William laughed.

"What is so funny?" The Duke asked from his perch within the carriage. William twisted around in his saddle to look at his master. The Duke's face was completely drained of emotion, and no amusement sung within his eyes.

"Nothing milord." William replied.

"Why have we stopped then? Haven't those beasts left? This part of the journey will go much faster if we . . . . KEPT MOVING!!!!" And the Duke smacked the drapery down with a slap. William sighed.

"He's right. We have to keep moving if we want to sleep at some point. The Shempshay Mountains hold our retreat and our safety. We must press on." William stated. Edmund nodded and followed Fivestar with dexterity.

William kicked Fivestar to a trot as he stared at the sky. He wondered if the dragons were to return along their same path, and if William were to see them again.

But something else was nagging at him and William's hand was firmly grabbing the reins of Fivestar, while his other gripped the hilt of his sword.

Edmund could sense William's uneasiness and he rushed his horse forward to be at his side.

"Sir William. Those beasts *are* gone right?" He asked timidly.

"Something feels wrong, and my senses will prove that theory to be correct." He said shaking his head. He urged them faster.

"How . . . how do you know? Are you certain?"

"Trust me. After all of the training that will do to achieve Knighthood, you learn to listen to your gut. You will learn how to feel it, what it means, and to trust it." William answered, then as if in reply, another bellowing roar echoed over the rumbling volcanoes, scaring Edmund half to death.

William slammed his heels into Fivestar's flanks, and he took off into the trees.

"Get them out of here!!" He ordered back at the men as he was frantically placing his helmet upon his head. Fivestar braced himself for battle as William drew his sword.

Lava pooled onto the ground, sizzling the earth. Fire was igniting at every angle, and bits of blazing ash were swirling around William as Fivestar plummeted forward.

Fivestar snorted in anger, shaking his head as the horned blade on his armored helmet gleamed in the light.

William's sword hung at his side at the ready as he charged forward. Fivestar skidded to a gut-wrenching stop, and he reared back in preparation of the attack. As the high levels of his stallion testosterone began to take over, Fivestar's front legs were kicking frantically in front of him.

A huge serpent slithered out of the pouring lava. It snarled at them, hissed and roared again. William stared meticulously at it, deciphering its weak points, and strategizing his future attacks in anticipation of those weak points being exposed.

Fivestar stomped his hooves into the earth, and clawed at the ground like a raging bull. The horse panted and screamed at the serpent.

Slowly, William let go of Fivestar's reins, and gently tapped the horse's side to signal that he had let go. Fivestar nickered in understanding.

William unhooked his shield from the horse's saddle and slowly slid his arm into the straps. Raising it to eye level, he tightened his fist and stared at the creature.

He saw the serpent's body as it coiled from out of the lava, steam was rising from its scales, and its muscles were tensing: it was about to attack.

In a blink of an eye, the serpent shot forward. Its teeth bared, it slammed the pointed fangs forward, and followed it with a slam from its tremendous body.

William slashed his shield up, and sliced his sword upwards as Fivestar knelt down to avoid the poisoned fangs.

William's sword sliced through the sensitive, soft underbelly of the serpent sending it wheeling back in pain.

William kicked Fivestar's sides, and squeezed his legs, which signaled Fivestar to gallop forward. The horse ran at full throttle towards the serpent and then twisted his head to the side and reared up.

The bladed horn upon Fivestar's shaffron, sliced through the underbelly of the serpent, while his spiked hooves stabbed into it again.

The creature roared in pain, as they continued to attack. William swung his shield upwards, and the shield's outer blades stabbed into the creature as well. Fivestar dropped back to all fours, while William yanked down at his shield, in an attempt to draw a long, deep cut into the creature's flesh.

But once it hit the rock hard scales of the serpent's back, it savagely yanked itself from William's grip, and spun violently onto the ground.

William grimaced at his mistake, and brought his sword up to attack. The serpent slammed its tail around, and splattered lava towards its assailants.

Fivestar jumped back as William ducked beneath the flying, molten rock; he glared up at the serpent. The serpent snarled and glared back.

Fivestar kicked at the ground, and snorted towards the beast. The serpent lunged forward again, but Fivestar ran towards it and jumped over the serpent's body with ease.

William pressed his right leg into Fivestar's side, and the horse wheeled around. The serpent hissed at them, then shot forward again.

Fivestar jumped again, only this time he bucked in midflight sending William soaring into the air. William twisted his body up and backwards, sending himself face first and back down towards the serpent.

Lowering his sword, he stabbed it through the backside of the serpent's neck while his legs caught him upon the serpent's back. William jumped to the side and twisted his body again, sinking the sword in deeper until, SNAP! A sickening pop echoed.

William slammed onto the ground, catching himself on one knee while using his free arm to absorb the shock of his landing. He crouched there as the serpent's head dropped next to him.

William panted as he tried to catch his breath, and the creature's body gurgled back into the lava, where it disappeared beneath its fiery surface.

Sheathing his sword, he stood and whistled for Fivestar. The horse trotted up next to him, and nudged him with his nose.

William patted his neck, and rubbed his ears.

"Good boy Fivestar. Good boy." His soothing words calmed the animal. Grabbing the reins, William led the stallion towards a thicket where his comrades were hiding.

His shield lay half buried in the earth, and Edmund had already begun to pick it up when William approach.

William sneered at the thought that he had even dropped his shield. The first rule that they taught him in his training was to never lose his gear. Yet he had made that mistake like a rooky would, it was not what a veteran Knight, as himself, should have let happen.

"That was amazing!" Edmund shouted in glee. "I have never seen the great Sir William in action before! The stories are true!" Edmund stated with a huge grin.

William nodded, as he unhooked the leather strap under his jaw and removed the helmet from his head. He shook his head violently, sending beams of sweat shooting onto the ground. It sizzled upon impact, and sent tiny streams of steam out into the atmosphere.

Fivestar gingerly trotted to the side of the wagon, and awaited his reward for his good deeds.

Luke snickered as he held out a handful of oats for the tired warhorse.

"Are we safe now?" The Duke asked from his window. William glanced over at him.

"Yes. For now we are." William said as he walked up to Fivestar and reached a hand into the barrel of water and began to drink it eagerly.

"But those creatures are always in pairs. No doubt its mate heard its cry of death. We must press on much quicker now." William said hesitantly as he swung himself back up onto Fivestar's saddle.

"If we move swiftly, we should reach the safety of the Shempshay Mountains by nightfall. And that is only if we run these horses like they have never ran before." He declared. Fivestar neighed and reared up kicking his legs in front of him. William kicked the stallion's flanks and Fivestar sprinted forward towards the dark, dragon infested mountains.

❖ Jenevy's consciousness slowly faded back as she was thrown towards the ground. She screamed as her eyes refocused and she saw the flaming ground beneath her coming quickly towards her.

She whipped out her wings and flapped them violently, shoving her into the air. But the burning lava below was too hot for her, and she couldn't gain enough altitude. She began to panic as she tried exhaustingly to fly higher but to no avail. She began to fall again towards the molten rock but Feau caught her mid-fall and soared back up into the sky.

Jenevy breathed a sigh of relief as they returned to the safety of the star filled sky.

"Are you alright Jenevy?"

"Yes . . .yes . . . But where is the other dragon?" She stammered. Feau looked back and Jenevy followed his gaze. The other dragon lay burning in flames within the lava below.

"But how?" She asked. Feau sighed.

"I barely caught up to him as he was about to dive into the dark cave of Sortea. I attacked him long enough to catch him off guard and then I killed him." Feau paused solemnly. "Thankfully he released you midflight instead of when he hit the ground."

Jenevy stared up at him in disbelief.

"And what if he hadn't?!" She wailed and Feau smirked.

"Then I would have ripped his arm off."

Jenevy half smiled.

"That doesn't make me feel any better." She stated.

"Trust me little one. I would not have let anything happen to you, I would never allow it. Not now, not ever."

Jenevy smiled, a very strong ally she had made, and a very loyal companion as well. If only she could find men like that! Jenevy smiled up at Feau; someday she would return the favor.

Once they had reached Feau's home safely, he released her. Jenevy stepped down and slumped into the grass. Feau laid down next to her.

"Dragon, what was that cave that you spoke of?" She asked once she was sure he was comfortable. Feau looked down at her.

"The cave of Sortea is the lair of the dark dragons of this world. They hide there, breeding and attacking one another. It used to be the prison where the evil dragons of my kind were sentenced to. But after the revolt, they all escaped." Feau said angrily.

Jenevy looked up at him in surprise.

"You mean, that dragon used to be a Shempshay Dragon?!" She asked bewildered. Feau shook his head.

"Somewhere down his bloodline there was one, but not one like me: one more darker and twisted. It was a more sinister, more evil creature. One your kind might refer to as a demon." He explained. Jenevy frowned. A demon? She laid her head back down onto the grass.

"I don't expect you to understand, not yet. Someday you will, but for now you must rest. We have to develop your powers more rigorously than you have before. And we will start tomorrow."

"What?!" She shrieked, jumping to her feet. Feau laughed.

"Yes. Your powers are similar to mine, if not the same. I have felt them and I believe that I can help." Feau suggested. Jenevy grinned in high spirits.

'Why hadn't I realized that before?!' She thought to herself. Even in that dark prison when she had saved Feau, and had felt the anger rise within her, she never connected it to have been caused *by* the dragon! She had experienced a new power, and a stronger energy ever since she had met Feau. She had assumed that her powers had changed for a different reason, but what?

'Maybe Feau was the reason for it?' Maybe they were connected more than she had realized. Maybe she was meant to meet him, and everything that had happened was all part of some giant puzzle piece, that connected them together?

It was mind boggling to imagine, almost exhilarating.

"I had thought the same thing dearest Jenevy."

Jenevy smiled up at him, Feau was feeling the same thing as her and it made her content in knowing that he felt the same.

"Somehow I have got to remember that you are able to hear me!" Jenevy said with a laugh.

Feau faced her, smoke twirled out of his nostrils as embers of fire glowed within his mouth. His tongue slithered out like a snake, and his eyes were firm and fierce. His legs braced himself in an attacking stance, as his tail whipped back and forth behind him.

Jenevy, a few yards in front of him, stood and watched him silently. Her mind remained clear as they severed their telepathy connection to help them focus more clearly.

Feau hissed at her, snarling as his nostrils grew brighter with flame. Jenevy watched as Feau braced himself for a strike. He sucked in a huge breath of air, and his mouth was wide open as he gathered energy within it. Sparkles of power gathered within his mouth, gathering together until a huge ball of energetic fire glowed. Snapping his head back, he sent the enormous energy ball whirling towards Jenevy.

The recoil of the blast had sent Feau skidding backwards, and he dug his legs into the ground, leaving skid marks in his wake.

Instantly, Jenevy retrieved her sword, and it began to glow red with power. She swung it forward, and sent out a sphere of energy hurdling towards Feau's attack. The two blasts collided, exploded, and sent shards of energetic light shooting into the sky.

Feau lunged forward with a snarl, and whipped his tail out. Jenevy flipped over it, and landed in time to block another attack from him.

But he had anticipated this, and had already shot out another sphere of powers. Jenevy struck out at it, batting it back at him.

Feau caught it with his clawed talons and threw it back, along with a stream of scorching fire.

Jenevy stepped back with one foot, and shifted her weight to her rear leg. She closed her eyes, concentrated and then screamed. A huge stream of water shot from her body, it twisted and coiled as it flew towards Feau. The water quickly extinguished the flame, Feau watched her with a sneer. She had only defeated one attack, and not the other. But within the water, an even larger energy sphere rested, and once the water had evaporated with the fire, the power sphere emerged. Jenevy opened her eyes and watched her sphere devour Feau's, and then it went careening towards him. Feau's eyes widened, and he ducked beneath the blast.

Jenevy raised her arms and yanked her hands behind her. Her energy sphere whipped back around and smashed into Feau, sending him soaring to the ground with a thud.

Jenevy ran forward and leapt into the sky. Drawing in her wings, she dropped down and sent her sword flying ahead of her. Gravity pulled her towards the dragon as she beat her wings to make her move faster. The sword stabbed into the ground next to Feau, and Jenevy clenched her hands together and slammed them down onto a boulder next to Feau's head.

The boulder shot into millions of pieces, sending dust and sand everywhere. Feau looked up at her, as bits of rock fell around her and she walked back over to her sword. She yanked it out of the ground, and sheathed it into her scabbard. She looked over at Feau, as she tried to catch her breath.

Feau was panting like a dog, and smiling with his huge, sharp-toothed grin.

"Your aim is remarkable. And your power has improved tremendously!" He said. Jenevy sat down next to him.

"So does this mean that I can fight the other dragons if I am forced to?" She asked.

"Yes and no. You are able to deflect their attacks and powers, with your own now. And even though your energy is the same as theirs, you should be able to knock them down without hurting them like you did me."

Jenevy looked at him apologetically.

"But, the only way to penetrate their armored hide is by powering up your sword. And whatever you do, don't lose your sword. A blow to their head won't turn out like that boulder did, even with all of the speed behind it." Feau finished.

Jenevy nodded in understanding.

"Come child. We need to rest before tomorrow's training begins." Feau rolled onto his feet and slowly stood up. He turned around and headed towards the disheveled buildings.

Jenevy trailed behind him, exited for what new things she was about to learn.

❖ Shempshay Territory and the Fenloré Mountains were all rock, sand and dead trees. William frowned at the heat reflecting back at him.

That part of the journey would be, by far, the longest three days of despair than he had felt in the whole journey itself.

Not only were they tired and miserable, but they were about to spend three days walking through a desert that was neighbored by tall, deadly looking mountains that were once, and might very well still be, infested with the deadliest dragons on the planet.

Not only was the heat unbearable, but also in knowing that their kingdom of retreat was also a kingdom of misery, it almost made them *want* to die on their voyage.

William groaned and Fivestar returned his gesture, the midday sun was unbearable. The sun felt hotter than it did near the volcanoes, and William was sure that blisters were starting to form on the nether regions of his anatomy.

William eagerly looked around for some shade, they had to rest during the day and travel by night or they would be the next skeletons that littered that route. Not to mention that their water supply was so exceedingly depleted, that death would befall them much sooner than destined.

'If the Duke plans on killing me after this trip, I wouldn't mind dying out here!' William said to himself as they walked past a towering cliff.

But then he thought of Jenevy, alone in that castle, and he felt a new desire to live. He wanted to live for her sake, to find a way to help her to escape to freedom. And if she would have him, he wanted to share the rest of his life with her.

William shook that thought from his mind; the *last* thing that she would want was him. She was a royal and he was just a knight, and a thief at that, who hand imprisoned her within a castle of terror.

Someday though, he wished that he could free her from the Duke's evil grasp, to see her happy and free once again. In fact, he had never seen anything *but* sadness and fear within her. But what did he expect, their circumstance for meeting wasn't exactly pleasant.

William still did wonder what had happened to her, he hadn't heard anything, from anyone. But he hadn't seen her leave, nor had he buried her lifeless body. So, unless the Duke had some secret burial ground, he doubted that she was dead.

A large ravine ahead disrupted his thoughts, it was north of them and a few large boulders were supported from an overhead collection of vines which provided the shade that William so desperately desired.

He led the party towards the small cavern and stopped them once they were all hidden from the sun's murderous rays. They all quickly unloaded the wagon, and pulled the water barrel from with the carriage, much to the Duke's dismay, and allowed the horses to drink.

"We won't have enough water to last us in this sun." Edmund stated.

"I know. There was a small pool of water just a few miles ahead. We have used it on every trip when we head towards Selfur Castle. Run on up and see if it is still there?" William ordered. Edmund nodded and climbed onto his mare. He trotted up the ravine and returned almost instantly.

"Sir William! Come quick!" He shouted.

William's eyes widened and he climbed onto Fivestar, the horse grunted in exhaustion.

"What?! What is it?!" William shouted. But Edmund had already sprinted his horse forward. William urged his stallion to speed up.

Within moments he saw Edmund ahead, the boy had gotten off of his horse and was standing still. William stopped Fivestar and ran up next to him.

"Edmund? What has gotten into y—" William trailed off as he realized what Edmund was staring at.

In front of them was one of the biggest, most terrifying remains of any dragon that William had ever seen. The dragon was bigger than anything he could have ever imagined, and it had the most gruesome claws and teeth. The dragon's body had to of been at least five times the size of the larger dragon that William had seen in the Monica Region.

But this dragon looked oddly similar to that same dragon. Granted, the dragon earlier had been alive with skin, flesh and muscles, but their bone structures looked identical.

The dragon remains in front of William, had the same spiked skull as the larger dragon from earlier that day. And it had the same shape of nose, horns on its spine, and almost the same kind of tail.

The tail was long, and had extra knuckle bones within it in order help it to be more flexible. When looking at the tip of the tail, William could see why that flexibility was needed. Bladed spikes lay at the end of the tail, the bones looked almost as if they had been sharpened to a blade.

William stared at the bones in wonder, and tried to imagine what that dragon might have looked like if it had been alive.

"What do you think killed it?" Edmund asked solemnly. William shook his head slowly.

"I don't know."

"What kind of dragon was it?" Edmund asked.

"Well, it's definitely not a dragon that we see anymore. So, it could be any number of different species. I'd say given its spiked skull and bladed tail, probably the Ingeo Tiat Dragon." He lied. Edmund nodded.

"Whoa. The Ingeo Tiat? That must have been a pretty serious dragon!" Edmund stated excitedly.

"That he was . . ." William said quietly. Edmund whistled and walked back to his horse.

"I'll head back for the water barrel, and I'll be back." Edmund said. William nodded as he knelt down next to the dragon skeleton.

"In all my studies, I never once thought that I was ever going to see any remnants of an actual Shempshay Dragon. But I guess I was wrong." William placed a hand on the skull of the dragon.

"You were truly a magnificent beast, and for what its worth . . . . I'm sorry. I am one knight that believes in you being the creator of our intelligent domain. And I am afraid that I might be the last." William bowed his head solemnly, and then stood back to his feet.

Fivestar approached him and William waited for Edmund. The stable boy trudged back over on his horse, with a pack horse laden with two empty water barrels being towed from behind.

"Sir William. Those dragons that we saw earlier, are they descendants of the Ingeo Dragon?"

"Yes. They are." He lied again.

"Really? So that large dragon that we saw chasing after that little one, could very well be a third generation blood line?"

William paused. His eyes widened in disbelief. That dragon that they had seen earlier looked identical to the paintings of the fabled Shempshay Dragons. Granted, it was much smaller, but it had the same attributes.

William looked back at the dragon skeleton. There was no way! Had the Shempshay Dragons found a way to live on? Did they have other wild dragons with their same characteristics?

William shook his head.

'No, if there were any Shempshay Dragons left, we would have heard from them by now. They would have tried to contact us, and not just eaten us.' He said to himself.

William groaned as he realized that the pool of water was a bit farther away than from the camp than he had expected. Hopefully by the time that they reached it, the sun hadn't dried it up completely.

The lands had changed a lot since their last maiden voyage to the Selfur Kingdom. It had been exactly five years prior to that day since he had trudged through the scorching lands of the Shempshay Territory.

But, even with time, the two small palm trees that had signaled the entrance to the small haven of hope still remained. Of course the *small* palm trees were no longer small, but they still stood unharmed.

"Sir William?" Edmund looked at William puzzled. William looked around, and realized that he had walked right into the pool of water without even realizing it.

"Oh . . . wow. Guess I was lost in my thoughts!" William said quickly.

Fivestar could smell the clear liquid from the drinking reservoir and instantly to shake William from his back so that he could get a cold drink. The pool still looked the same, not even a pebble was misplaced.

William jumped off Fivestar and led him towards the spring; he let the stallion drink his fill, while William brushed his hock. Fivestar exhaled air out of his nose, indicating that he was content and happy.

Edmund did the same with the horses, but while the animals were drinking he was quickly un-strapping the barrels and dropping them into the water with a splash.

Unhooking the lid, Edmund silently filled them. William unfastened his leather helmet strap from beneath his chin and lifted it from his head. He hung the shiny helmet on the horn of Fivestar's saddle and began to run his fingers through his hair.

His black hair was becoming longer and longer with each passing day, and with his constant wearing of his helmet it was getting matted from all of his sweat.

William was half considering chopping it off with his sword if it weren't for the fact that he would appear as a rookie Knight again.

So, William concluded with just pouring water onto his scalp to replenish the coolness that it lacked. Kneeling down next to the stallion, he cupped his hands and scooped up the water and let it run down his head.

The water instantly cooled him, and William began to feel rested and relaxed. Fivestar paused in his drinking to perk up at William, and then nickered at him.

William smiled and reached out a hand to stroke Fivestar's neck.

"I don't know how you do it boy. But you seem to get younger everyday that I am getting older." He said solemnly. The horse grunted in reply. William smirked as he reached down to get more water. They both drank in silence; two lifelong friends who had lived through hell on earth were instantly calmed by a drink from a fresh mountain spring.

"Are those the Fenlore Mountains?" Edmund asked interrupting the silence. William looked up at Edmund and watched the boy as he rolled the barrels back onto shore. William glanced up at the mountain pass to the north.

"Yes and no. Those are the beginning of the mountains, intermingled with the Shempshay Mountains." He replied. Edmund looked confused.

"Alright, let me explain." William said with a laugh. "According to legend, the Shempshay Dragon's of old lived within these mountains." William said as he guided Edmund's direction towards the steep mountain faces that surrounded them.

"You can see their homes on the peaks up there. But Fenlorè was where the ancient Shempshay Dragons dwelt. Well, where their royal family dwelt I should say." William said as he pointed back towards the northern mountains. He continued.

"Somewhere, on the other side of that ridge the Shempshay Mountains end and the Fenlorè Mountains begin. They are intermingled, almost like fingers that interlace, it's a bit confusing. But no one can climb up those mountains to distinguish the two, we just know that they are there." William finished.

"How?" Edmund asked, still confused.

"I guess we *believe* that they are there. Whether it is true or not, it cannot be proven otherwise. Maybe that is why it is a legend and not history. It is not a fact, only a long believed thought that everyone shares." William concluded. Edmund frowned, and stared at William bewildered.

"Am I to know as much as you?" Edmund asked baffled. William grinned at him and then sighed.

"Perhaps someday. But most you will have to learn through your own studies just as I did. I can teach you the sword, how to battle, and help to train your horse to fight as well. But by being diligent in your readings, you will gain far more knowledge than I could ever hope to teach you. Just be patient." William replied and he smiled up at Edmund.

"Drink some water and rest for a bit, but we must be heading back soon." William instructed as he stood to his feet. Edmund nodded and headed over to the mule. But before he had time to lower himself down for a drink of water, a loud crack echoed through the area, followed by an even louder explosion.

In a blink of an eye, both the pack horse and Edmund's horse had bolted away with fear, and took off into the desert plains. Edmund ran after the spooked animals, yelling for them to stop.

William, whose hand was already on the hilt of his sword, had jumped upon Fivestar and kicked the horse into action. Fivestar was barely startled by the explosion, and quickly galloped after the frightened equines.

"Edmund wait! You'll never catch them!" He shouted as he circled around the stable boy.

"Stay here, I'll bring them back!" And he sent Fivestar soaring in fast pursuit of the horses, leaving a trail of dust behind them.

They caught up to the draft horse first, and William reached down to grab the reins and urged it to stop. William tied the horse to a tree and kicked Fivestar forward again.

Edmund's horse was much faster than the draft horse, but was no match for William's Andalusia Stallion. Fivestar sprinted forward as soon as he caught sight of the spooked horse. Once they were running alongside the horse, William jumped onto its back, and pulled on the reins. Fivestar pressed up against the mare's side, urging it to stop.

"Whoa girl, easy easy!" William said calmly, the horse snorted and began to slow down. Once it had stopped, William leapt back onto Fivestar and pulled the other horse behind him.

Edmund saw them approach, he had reached the tree where the draft horse was tied to and rushed over. William instantly handed him the horse's reins.

"What was that?" Edmund asked bewildered.

William looked up at the mountains in confusion. The mountains were quiet; nothing looked different except for a thin line of smoke coming up from the back side of the ridge.

"I'm not entirely sure. But I'm not going to wait here to find out." William stated.

"Was it a dragon?" Edmund asked.

"Possibly, I wouldn't be surprised! Those caverns were made for dragons at one point in time, so why wouldn't one still be living there?" William posed.

"Come on. Let's head back." Edmund suggested.

❖ Jenevy coughed through the dust and smoke that had clouded around her.

The blast had been a bit overpowering as she had shot it out, and it had hit the mountain face with immense force.

Feau had taught her a new power to harness and had insisted that it was easier to control despite its huge magnitude of destructiveness. Jenevy fanned the smoke away from her face and glared at Feau.

"That was a surprise." She stated.

"Yes, a much bigger surprise than I had expected." Feau responded.

"What went wrong?" She asked while stifling back another cough.

"Nothing. Your powers are much stronger than I had originally predicted."

"What do you mean?"

"They are on a stronger level to even that of mine! That blast should not have had that type of energy. Let alone that strong! It was a short-wave energy cannon. You practically took out the rock wall! With a blast that should of only have destroyed a small tree, I am curious as to what other surprises your powers may hold." Feau said with a gleam in his eye.

"Wait, wait wait. Are you saying that if I were to have done that same attack, only on a higher degree of power, I—"

"—Would have flattened that mountain ridge." Feau finished, cutting her off. Jenevy looked at him in astonishment.

"Well, I'd say that's enough for today!" Jenevy declared as she started to walk away. Feau stopped her with his tail, and spun her around to face him.

"Here yes, but elsewhere no. We shall continue this at a safer location. How would you feel about the ocean?"

Jenevy looked up at him with a huge grin on her face.

"I've never been to an ocean before!" She said enthusiastically.

The waves echoed off of the rock cliffs bordering the small alcove of water, and brightly colored rocks glistened beneath the frothy water. The saltwater hissed as it was dragged back out to sea, almost as if it sighed in disappointment.

Tide pools imprisoned small, sparkling fish and vibrantly colored coral. The setting sun outlined the horizon, shining its golden colors upon the wavy water, and made the fish and coral even brighter.

Jenevy landed upon the sand as gracefully as possible. She was afraid that she would shatter the beach as if were a painted glass menagerie.

She stood there, mouth gaping, staring in wonder at the place she never knew existed. Feau walked up behind her.

"Imagine beauty like this existing on every place upon this earth." He said whimsically. Jenevy broke her trance to look at him.

"The world looks beautiful to me!" She said cheerfully.

"It used to be a even better than it is now, before men took their reign upon this world. Back then it had many flourishing plants, and bright, crisp water and countless numbers of creatures. Shempshay Territory was a green forest filled with small creatures of every species. But then the land died, and became what it is today."

Jenevy's grin faded and she stared down at the ground.

"Were the dragons what had kept it alive?" She asked quietly.

"In a magical sense, yes. But it was mostly the fact that the land was never touched. Mankind, once leaving our protection, took grip upon the lands like a vice. They began to strip it of all sustenance and life. We never knew whether it was a coincidence or not. But we had always assumed that the earth began to die once our alliance had been broken. It was as if the earth knew of the treachery afoot, and killed itself before anything else had a chance to." Feau finished solemnly. He looked out to sea, and sighed as the ocean breeze swept over him.

"Now come child. There is much more to learn and I feel that our powers would be best used far out of sight and over the water." And with his huge, massive legs he bounded into the sky, as Jenevy followed closely behind.

Chapter Eleven

Fate

THE EVIL CASTLE lured ahead of them on the twenty-fifth day of their horrific excursion. Its gloomy presence brought despair and death to its neighboring cities, and cries of agony echoed throughout the streets.

William groaned in sadness, regretting having to enter within the walls of that desolate kingdom. Edmund could feel William's uneasiness, and trotted his horse up next to the knight.

"Sir William, you seem tense."

"I'm not tense, I'm tired." He lied. The last thing that he needed to do was to explain his nervousness within earshot of his master.

'God help me.' William said to himself, as they approached the gates.

"Halt! Announce your business at Selfur Kingdom!" The guard from within the tower barked down at them. William glared in agitation up at him.

"I am Sir William, Knight of Albastson von Juefel. I am escorting the Duke of Greenwiche, whom has important affairs with the King. The other two are his carriage orderly and my squire." William shouted. The guard nodded and quickly waved to the gate-guards to raise the gate.

As the two gate-guards lifted the gate with an ear-splitting screech, the group walked through. The two guards bowed in respect at William, and then as the Duke passed they hid their faces as they showed expressions of disgust.

William almost laughed; at least he wasn't the only one who felt that way about the Duke. It was amazing that the Duke's reputation had reached that far.

William urged the party up the hill, one more gate and a drawbridge before they reached the very fire of hell itself. The villagers outlining the street held solemn expressions, their faces symbolized their feelings of despair, eyes of hope stared at William as he walked past. William frowned at the emancipated bodies of the people; there wasn't a single healthy human amongst that populace.

What kind of a King would let his people become so disheveled, so famine, and so weakened?

The guardsmen within the streets walked with strength and power as they beat everything and everyone within site. What was worse was that the guards showed no remorse in their acts of despair.

It angered William so much, that he had to firmly grip the horse's reins in order to restrain himself from lashing out at the cruel guards. William could sense Edmund's anger as well, so William quickly raced all of them up the hill towards the castle.

The drawbridge into the King's lair lay before them. They crossed the rickety bridge with ease where they were met by yet another iron clad gate. Only this gate was much different than all of the other ones within the kingdom.

The gate had deadly spikes that coiled up the front of the giant swinging doors. Each spike was tipped sharply towards the sky, and had matching barbs that speared their way off of the gates in a horizontal matter. It prevented people from climbing over the gate, but in case one were to make it past the sharp vertical spikes, then they would be diced and shredded by the lower barbs.

As a symbol of what freedom might bring to the castle slaves, the rotting flesh and bones of prior escapees were trapped all over the gates barbs and spikes.

Flames licked their lips from atop two large gate towers that guarded the entrance through that gate. Paired by two guards in each, and both armed with a spear and a crossbow.

The guards stared down at the company as they approached. William caught the eye of the guard to his left and waited for acknowledgment.

The guard on the left stood with his arm raised, waiting to signal the raising of the bridge. The guard to the right looked down at them and demanded introductions.

William yelled the same lines that he had said when first entering Selfur Kingdom, and the guard nodded and waved at the left sentinel to raise the gate.

The iron gate cranked to life, as it grinded and creaked from the chain pulling to raise the enormous door.

Fivestar waited until there was just enough room for him to enter and he eased himself underneath. The smells from the decaying land invaded the stallion's nostrils as the gate created a current of air, the horse snorted in abhorrence.

"William!" It was the Duke. William yanked on Fivestar's reins and waited for the coach to catch up.

"Yes my master." William said as he firmly gripped the reins, and bowed his head.

"Once I am inside of the castle, I will not be disturbed." The Duke demanded. Luke whipped the horses pulling the coach to life; they whinnied and took off into a gallop up the hill towards the castle.

'How long will that be?' William mused. He urged Fivestar up the hill towards the coach just as Luke was jumping down to open the door for a fast moving dignitary.

The Duke stormed inside of the castle with Luke hot on his heels. The castle doors slammed shut and the horses jumped in reply.

Sighing, William led his horse behind the coach, jumped off, and then tied the reins to the back railing. Walking towards the front he leapt onto the coach seat and urged the lead horses towards the neighboring barn.

Edmund brought his horse up to a trot alongside William as he looked around leery.

"Be prepared for a smell from hell when it's time to clean this thing out." William said as he motioned towards the carriage.

"How so?" Edmund inquired curiously. William looked at him with doubt and then smiled.

"Think about it. The entire excursion, did you ever see him leave this thing?"

Edmund's eyes widened and he grimaced in disgust.

"Oh Jasmina! Couldn't we have one of the stable boys do it?"

"You are a stable boy!" William shrieked.

Edmund groaned and raced his horse towards the barn.

"I better get the supplies." He shouted back as a puff of dust shot into the sky from the horse's hooves.

It took the rest of the day to clean out the Duke's carriage. When they had first opened the door, a wave of human secretions and sweat nearly knocked them off of their feet. Once they had actually begun the lengthy process of cleaning, they had had to stop twice due to their gagging from the putrid smells.

Eventually, they were able to restore its shine and splendor and had everything put away, animals fed and were heading up towards the castle before nightfall had fully set in.

"Now what?" Edmund asked panting. William glanced over at him.

"Not sure. This is the *first* time he has not required my assistance. Nor do I know how long he plans on being here." William said matter-of-factly.

"Where do we stay then? In the barn?" Edmund asked worriedly.

"Doubtful. But by all means stable boy! If you feel more comfortable in the hay, then turn around now!" William replied with a chuckle. "Although a large pile of hay doesn't sound too bad right now."

A maid unexpectedly appeared at their sides, where she proceeded to curtsey and then addressed them.

"Your rooms are ready if you wish to retire for the evening. If you please, I shall direct you towards them." She said quickly without making eye contact.

A huge grin spread across Edmund's face as he rushed forward after the maid, while William slowly brought up the rear.

But as they were barely into the grand hallway of the castle, William began to get a sick feeling in the pit of his stomach. It was the same sour feeling that he had felt when the creature from the Monia Region had appeared. William knew that he needed to follow that feeling and to turn around.

"Edmund head inside, I left some things in the barn." William said as he rushed outside without even a moment's glance backwards.

"Oh, alright! Do you want me to save you some supper then?!" Edmund shouted in reply.

"Sure." William replied. He rushed down the hill towards the barn and breathed a sigh of relief once the feeling had subsided.

He stopped and looked back at the castle. Its dark towers were sending gloomy shadows onto him. The Dark King's castle always sent shivers up William's spine, but the one he had just felt was different: frighteningly different.

William was actually scared! Not of the castle, the Duke, or the King, but of the unknown. What had caused that gut wrenching fear to overpower him?

William pondered for a moment, trying to decipher what he had felt and why. He didn't know, but one thing that he was most positive about was that he was *not* going back into that castle . . . ever.

He felt better sleeping with Fivestar than in the King's death trap where his death slave sat waiting in the corners.

William shook the fog from his head and swung open the barn door. Fivestar was in the back stall and was instantly nickering in excitement. William smiled as he got closer to his beloved friend.

"Hey boy, you miss me?" He asked with a whistle. Fivestar snorted and nibbled at William's face with his lips. William laughed and he scratched the horse's forehead.

William instantly had a memory of his childhood flash before him. He was a small boy, and his father had first begun in training William of the ways of a knight. William's father had given him a small, black Andalusia filly.

They were inseparable as they grew and trained together. William remembered choosing to sleep next to Fivestar than in his own bed at every chance that he could get.

William's father was pleased with William's choice in sleeping accommodations. For in his father's eyes, a warhorse and his knight must sleep, eat and train together so much, that being apart would be utter chaos for both man and beast.

William's father revered horses, and had taught William words and phrases that horses could understand and would be soothed by. He remembered practicing those words so much that he said them in his sleep. William's father was a very formidable, respected and talented knight.

He too, had been raised in the training of knighthood, and taught all that he could to his son William. William's last memory of his father was when William had left at the age of fifteen to attend the coveted Warfare Elements Convent. An academy that only a few knights in training were invited to attend. It taught him everything about spells, potions, fighting and many other scientific properties that were greatly associated with being a knight and the foes that may cross his path.

But five years into his training, William received word that his father had passed on. And to that day, he still had not found out why or how his father had died.

Fivestar nickered at William, interrupting his thoughts, and William smiled back at the horse and continued to rub his muzzle.

"Hey boy, sorry I got lost in my mind. How are you doing? You getting along with the other horses?" William asked. Fivestar snorted and kicked his front feet at the gate. Then he squealed loudly, sounding more like a scream rather than a squeal, to which he finished with a snort.

"Guess not!" William said with a laugh. He stroked the stallion's neck, and the horse bumped his head against William, while blowing air out of his nostrils. It sounded like a hollow wind tunnel.

"Well boy, I'm sleeping with you tonight. I just don't have it in me to be within those walls of evil anymore." Fivestar lifted his head to look into William's eyes, then shook his head and snorted again.

"We're getting too old my friend. We can't be living on the edge anymore." William said sadly. Fivestar hit William with his head again, practically knocking him over and shrieked at him once more.

"Okay, okay. I'm just getting old alright?" William corrected. The stallion whinnied his approval, and William smiled.

William grabbed the edge of Fivestar's stall door, hoisted himself up and jumped over the wall. He landed next to Fivestar with a thump and headed towards the back of the stall. Once finding a suitable pile of hay, he plopped down onto it and stared up at the ceiling.

Fivestar walked over next to him, and lowered his head down. The horse blew air out of his nostrils at him, ruffling his hair and then nibbled at the ruffled strands. William reached up a hand and stroked the horse's muzzle.

William placed his other hand behind his head, and closed his eyes. Sleep fell upon him within seconds.

To feel the cold, stabbing sensation of that salty water would take anyone's breath away. But to feel it, at the same time as a wave of panic is washing over you, is an entirely different sensation.

Was death near? It had to be, for Jenevy's power had diminished just as quickly as the demon had evaded her. It had been stripped away from her with so much force, that it brought a pain upon her that that very water she was sinking into held no comparison to.

She felt no feeling in any of her extremities as she sank deeper into that cold water. At first it was a stabbing sensation as the ice cold water invaded her lungs. But then her limbs had gone numb, and it was nothingness, just pure emptiness. The only emotion that she still felt was the pain of her power as it had been so violently ripped from her.

She sank further and further down; it clouded her thoughts as she drifted downward into that dark abyss of death. She tried to call out to Feau, but it was useless; he couldn't hear her now.

Her mind was blank, her vision was fading. Or was it just the blackness of the ocean as the sun's rays could go no further? Jenevy couldn't tell, she only knew that someone, or something was coming, but what?

Straining, Jenevy tried to regain control of her limbs by slowly moving her arms, and then her legs. But with every movement, came a wave of pain and it washed over her like the shadow of a bird as it flew across the sun.

She tried again, over and over, until at last the water lightened and the sun began to shine through. With one last wave of strength, she emerged from the water onto the surface as her lungs burned for air.

Jenevy yelled into the sky, a yell so full of anger, despair and pain that every creature in that water ducked away in fear. Jenevy leaned backwards and floated on her back. She was in agony, in shock, and her body was rapidly deteriorating. It was shutting down as the frigid ice water consumed her, taking hold of her vital organs and diminishing them.

She floated, wheezing, thinking of death and the relief that it would bring, if only it would come faster, if at all; but she knew that it would not. She couldn't let it, not with all of those souls that were trapped within the Duke's evil castle walls. Not with William imprisoned in a life of servitude that made him do unspeakable things, and not with the thought of future women that the Duke would destroy.

Jenevy's eyes snapped open, she had to move, had to press on to endure for just a moments longer; for them. They were depending upon her! A new wave of energy surged through her; she rolled to her stomach and began swimming. To where? She did not know.

After her spiraling fall from the sky her bearings were off, but she knew that land was somewhere. It had to be, she came from land, from solid ground, from tiny dark specs of sand hidden amongst white siblings sparkling in the moonlight.

Night? Was it night when she had fallen? Yes, she was attacked at night, as she flew from her home at the Shempshay Mountains. A home she had to find, at all costs no matter what.

Then she had to find that demonic beast and reclaim her powers that had been trustingly bestowed upon her. But how? She had no idea. But if she could find Feau, he would know, and hopefully they could find that demon before it consumed her powers entirely.

She swam, with everything that she had left in her and then screamed out for her beloved friend Feau, the last loyal, protective, noble and civilized dragon in the world. Surely, she had not lost all of her abilities. Maybe he could hear her, and would find her! He had to!

She swam faster, causing ripples and currents of pain coursing through her. She had to pause when the pain became too unbearable, and tread water as she frantically searched for any signs of land. A bird, an insect, anything! But there was nothing.

"I don't believe this!" She shrieked as she thrashed out her arms in frustration.

"Ow . . ." She grimaced. "That was a bad idea." She said wincing in pain. Jenevy looked up towards the sky, and then froze. She was getting that feeling again, that uneasy, nagging feeling of the unknown that was sending shivers up her spine!

She twirled around in the water to look around her. But there was nothing.

"Something . . . is not right." She said uneasily to herself. A pressing feeling of alarm crushed down upon her. She looked around her again, and a look of realization hit her face.

"Oh no!" She quickly dove underwater and looked around. Once her eyes adjusted to the saltwater she stared at the depths below her. Everything was fuzzy and out of focus. She twirled to the other side and let out a scream. A scream that rumbled from beneath the waves and no one could hear.

Floating in front of her was a giant, toothy grimace of a grin, belonging to the face of an enormous, sinister looking creature from the depths of the ocean. Its fangs were twice the size of her body, and its large oval eyes carried a yellowish-green tint with dark blue slit pupils.

Its body was a combination of a lizard and a shark. But instead of wings, it had one large dorsal fin, followed by two smaller fins running parallel. Two huge arms, equipped with razor sharp claws, extended out from the creatures massive shoulders. Its hind legs resembled his arms, only larger, *much* larger. And coiling behind its massive body lay a long tail with a spiked fin on the end.

Jenevy stared dumbfounded at the creature. Was it smiling at her? And if it was, why was it smiling?

They both stared at one another with intriguing curiosity; Jenevy could feel the burning in her lungs return as she ran out of air. Reluctantly she broke eye contact and rushed for the surface.

No sooner had she broken the waves, than she was yanked violently back down underwater. Her head snapped backwards, smacking the water and whiplashing her neck forward, as the creature hurled her under, making a current with her body as he swam.

Jen moaned as the pain returned, and again her lungs began to burn. She struggled within the creatures hand to get free, but it only tightened its grip. She clawed at its fingers and it released her, and she frantically scrambled for the surface. But she was grabbed again, only this time by its tail.

She hysterically tore at its skin trying to escape, but it was of no use. Her vision blurred to red, accompanied with a painful ringing in her ears. *'This . . . is the end.'* She thought, and she gave in to the frigid temperatures of the salty sea.

Feau's mind was racing with emotion. How could he have been so blind? How was he helpless in stopping that creature from destroying Jenevy? He snorted in disgust at himself, as he flew over the moonlit water. She had to be there somewhere, that creature was finished with her. Once it had devoured her energy and powers, it had sent her plummeting into the water and took off into the sky. But where had it thrown her?

Feau searched the underlying waves, scanning them as his wings beat into the air. He kept listening for her thoughts, in hopes of her being alive, but there was nothing. But her being alive might not be plausible, especially when Feau thought of the devastating effects that that demon inflicted upon its victims.

He still couldn't understand why the demon had attacked. Jenevy and Feau were flying, aiming for home when it appeared out of nowhere. At first, its sights had been on Feau, but once Jenevy intervened it changed its attacks and zeroed in on her. That meant that Jenevy was much, much more powerful than either of them had realized.

That demon, known to Feau's kind as the Engulfer, lived off of the energy of life forms. But, if that life form had powers of creation and destruction, than the Engulfer would drain them completely dry, ripping away their very souls. And when it had attacked Jenevy, Feau had seen her life fade right in front of him.

Her pain was so fierce, that her thoughts had blinded Feau, leaving him helpless in defending her.

Once the Engulfer had drained her, she fell to the earth, and slammed into the icy water. By the time Feau had gained full awareness, both the Engulfer and Jenevy were gone. And Feau had spent the entire night searching and praying to find her alive.

The moon was full, which aided in his search, but the moon also had an evil glow to it. A bad omen by his standards, and Feau snarled in outrage, the last thing that he needed was bad luck.

Feau listened to the waters below, as whales sang to one another, dolphins' songs of communication to locate their pods echoed, and somewhere even deeper booming sounds of two creatures dueling out a feud of power raged.

Feau snorted in frustration as nothing was even remotely close to his lost friend. Feau beat his wings, shooting himself high into the sky. Once the ocean was just small glitters of reflection beneath him, he stopped and flapped his wings to stay stationary.

Closing his eyes, he cleared his mind, and focused only on the world around him. Floods of sounds rushed in on him, sounds from the air, the land and the sea. Straining harder, he focused on the sounds from the ocean below. Fighting over their recent catch, he heard the minds of small fish as they scattered for food. And then he heard the voice of a large creature laughing incessantly over the small human that had so eagerly allowed him to catch it.

Feau's eyes snapped open. A rage built up inside of him as he thought of Jenevy within the clutches of that creature. His mind instantly filled with anger and death and he let out a loud, ear splitting roar that sent shockwaves upon the sea below.

Feau dove towards the water, flame licked their fingers out of his nostrils as the rush of wind zipped past him. He slammed into the icy water, sending clouds of steam into the air.

He held onto the thoughts of that creature as he swam with all his might. The thoughts were growing louder and louder as he approached until at last, the creature floated in front of him.

Feau sneered at the beast, as it spun around to look at the intruder. The creature's tail floated around towards them, coiling the lifeless body of Jenevy.

"I believe you have something that belongs to me." Feau said telepathically to the creature. The giant predator looked at its captive, and then back at the dragon.

"A human?" It pondered. "Now what would a Shempshay Dragon have to do with the ruthless prospects of a greedy human?!" It mused.

"That is of my concern, and mine only." Feau snapped back.

"Our kinds have never dealt with one another in the past, and I do not wish to start now. But, if this human is so precious to you, then enlighten me of its importance. And I might be willing to part with such a treasured treat." It said, licking its lips.

Feau loathed the creature; he hated sea-beasts and their entire clan. And he wanted nothing more than to destroy it where it was. But he felt his instincts as it nagged at him not to, warning him that their destinies were to be entwined somewhere in the future. Regrettably, he fulfilled the creature's wish.

"She and I are connected in a way that no two minds should be. She is as much a part of me as I am of her." Feau solemnly stated.

The creature's wicked smile faded, and it stared curiously at the human.

"You, actually care for this human?" It asked bewildered.

"She . . . saved my life. Her destiny is far too valuable to waste. You, of all things, should understand that." Feau remarked boldly. The creature brought his tail forward to look at her closely.

"Alas, my kind has always believed in a greater fate than that which is known. But then again, I have never known of a human to possess something as precious as a bond between a dragon and its beliefs. Not since the great war that is." The creature let go of Jenevy, nudging her towards Feau. Feau reached out to her, and yanked her to him, like child holding a precious toy.

"Tell me dragon. When that day comes, where her destiny is revealed, will you be ready for it?" Feau looked up at the creature curiously.

"When the consequences of her actions, bring forth the end and the beginning, of what you hold dear, will you still stand beside her?" The creature asked with endearment. Feau really hated sea creatures and their twist of words, but his expression became stern nonetheless, and he looked down at her.

"We will know when that time comes." He replied. The creature smiled in return.

"Perhaps . . . . Either way, we *will* be meeting again." And it sank back into the depths of that dark sea. Feau sneered, and then kicked his legs launching him through the water and towards the surface. He lunged into the sky like a shark jumping out after its prey.

Feau spread his wings and flew as fast as he could. Land was near, and to revive Jenevy it would take whatever strength and power that he had left. Yet, the dark sea creature's words were still echoing in his ears, Jenevy's destiny had to be far more important than Feau had originally foreseen.

❖ *"William—"* A whimsical voice echoed his name. William turned around, looking for the source of the noise. But nothing was there, except for darkness and fog.

"Yes?" Came his confused reply.

"*You must leave here William.*" The voice responded warningly. William strained his eyes into the blackness around him.

"What? To where?" He asked. There was no reply.

"Who are you?!" He demanded. Still nothing. William walked forward a bit, and nearly stumbled over something. It was the edge of a cliff; William stared down it, and leaned back wards to turn around. But before he could, the area whirled around him in a blur of colors, it stopped and a man refocused in front of him: a knight, lying dead upon the ground, with a beautiful horse lying at his side.

"What the—?" William exclaimed. He knelt down and reached for the helmet of the knight. But before he could reach it, the man disappeared in a wisp of smoke.

"*You will not be the first who dies if you stay!*" The voice said louder. William stood up.

"I know this! You don't think that I don't?! I know what these men do! I have seen them do it!" He shouted angrily. He swung out at the mist. The clouds rolled over his arm.

"*No William. You . . . will* not *live to tell this tale if you do not leave at once.*"

William frowned. He looked again for the person speaking to him.

"But I cannot leave. I am bound to the Lord of—"

"*—So was your father.*" The voice interrupted. And again the dead knight appeared before him.

"*And he too was deceived.*" The voice stated. William looked again at the man. His father? How could it be?

"*William. You have a greater purpose in this world, than to be a slave to the Duke of Greenwiche. You must leave, tonight. Or all will be lost.*" A woman emerged from the darkness. William stepped back in awe, she was stunning. Clothed in expensive silk and jewelry, the woman practically wreaked of royalty and power. William gulped.

"Who . . . are you?" He asked once more. She held no expression, but her eyes held a story of sorrow within its depths.

"I am one, who too was betrayed by your master." She rang. William looked back at the knight on the ground.

"How . . . do I know that you speak the truth?" William asked skeptically. The woman's face sank, and she reached up, and with an outstretched arm pointed towards the castle.

"In the woods, behind the castle, you will find your answer." She said sadly. *"But you will not have time to reach it."* And she disappeared.

"Wait!" William rushed forward." I must know!!" He wailed. Her voice echoed into the darkness:

"You must hurry William. For I fear, that you will not reach your answer before the fate of death comes upon you."

William sprang straight up, startling Fivestar so much that the stallion broke the door to the stall. Fivestar grunted his outrage as he walked back over to be beside William. William breathed in heavily, sweat poured down him. His eyes searched around him, frantically darting from one object to the next.

He instantly jumped to his feet, jumped onto Fivestar's back and kicked the horse's flanks as hard as he could.

Fivestar reared back, whinnied with rage, and then raced out of the barn heading towards the castle. William wiped the sweat from his brow, that dream had been so vivid, so real, that her words still rang in his ears.

His father? It wasn't possible! William looked to the sky; he saw the faint lines of light appearing over the rim of the mountains, dawn was approaching and fast! The woods lay in front of him, and he kicked Fivestar faster towards them.

He *had* to find out if his dream was real, he *had* to know! He kicked Fivestar faster and faster, where the hell was he supposed to look in the woods? William huffed in frustration.

William strained his eyes, looking at everything for signs of what he was looking for. He had an image from his dream of only a man and horse, but nothing else. Were they in a clearing? Where was he to look?

William urged Fivestar faster, the horse grunted at the speed, sweating more and more at every step. The stallion's testosterone was building at every step, and William knew that the horse was about to explode into a new aura of speed at any moment. William leaned forward and gripped the horse's sides with his legs, and held onto Fivestar's mane for dear life.

With a squeal the horse exploded into an engine of speed. Its muscles rippling beneath William's body as the horse was surging forward. The trees were passing in streaks of color, and the ground was turning to a blur.

'Turn right' it was her. William blinked in dismay. It couldn't be! He yanked on Fivestar's mane and squeezed the stallion's right side causing the horse to careen sharply to the right. Fivestar dove through the trees, racing forward in fury.

The stallion snorted and wisps of fog were fuming from its nostrils as it jumped over logs, rocks, and creeks. It barely missed the trees as they surged blindly through the dense foliage.

"There . . . in the clearing . . . " Her voice echoed in his head. William squinted and looked forward, the trees began to thin and he saw a clearing a few yards in front of them. William squeezed his legs on Fivestar's sides, causing the horse to skid abruptly to a stop. William jumped off of the stallion's back and walked towards the darkened objects lying on the ground in front of him.

Before him lay the remains of a knight and his horse. The scavengers had picked off any living tissue and all that remained were the skeletons of the two fighters.

"Father—" William whispered, as he knelt down beside the dead knight. William stroked the armor of his dead father, the metal plating held the same resemblance to William's own armor. William looked over at the horse skeleton and his eyes filled with tears.

"Firestorm." He said slowly. William hung his head in agony, as Fivestar nudged him, brushing his snout beneath William's arm. William yelled a scream of anger into the night, echoing it into the heavens. William stopped his scream to breathe deeply, as he remembered his dream: that woman had been right.

"Wait!" William snapped his head up, and gazed out at the forest. "If the dream were right, than that would mean that—"

"So . . . you have found your father. How ironic that your death befalls you within the same place, in exactly the same way." William jumped to his feet and spun around to look at the man speaking. Fivestar squealed in anger and scratched at the ground in irritation.

The Duke was standing staring wickedly at William, the King stood at his side as well as Edmund.

"You . . . you monster!" William reached his hand instinctively towards his sword, but looked in shock at his waist. In his rush to get to the clearing, he had left everything in the barn. William grunted in frustration at his clumsy mistake, knights *never* forget their armor let alone their weapons!

Edmund gazed at William then looked up at the Duke hesitantly. The Duke stood perfectly still, as he stared at William.

"Kill him." The Duke ordered.

"Master?" Edmund stared up at the Duke in shock. The Duke glared at Edmund then ordered his directions again.

"Now slave! Or suffer the same fate!" He barked. "And make sure you dispose of his beast!" Fivestar shrieked an outcry of anger and stood cantering in place. Edmund sighed and stepped forward as he unsheathed his sword. William raised an arm gesturing to Fivestar to ease his emotions. The horse stopped moving and waited for William's command.

William turned his attention to Edmund, raising both arms instinctively as if getting ready for unarmed combat.

"You don't have to do this." William said calmly. Edmund paused mid-step.

"Ignore him!" The Duke shouted. Edmund jumped startled and continued forward.

"I'm sorry. But I have to—" Came Edmund's shaken reply. William frowned, and then he sighed in despair, Fivestar ninnied and pranced at William's side.

"Run—" William whispered to Fivestar, as he dropped his arms in defeat. Like a bolt of lightning, Fivestar bolted into the woods as Edmund lunged at William blindly. With eyes closed, Edmund felt the sickening metal of his sword, impaling flesh.

Reaffirming the sound of Edmund's sword striking its target, Edmund opened his eyes and watched as William groaned and then slid backwards. William slid from Edmund's blade, and the stable boy watched the metal reappear from beneath William's torso. William slammed to the ground with a grunt.

"I'm . . . so sorry." Edmund apologized under his breath. William half smiled up at him, shielding the pain that was radiating through him.

"I . . . . know." William replied sadly. Edmund watched William, his friend and mentor, drop his head for the last time. One final breath escaped his lips, and the knight moved no more.

The Duke smiled wickedly, stepping up alongside Edmund and he laughed a very sinister and evil cackle towards the fallen knight.

"Clean off your sword." The Duke commanded. Edmund grimaced at the sight of William's blood upon his blade. Edmund didn't know what was worse, the fact that he had killed William, or the fact that he had killed William with the knight's own sword.

Edmund wiped the blood off of the metal by wiping it on his cloak, and sheathed it in its scabbard.

"Leave him there to rot alongside his father." The Duke said as he turned to walk away. Edmund stared down at William; he could hear the Duke's footsteps as he walked back towards the castle. Edmund knelt next to William and smiled.

"You are free." He said quietly, and then grabbing the sword once more, he slammed it into the ground next to William's head.

Edmund stood up, and rushed back to catch up to the Duke.

"Make sure that you dispose of William's armor, belongings and his horse before we leave. I want no one to know of his existence."

"Yes my master." Edmund said as he walked side by side to the Duke. Edmund hung his head down in despair, he had killed a knight and not just any knight, a knight well known throughout the region and possibly further. William's disappearance would not go unnoticed for long, and Edmund hoped that they would find William's dead body and seek justice for his death.

Slowly, William opened his eyes, as Fivestar gently nudged William's side. William groaned in misery as he looked at Fivestar. The horse's eyes were filled with concern as it made a quiet grunt at William.

"Easy boy." The words were painful to say, as his stomach sent waves of pain throughout his body. Fivestar knelt down next to him and leaned gently onto the knight. William closed his eyes, and tried to regain his composure.

Fivestar nudged him again, insisting that William should open his eyes.

"I know I know." William said hoarsely. Wincing, he grabbed the stallion's mane and then hoisted himself onto Fivestar's back. The horse pushed William further up with his head, and gently stepped to its feet. William groaned once more, and panted from his position.

Once Fivestar was sure that William was balanced, he carefully stepped towards the darker parts of the forest. Every now and then, Fivestar would use his head to readjust William so that he remained firmly upon the stallion's back.

William hung over Fivestar's hock, and felt his strength leaving him. He slowly started to lean towards the stallion's left shoulder.

"Hurry boy. I can't stay awake much longer!" William pleaded. Fivestar ninnied a reply and quickened his step. Everything that William saw was getting blurrier and blurrier. The haze was unsettling as William's blood was being drained. What was even more unnerving to him, was the fact that if and when William closed his eyes, he knew that they might not open up ever again.

William shut his eyes hoping that re-opening them would clear his eyesight. But he had a hard time trying to reopen them, and when he did his vision was worse. He instinctively grabbed Fivestar's neck and squeezed, and tried to hoist himself to sit upright.

Fivestar quickened his step, rushing carefully through the trees. William knew that the wild creatures of the forest were about to emerge, they probably could already smell William's blood and were trying to desperately to find him.

Fivestar could sense it as well, and his sure footing instantly became rough and unplanned. William tried to calm Fivestar, but it would be in vain, because the creatures that were about to emerge were much stronger than any warhorse could fight.

Fivestar's uneasiness spread through the horse like a wildfire, the horse made nervous whimpers at almost every step, and it began to tremble in fear.

"Fivestar! Calm yourself, your fear will only lead them straight to us!" William chided. Fivestar snorted and tried to calm himself, but his ears darted like a bird at every sound, accompanied by his head as he would look towards it.

At last, a ray of hope lay within view: a tall, rocky cliff loomed ahead. If they could make it safely to the top of the cliff, the setting sun's rays would keep that cliff free of creatures. Plus, it would give William enough time to start a fire to thwart off the creatures for when the night fell upon them.

William diverted Fivestar's attention towards the cliff, and urged him towards it. William felt Fivestar's muscles ripple and held on tighter as he knew that the horse could take the suspense no more. The stallion reared back, landed, and then lunged forward into the fastest gallop that the horse could muster. William saw the world speeding past him in more of a blur than it was before, and Fivestar was sprinting so fast that he was tripping and stumbling in the gradually darkening forest.

"Whoa boy! You break an ankle and neither of us will survive!" William shouted. Fivestar snorted, he understood but didn't slow down. The stallion was going to take its chances with the uneven earth, opposed to the murder-seeking beasts. However, despite Fivestar's speed increasing, his footing did seem to improve.

After what felt like ages to William, they finally reached the base of the sky towering cliff. Fivestar paused to stare up at the precipice of the mountain, and then looked around for a path to the top. With a leap, the horse landed upon a pile of huge boulders and began his trek up the peak, while William guided the stallion towards sturdy footholds.

Once reaching the top, Fivestar stopped and panted for air. The horse's sweat had soaked its hair, mixing with that of William's blood. The stallion shook its body in short spasms as it tried to flick the moisture from its hair.

A wave of nausea followed by a headache coursed through William's body that caused him to groan and snap his eyes shut. William felt the gravity pulling at him as he began to lean to the side of Fivestar, and he was powerless to stop it. He slumped to the ground with a thud, as the stallion jumped to the side startled. Fivestar lifted its hooves trying to avoid stepping on him.

William groaned and rolled to his side, he breathed deeply hoping that the pain would subside. But the more he breathed, the more the pain increased and the nausea as well. William moaned in agony and Fivestar rushed to his side. William reached a hand up as Fivestar dropped his head to William's stomach. William wrapped his arms around the horse's neck, and Fivestar pulled him gently to his feet. As he felt his legs wobbling beneath him, William leaned against his stallion for support.

"Thanks boy." William said weakly. Wincing, William forced his legs to step forward. What he was about to do, was going to take all of the strength that he had left and was going to be harder than anything he had done that day. But it had to be done, or else the creatures of the night would devour them in a ravish hunger.

Clenching his hands into a fist, William brought them to his chest. Closing his eyes, he concentrated and stood firmly upon the ground.

Slowly, his body began to glow. At first it was green, and then once enough energy had been collected into William's body, it turned blue and absorbed into William's fists.

By pulling his arms to his side, the blue ripples of energy streaked into a long line extending as an arc from one arm to the other. Yelling, William surged the energy onto the ground. It engulfed the rocky ground in flames, encircling him and Fivestar in a shroud of protection. The cliff lay at their back, and the flame lay at all sides surround the edge of that steep pitfall.

Weakness invaded William's entire body as he dropped his hands; his knees buckled and he slumped over falling backwards onto the ground. Fivestar ninnied in panic, and rushed over to William, the stallion nudged the knight's side in hopes of reviving him, but William didn't move.

The horse pushed him again, over and over, but William wouldn't budge. The horse breathed out loud gusts of air as it grunted in agitation and despair. It looked towards the cliff behind William, and then at the flame in front of him.

The last rays of sun set, and the darkness dawned upon them like a shroud of mist, unleashing the realm of the creatures of the night. The blue flame licked its lips towards the sky, glowing an eerie shade of blue onto the mountainside. With a screech, the creatures emerged from the shadows, Fivestar screamed in anger and pranced in front of William. The stallion glared at the beasts in outrage as they surged forward in hunger.

But once hitting the flame, they instantly ignited and dissipated into a pile of smoke. Another wave of creatures raced forward and they too followed the same fate, as the fire glowed brighter at every strike. Fivestar snorted at the beasts, and watched as another group cautiously stepped forward. They sniffed at William's fire, and stepped back in defeat. Fivestar snorted in disgust and watched them leave.

Glancing back at the cliff, Fivestar's eyes softened in relief, and he laid down gently next to William. The stallion shielded William from the hot, blue flames as he hung his head in exhaustion. Fivestar let sleep claim him, and he dropped his head and fell asleep. He remained beside William through the entire night, ever guarding his closest friend: Sir William, the Knight of Albastson von Juefel.

Chapter Twelve

Reinstatement

JENEVY'S EYES SNAPPED open and she gagged at water that was climbing up out of her lungs. She sat straight up and began coughing, straining to free the fluid and to entrap the oxygen from her breath. She sucked in the air to breath deeply, wanting the soothing feeling of breathing again. She closed her eyes and smiled as the last of the fluid had almost dissipated from her lungs.

Wheezing, she coughed again and waited for the stars in her eyes to retreat. Slowly opening her eyes, she looked around her. At first she couldn't figure out where she was, and she frowned in confusion. That was when she saw Feau, as he lay asleep at her side. She strained her eyes and looked around her again. Where was she? What had happened?

Then it hit her, and the memories rushed at her, practically knocking her senseless. The beast! Her powers! The creature from the water! Then nothing?! She began to shake in panic, she jumped to her feet only to fall back to the ground as her knees buckled. She decided to crawl towards Feau, but that hurt even worse. Jenevy moaned in frustration, never had she felt so helpless in her entire life!

She resorted to dragging herself towards the dragon, but then shrieked when she touched him. Feau was sleeping, or so she had thought, but upon further inspection it had dawned on her that he was not!

"Oh no, no, *no!!*" She shrieked as she struggled to her knees to slide over to him. She fell upon his side and listened intently.

"Oh thank god!" She gave a sigh of relief, and rolled over to her back. She skidded down to the ground, and sat propped up against Feau. There had been a heartbeat, faint, but a beat nonetheless. Jenevy smiled, happy that he was alive.

Sleep called her name; in fact, sleep was all that she could think about.

"When I wake up, Feau will explain everything!" She reaffirmed herself. Although, she highly doubted it, he was probably just as confused as her. Her head dropped and she was asleep instantly.

Feau woke her up the next morning. Jenevy reassured him when she saw and felt the relief in Feau's eyes. She smiled up at him, and reached out to him as he purred rubbing his forehead against her hand.

Jenevy felt the warmth in her rise in delight.

"What happened?" She asked. But there was no response. Jenevy frowned and looked at the dragon in concern.

"Feau?" She asked bewildered. The dragon's face dropped in sadness. A wave of panic rushed through her.

"*Oh no!*" She thought, as she realized that the draining of her powers had also resulted in the severed connection of their minds. Jenevy's eyes filled with tears at the realization of her being unable to communicate with her beloved friend.

"I thought that whatever spell I cast, was to remain permanent!" She shrieked. She felt something touch her, and she jumped. She looked behind her and her face filled with wonder.

"My wings?" She said dumbfounded, as she reached out to touch one.

"But . . . . how?" She mused. Feau touched her with his tail, and she looked up at him. By using his flame he painted a scene of pictures onto the sky, just as he did when they had first met. He explained everything that had happened over the past few days, and Jenevy watched intently.

The fire show ended, and its sparks licked at the sky as it disappeared. Jenevy looked down in sorrow, her tears were building up again in agony. She remembered the pain of her powers being ripped from her, the fear of her falling paralyzed into the ocean, and the terror of that sea creature that had nearly devoured her. She instantly burst into tears at Feau's side as she wrapped her wings around herself protectively.

Feau wrapped his tail around her and pulled her to him. Jenevy cried for a very, very long time as her body shook in spasms of pain. Feau was growling in anger at seeing her in that manner. He desperately wanted to help her, and finding the Engulfer to kill it would be the only way. But he would risk losing his own powers in the process, and then Jenevy would have to fight it off as a mortal.

Feau grunted, flaring his nostrils in frustration, and then stood up to stretch out his wings to fly. Feau shook his head in confusion. What was he thinking? He *had* to get her powers back! She was to bring about a new peace upon the land! Besides, hadn't she saved his life and would do it again with no questions asked? He owed his life to her, and he *had* to do it!

Jenevy stared up at him; she desperately wished to know his thoughts. But once seeing his wings spread, and saw the anger coursing through his body, she instantly jumped to her feet. There was only one thing that he was preparing to do, and she had to be with him. In wobbly, feeble attempts of walking, she rushed over to his side. She flexed her wings, and stretched them out.

"No Feau! We are in this together! I don't care what happens! I will not stand idly by while you go off alone!" She announced firmly.

Feau growled again, and Jenevy raised an arm to silence him.

"You don't have a choice in the matter! I'm coming with you!" And she leapt into the sky. Feau watched her take off, shrugged and jumped up after her.

The Engulfer's lair took most of the day to reach, and its lair was exactly as Jenevy had visualized it. It was a dark, smelly hold, filled with the foulest stench that either one of them had ever smelled. Feau paused to look at Jenevy, she too was having a hard time trying to stay focused. Feau swallowed and dove down into the crevice, as Jenevy stayed close to his side. Once it became too dark to see, Feau felt her silently climb up onto his back for the duration of their pursuit. He could feel her heart thundering in her chest, she was scared, but could he blame her? She had been downgraded to a feeble human, a spec of a creature that was nowhere near formidable to the Engulfer. A roar interrupted his thoughts.

"He's sensed you!" Jenevy shouted. The walls of that dark cavern shook violently as the Engulfer made its ascent out of its den. Feau veered around, and took off into the daylight. But the Engulfer was hot on Feau's tail, moving much, much faster than the dragon. Jenevy looked behind them, the cornea of the demon was getting bigger as it got closer.

"Feau! Hurry!" She wailed, as the sun's rays began to shine brighter from the mouth of the cave. The dragon roared as he slammed his wings harder, shooting him faster towards the cavern's exit. Jenevy leapt off of his back, and Feau exploded out of the cave, sending rocks flying all around him. Jenevy landed softly upon the ground, watching Feau as he screeched to a halt in front of her. His claws were extended, digging straight into the ground.

Bearing his teeth, he awaited the demon from the underground. The Engulfer tore out of the ground with such speed that the ground cracked around the opening to the cavern. Jenevy fell to the ground from the aftershock of the Engulfer's quakes, catching herself with her arms. She grunted in annoyance.

The massive body of the Engulfer coiled out of the cave like a snake. Jenevy stood up staring dumbfounded as the creature from her memories emerged. It was even more terrifying than she had remembered. From the front, the Engulfer resembled that of a decaying, skeletal body of a bull. Equipped with fangs, and dark, lifeless eyes that penetrated her very soul. It had four enormous arms, with large clawed hands. But the rest of its body was that of a viper, that coiled down into the crevice underground, with the extent of the Engulfer's body unknown.

Somehow, Jenevy knew that that creature was able to take flight to attack its prey from virtually any angle. Or, it could just jump really, *really* high! It was possible too, that maybe it lashed out like the viper part of its body's ancestral roots did. Either way, that demon was an indestructible, killing force that loomed above Jenevy's vision, like the worst nightmare from her childhood memories.

Feau snarled up at the demon, reminding Jenevy of a territorial cat. The Engulfer growled in return, or rather it gurgled, as huge droplets of acidic saliva fell upon the ground hissing as it ate through the soil.

Jenevy stared at the small craters of sizzling earth, and she slowly looked back up at the demon. That was when she realized how much danger she was in. Frantically she jumped to her feet and ran as far from the Engulfer as she could. But the creature was fixated on Feau; it was the powers that the dragon possessed that enticed the Engulfer, not Jenevy.

Jenevy's heart sank as she realized the degree of damage that was about to befall upon Feau once the demon attacked.

Entranced by the demon's glowing eyes, Feau was unable to focus. It hypnotized Feau, and the dragon was powerless to resist. Jenevy madly raced towards Feau, she had to break his stare, and she had to wake him from the Engulfer's trance. She hesitantly crept in between the Engulfer's massive arms, ducking underneath its large abdomen, and slowly reached Feau.

Both creatures were frozen in their spots, one focusing on entangling its prey, the other on withstanding the spell.

"Feau!!" She shrieked. She jumped up and grabbed a hold of the horns on his head and pulled herself up to be within eyesight.

"Feau please! You'll die!" She wailed, as she attempted to pull herself higher only to lose her grip and fall to the ground.

The wind was knocked out of her, and she grunted in pain. Jenevy pushed herself back up, and Jenevy looked around. There had to be something that she could do to awaken Feau's alertness. Then she saw it, an elongated piece of stone that had a sharp point on its end. She rushed over, grabbed it, and then raced back to Feau.

"Forgive me!" She said as she raised the stone over her head. With eyes closed, she swung it down stabbing it into Feau's side. The stone barely pierced through the dragon's thick-scaled armor, but it was enough. Feau roared, and shook his head. He looked over at Jenevy, and then back at the Engulfer right as the Engulfer swung out its arm to grab the dragon.

Feau leapt to the side, grabbing Jenevy in the process, and hurdled into the sky. Swinging her onto his back, he yanked out the stone from his side; he tossed it back at her, and then wheeled towards the demon.

Jenevy caught the stone with a confused expression, but as Feau soared towards the Engulfer's head, she understood. Leaping from his back, she spread her wings and took flight. Feau steered back around towards the ground to divert the Engulfer's attention, as it slithered after him.

Jenevy flapped her wings, pushing herself towards the demon and held onto the stone like a blade. She launched herself in front of the Engulfer's gaze, and looked up at it.

It barely noticed her, which Jenevy had intended, and she slammed the stone straight into the demon's eye. It sliced through the thin, jelly like substance of the demon's eye like butter, wedging itself deep into the Engulfer's retina. The creature screeched in pain, flailing its arms up towards its face.

Jenevy ducked down, diverting the demon's swings of despair and swerved towards the ground. She barely landed as she used her legs to bounce her into the sky. The Engulfer hurriedly tried to find and release the stone from its eye, but it was too small for its grip which only angered the creature further. Jenevy used that opportunity to find another weapon to permanently blind the creature as Feau commenced his attack at the startled demon from below.

Jenevy surveyed the objects beneath her as she flew, and then stopped mid-flight to look harder.

"There!" She said excitedly as she dove towards the ground. She landed so fast, that she had to run to keep herself from tumbling. She rushed towards a smashed boulder; she grabbed pieces of rocks throwing them behind her until she found the perfect fragment. She yanked the rock free and stared at it for a moment. It had a serrated edge, sharp point, and was razor sharp. She held it to her and jumped into the air.

Feau was still slicing away at the demon's soft underbelly, and he paused once he saw Jenevy approaching. The Engulfer swung out at her, but she averted his attack with ease. The Engulfer was slow, too slow due to its bulky body. But his mammoth arms created a current in the air, almost like a vortex which caused Jenevy to tumble unable to regain stabilization. Feau raced up and caught her, but unfortunately his claws caught her, and they dug into her sides. Jenevy winced, and tried to ignore the pain.

Feau tossed her forward, right as the Engulfer swung out to catch them. His hand passed between them, only this time it created a gust of wind that boosted Jenevy faster towards the demon. The Engulfer turned its gaze towards her, and opened its mouth to release a spout of acidic saliva towards her. Jenevy continued forward and grimaced in anticipation of the sting.

But before the Engulfer could spray its acid, Feau flew in front of her shooting out a huge billow of flame at the demon's face. Jenevy flew through the flame and slammed into the Engulfer with the stone pointed outwards. The pointed tip stabbed into the demon's eye, as the serrated edge sliced through the outer layer shoving it deeper into the center of the retina. Gripping the stone harder, Jenevy twisted it and pulled it to the side of the Engulfer's eye socket.

The demon roared in pain, and dropped down to the ground as it reached up, to scratch at its face. Jenevy saw the Engulfer's hand heading towards her, but just as he was about to reach her, she used the rock as a stronghold to leap off of the demon. She propelled herself skyward and Feau rushed towards her. They flapped their wings to remain stationary in the air, as they watched the demon writhing below them.

Feau snorted at it, and Jenevy looked over at him and then back at the Engulfer.

"No way . . ." She said as she looked in horror at the demon as it pushed itself back up. " . . . now what?" She said breathing heavily. Feau looked at her bewildered.

"How do you kill a creature that is blind and impenetrable?!" She shrieked. But before she had time to think, Feau was already diving towards the ground. Jenevy folded in her wings to her back and plunged after him.

Feau lit up the ground beneath him with flame. The underbrush ignited, sending fire to every dry piece of shrubbery that was around it. Feau soared to the other side of the Engulfer and did the same to the plants on that side of the ground. Then flew to the front of the demon and whipped at it with his tail.

The Engulfer stopped moving and turned its body towards the dragon. It lashed out its arms trying to catch the dragon blindly. Jenevy stopped and watched Feau as he continued his charade, keeping the Engulfer focused only upon him.

That was when Jenevy saw it, the fire from Feau was heating up the Engulfer's sides, making him glow red. It was softening his armored scales like the melting metal of a blacksmith. Jenevy knew that this was how they were to destroy the Engulfer, but how was she too kill it? She did not have any weapons, no powers, nor did she know of where the demon's vital organs were in order to stage a proper attack.

"Oh! Curse me and not being stronger!" She yelled towards the sky. Jenevy closed her eyes in shame. There had to be something that she could do! Perhaps should could replace Feau, and keep the Engulfer preoccupied with her long enough for Feau to kill the demon? But, she would not be able to fly fast enough out of its way if it were to attack! It may be slow, but she would have to be directly beneath the Engulfer in order to attack it with enough force for it to feel her! Jenevy was getting frustrated, if only she had a sword!

But it had disappeared, along with all of her armor when she—

"It can't be!" She screamed, and stared at the Engulfer's side.

"The last time that I had my armor and my sword, the Engulfer had me within its coils!" She shrieked. Staring at the red, glowing scales she watched as smoke began to smolder out from the demon's flesh.

She had to hurry; soon the Engulfer would feel the flame and would more than likely come after her.

Swallowing her fear, she breathed in deeply and tore out of the sky, diving straight towards the Engulfer's side. She pulled her wings in tightly to her back, and point her arm straight out as she tightened her hand into a fist. The wind tore at her as her velocity increased. She aimed at the Engulfer's red glowing abdomen, closed her eyes, gritted her teeth, and prayed that she was right.

Feau looked up at Jenevy and watched her slam into the demon's side, her body slicing through its now soft scales and disappearing within the demon's body. Feau roared in fear, what was she thinking?

The Engulfer reared back in torturous agony, flailing its arms and crying out in terror. Feau jumped back and watched the Engulfer rise upwards, as it frantically clawed at its stomach.

Within moments of Jenevy's perilous dive and disappearance, the creature stopped moving. Feau heard the demon's heart beat one last thunderous boom, and then it stopped. The Engulfer remained motionless for a moment until gravity took over and pulled the demon to the ground like a tree being cut at its base. It slammed to the ground with a thud, and its last breath was forced out of it.

Feau rushed over, skidding to a stop next to the demon. The Engulfer's lifeless body twitched as its nerve endings slowly died.

'Jenevy!' Feau thought to himself. He raced alongside the demon, looking up and down the demon's body hoping for some sign of her. The Engulfer started to move once more.

'Impossible!' Feau thought bewildered. The demon's body began to glow a dark, turquoise blue. Sparks of energy gathered from all around it, and then retracted into the demon.

Feau's eyes widened, and he stepped back in surprise. A loud whirring sound filled the area, growing louder and louder until BANG!! The Engulfer's body exploded, shooting pieces of flesh, blood and bones for miles.

Feau grimaced as he bent his head down, waiting for the explosion to clear. When he looked up, his eyes filled with wonder. Jenevy stood, with arms ablaze with a blue flame. She breathed in a deep breath, and re-opened her eyes.

"I'm back." She said with a smile.

"And I can hear you once more." Feau said, returning her grin. Jenevy stepped forward.

"And it appears that my power has doubled since I had lost it." Her voice echoed with a metallic chime. Feau paused for a moment, as he felt her power within his mind. She was right; her power had since tripled and was combined with new strengths both dark and strange.

"It seems that you have acquired all of the powers that the Engulfer had stolen." Feau said in disbelief. Jenevy stared at her hands, changing the flame from blue, to that of red, green and then a dark, black flame that had a deep, scarlet red in its center. Her eyes also reflected the colors of power that she activated. She shook her hands, returning them to normal. Then she froze.

"I sense something." She stated, and looked at Feau. But he too had already felt it. His lips curled up in a snarl, his spikes, horns and elongated spines stuck out like a rooster that was about to attack. With a puff of dust, he ran towards the forest, jumped up and over the trees and spread his wings to take flight. Jenevy jumped up after him and was hot on his heels.

Chapter Thirteen

Fivestar

THE RISING SUN sent away the evil creatures of the night. Their horrific sounds echoed against the cliff face as they retreated into the forest, where they would await their time to hunt again.

Edmund watched the cliff from his window, as the suns rays brought color to the world again. Earlier that night, Edmund had seen a blue hue radiating off of that same cliff. Perplexing him, he had stayed up most of the night to watch it. But once daylight hit, the blue hue had vanished and Edmund still did not know of what was its creator.

He sighed and pushed himself back inside of the castle. What had he done? He had killed his only friend, and for what? For the acceptance of the Duke? Or was it because of the fear that the Duke had imposed upon his slaves if they ever refused his orders? Edmund was filled with regret and remorse for his evil decision of the day before. He should have just let the Duke kill both of them, it would have been better than dealing with the pain that was ripping through Edmund's insides.

Edmund silently dressed, and walked out of his room. The Duke needed him in the courtyard, he wanted Edmund to be hard at work while the Duke would continue his careless charade of tyranny and abuse while aboard the King's requests.

Edmund was deep in thought when he arrived at the courtyard. He practically tripped over something on the ground as he continued his movement. Edmund halted midstep, and cursed at the items that had interrupted his thoughts. He looked back and then frowned upon seeing William's armor strewn out upon the stone. Edmund knelt down beside it, and picked it up piece by piece.

Edmund then knew of what *errand* that the Duke had in mind. Edmund gathered up the last pieces of metallic armor and brought in into the stable to load upon a mule. Moments later, Edmund emerged from the stable seated upon his horse with the reins of a load-packed mule tied snugly to the horn of Edmund's saddle.

Edmund eased the animals forward, leading them into the woods. The mule started to pant as the load of William's armor and belongings weighed down upon him.

"Already?" Edmund stated in disbelief at the mule. "What kind of pack animal are you?!" He added bewildered. The mule snorted in annoyance at Edmund.

Edmund looked around the forest as they walked through, he was unsure as to where he should dispose of William's armor. Should he leave it with the remains of the Sir William? Or just toss it off of the cliff and let it fly to the winds? Edmund decided on the latter of his ideas, and redirected his route towards the cliff. Besides, Edmund was hoping that he might get to investigate the source of the blue hue from the night prior.

Edmund urged his horse forward, dragging the already exhausted mule behind him. The forest was a lot darker and the route much longer than Edmund had presumed, but eventually the trail to the top of the cliff emerged. Edmund paused, stopping the animals to look up at the cliff. He estimated the safest possible route to its peak, and then searched the trail for strong footholds that his horse could follow.

Upon seeing a gentle, winding slope leading up the backside of the cliff, he kicked his horse forward and guided them up the path. The horse began to climb, but stalled once the weight of the mule stopped him. Edmund looked back at the animal, and it refused to move. It brayed in protest.

"Alright mule. Either you make it up this trail, or I'll kill you now and eat you for supper!" He shouted. The mule seemed to understand and gathering up every bit of strength and energy left, it rushed up to be alongside Edmund and his horse.

"That's better." Edmund said while patting the mule's forehead. He kicked his horse forward again, and the mule, surprisingly, kept up.

The slope was getting steeper at every step, but the mule tried his best to not slow down. It would dig its hooves into the ground, pushing itself faster. Edmund kicked his horse's flanks, making sure that it would not get out sped by the mule. The last thing that he wanted was for the two animals to falter in their footing and tumble to the bottom.

Looking ahead, Edmund could see the tip of the cliff and could also see the ground begin to level out a few paces ahead of him. The mule could see it as well and began to trot forward eagerly, yanking Edmund's horse forward. That sudden movement caused Edmund's horse to rear and buck in protest.

"Whoa! Easy girl!" Edmund shouted, trying to calm his mare. But it was of no use, and Edmund was thrown to the ground. Fortunately, he did not topple down the side of the mountain, but instead used the momentum to roll to his feet. He ran forward, taking off after the spooked animals hoping to catch them before his mare yanked the mule off of the cliff.

The animals disappeared from view once they had reached the top, and Edmund tried to pick up speed. What he saw when he reached the top of the mountain, was something that he did not expect. Instead of seeing the two animals running towards their doom, he saw Fivestar halting the creatures and saving them from plummeting to their deaths.

The horse had Edmund's mare's reins firmly in his teeth, as he circled the animals in a trot around the edge of the cliff. Edmund's mare was calmly following the stallion, as the mule inexplicably followed. Edmund breathed a sigh of relief and walked casually towards them. But something else caught his eye, and he stopped dead in his tracks.

"Sir William!" He shrieked. There was the knight, lying dead upon the ground. Edmund then noticed a dark, chiseled circle of ash surrounding the edge of the cliff. Upon closer inspection, Edmund recognized the remains of a blue ash, which was the signature of William's unmistakable power. Edmund stared back at William.

"He was alive!" Edmund cried in disbelief. Edmund started to walk towards William, but Fivestar shrieked and ran in front of him. The large stallion growled at Edmund and clawed at the ground with his hooves. Edmund looked up into the horse's eyes, and saw the anger building up inside.

"Its alright boy. I won't hurt him." Edmund said calmly. *'Again.'* He added to himself. But Fivestar wouldn't budge; his distaste for Edmund was clearly eminent upon the stallion's battered face. Edmund attempted to go around Fivestar, but the stallion reared and kicked out its front legs in warning. Edmund jumped back and Fivestar slammed to the ground. The stallion lowered down, putting all of its weight on its front legs and screamed the loudest neigh it could at Edmund's face. Edmund raised his hands in alarm.

"Please Fivestar. I know that I am the reason for your pain, but you have to trust me now!"

Fivestar growled at him again, and wouldn't budge. Edmund reached out to the horse, aiming for his muzzle.

"I know that you and I have never gotten along before, even more so now." He gently touched the nose of Fivestar.

"But I promise you. If you let me by, I can save William and bring him back to be with you." Edmund stared deeply into the stallion's eyes, Fivestar glared back at him. They stood there for a while, as Fivestar read into Edmund's soul through his eyes. Horses have an unnatural canny about them, especially when it comes to deciphering the meaning from one's words. They can sense fear, betrayal, loyalty and love. A horse's spirit is what connects a knight and its warhorse together. They are able to read one another, and to anticipate each other's moves. And a stallion was far more superior in intellect than any other horse, especially an Andalusia stallion. Their instincts are to protect and to save their herd, and when a stallion is used as a warhorse their instincts turn towards being the savior of their knight. Plus with their easily angered temper, they make an exceptional warhorse.

Edmund knew this, so he restrained from blinking, knowing all too well what would happen if Fivestar read something completely different than what Edmund meant. The stallion's nostrils flared, but Edmund stood his ground. With one final stare, the stallion calmed down and allowed Edmund to fully touch his head.

"I wish to make right, what I have caused to go wrong." Edmund said as he stroked Fivestar's head. He stared into the stallion's eyes unfaltering; Fivestar blinked and then bowed his head and stepped to the side.

Edmund rushed forward, and knelt down next to William. William's eyes were closed, as he lay motionless upon the ground. Edmund looked for signs of breathing, but there was none. He reached down and placed his hand upon William's throat and felt for a pulse.

"He's alive!" Edmund shrieked excitedly. Fivestar ninnied and bounced his head up and down. Edmund looked over William; the wound that Edmund had caused was still bleeding. Edmund knew that he had to stop William's blood loss if he was going to have any success in reviving him.

"Hurry! We must do this before the Duke discovers my whereabouts!" Edmund shouted as he jumped to his feet. He ran to the mule, and unloaded the gear from its back. The mule shook its body in relief of the weight being retrieved.

William's armor dropped to the ground with a clank, and Edmund quickly dug through the items. Somewhere in that heap of gear, laid William's satchel and within that satchel would be the knight's collection of potions and spells for healing that he had obtained from multitudes of wizards.

Edmund sifted through things sporadically, and Fivestar helped him by picking up things with his teeth to show to Edmund. Fivestar moved things around with his nose until he found what Edmund was looking for. The stallion picked up a leather pouch in his teeth and then hit Edmund in the back of the head with it.

"Ow!" Edmund said, rubbing his head. He looked up at Fivestar as the stallion waved the satchel in front of Edmund's face.

"That's it!" Edmund yelped with enthusiasm. He yanked it from Fivestar's mouth and ran back to William. He opened the flap of the small purse, and sorted through its contents.

"Oh, I wish that I had paid better attention to the potions part of William's training!" He said with dismay. Edmund grabbed two bottles, and stared at the liquid. Neither bottle was labeled, but they each had a different color of fluid within its depths, which signified its type of potion.

"There must be something—" He went to look back at the satchel, but Fivestar stopped him. Edmund squinted up at him.

"Yes! That's it!" He said excitedly as he grabbed a scroll from the stallion's mouth, and quickly unraveled it.

"I see why William chose you. You are much smarter than my mare!" He remarked fondly. Fivestar ninnied in giddy and his mare snorted in offense.

"Sorry girl!" He yelled to her as he read the text upon the leather bound parchment.

"Alright, we need sage, black moss to put into the wound, then . . . ." He silently read to himself. He stopped and looked at the potions sprawled out around him.

"Now which one is . . . . Dragon's Breath?" He said confused. He read the scroll again, and then looked up at Fivestar.

"How do I know which one to use?" He asked the stallion with dismay.

"Dragon's Breath is the blue one."

Edmund shrieked in delight, and grabbed the blue liquid.

"Thank you!" he said excitedly, then froze in sudden realization that he was not alone. He spun around jumping to his feet.

"I must thank you again Edmund. For now I have the pleasure of killing him myself." The Duke said coldly as he touched the tip of his sword. Five guards sat on their horses behind him with weapons drawn, ready for anything.

Fivestar shrieked in fury and ran towards the Duke.

"No Fivestar! Don't!" Edmund yelled as he jumped out to stop the enraged stallion, but Fivestar was too fast for him. Fivestar grunted, screaming out as he aimed for the kill. But the Duke had anticipated an attack, and his guards kicked their horses forward and rushed towards Fivestar. As Fivestar was ready to lunge out at the Duke, the guards dropped a net over the stallion and pulled back hard, the stallion slammed to ground with an outcry of shock. The guards kicked their horses backwards, and they drug the panicky stallion with them.

The Duke smiled wickedly at the stallion and then back at Edmund.

"Master!" Edmund exclaimed. The Duke walked forward, as Fivestar flailed in the background.

"You know, Dragon's Breath shouldn't be used on a wound that severe. It might kill him. Not that I mind. But Bluemist would work better, and you wouldn't need sage or anything. A simple drink would suffice. Then again, maybe you should use the Dragon's Breath." The Duke said monotonously as he continued to groom his nails with his sword tip.

Edmund shivered in fear as he looked at the Duke. He glanced back at William and then at the potions lying upon the ground. Bluemist was the greenish-blue one, of that he was certain. And the Duke was right, Bluemist was the only potion that Edmund had remembered from his lessons. Edmund frowned at himself, how could he have been so stupid?

The Duke continued forward without looking up from his task at hand.

"Edmund, Edmund, Edmund . . . . What am I to do with you? Here I had thought of you as an obedient slave." The Duke said snickering.

Edmund watched the Duke closely, as Edmund's hand slowly reached towards the Bluemist.

"But slaves are so unpredictable. They disobey their masters at every opportunity that they get." The Duke looked back at his guards, Edmund used that opening to quickly kneel down and grab the Bluemist, he then hid it within his palm. Edmund jumped to his feet as the Duke glanced back at Edmund.

"Now, what should I do with such a disobedient slave?" The Duke asked rhetorically. Edmund swallowed nervously. The Duke looked down at his sword again.

"I should kill you." The Duke stated, Edmund's eyes filled with fear.

"But . . . . then again . . . ." The Duke sheathed his sword and then continued. " . . . I am one more for capital punishment, especially in regards to torture." He finished coldly. Edmund leaned back in panic. The Duke smiled and walked back towards his horse. He pointed at his guards and gave them instructions on what to do with Edmund and then with Fivestar.

Edmund drowned out the Duke's words, using that moment while they were distracted to open the bottle of Bluemist. He slowly crept towards William and poured the liquid into his open mouth. Edmund recapped the bottle, and hid it in his sleeve.

"Come on William, you need to get up and run! Come on!" Edmund urged quietly. Edmund paused to look back at the Duke and his guards. He stared at them, as they continued their discussions of Edmund's demise. William groaned. Edmund quickly knelt down and covered William's mouth, and looked down at him. His wound was quickly healing, and warmth was returning to William's face. Edmund gazed back up at the Duke.

"William. If you can hear me this is Edmund. The potion is healing you fast and Fivestar is trapped by the Duke, and we are all about to die. You need to awaken before the Duke returns!" Edmund quietly pleaded. Edmund could feel William's heartbeat quicken, Edmund turned his gaze to look down at the knight. William's eyes were open, and he was staring up at Edmund. Edmund uncovered his mouth and smiled faintly at him as he stood back up.

His attention was diverted back towards the Duke as he heard Fivestar shriek. The guards had retaken their aim at Fivestar, and their spears were up and ready to strike. The Duke had gotten upon his horse and was heading towards William and Edmund.

A double ball mace laid hanging at the Duke's side as he clenched his fist in preparation of wielding it. Edmund knew what was about to happen, and William grabbed his hand and squeezed.

"Don't . . ." He whispered to Edmund. But Edmund was frozen in place, watching the Duke approach. The Duke smiled wickedly, pulling the mace up and he started to twirl the chain and spikes.

"You should have never disobeyed me!" The Duke yelled and he kicked his horse's flanks. The horse reared in outrage, landed and took off in a dead sprint at Edmund. The horse's hooves beat the ground like thunder.

Edmund leaned back in fear; a look of terror was drawn on his face. In an instant William was on his feet, and he threw Edmund behind him. William stared down the Duke, as the Duke yanked on the horse's reins. The horse skidded to stop just inches in front of William. The Duke stared fiercely at William.

"What's the matter? Are you afraid of what you can't kill?!" William shouted. The Duke sneered at him. "Or is it you're afraid of dying yourself!" William added smugly.

The Duke stared at him intently, and laughed wickedly into the sky.

"You can't kill me! Back from the dead or not, you have nothing!" The Duke said viciously. William glowered at him.

"You forgot about one small thing! I can't die! Your father learned that the hard way, as you are about to . . . . again!" The Duke said hysterically. William clenched his teeth, folding his hands into a fist.

"What? Do you think that you can kill me with your bare hands? Ha! No substance of man can destroy me! Unlike you, who is dead where you stand! Dead . . . like your father!!" The Duke added maliciously. William's anger was rising; he could feel it pulsing in his temples. The Duke slid off of his horse and he approached William, stepping right up into his face.

"Dead . . . . just like Jenevy." The Duke added with a spiteful smile.

William's eyes widened at the Duke's last statement.

"Oh . . . you haven't heard?" The Duke took satisfaction in seeing that his words were affecting William. "That sweet, delicious girl gave it up to me right as I was about to kill her! Her naked body was so tender, so warm. I had my way with her, and then I killed her." It was like adding fuel to the fire. Only the fire was William's temper. He was lying, he had to be lying!

"You lie!" William shrieked through gritted teeth. The Duke laughed.

"Oh no! It's true, as true as the sun that sets every night. You can even ask Edmund."

William looked back at Edmund in disbelief.

"Is it true?" He asked. Edmund silently nodded. William closed his eyes. So that was why he had not seen her. But where was her body? There was no way that he had missed her dead body, not within the last three years! That was when William remembered the tower. That dark place where the Duke sent the women he wanted to suffer the most.

The thought of Jenevy being up in that tower, dying, while the whole time William could have saved her made his anger grow even stronger. If only he had known, if only he had known!! So the Duke knew of William's love for Jenevy, and now she was gone. William's blood boiled, and with out thinking he reached up and uppercut the Duke sending him flailing to the ground.

The guards turned towards them as they heard the Duke's painful cry, and they rushed their horses forward with swords drawn. William panted, as he stared down at the panic stricken Duke.

"Understand me now, before this year has ended, your life will be mine!" William shouted arrogantly. The Duke's eyes filled with shock, he felt fear that he had not felt since the incident with the troll. He shivered in response.

"William! We must get out of here!" It was Edmund.

"That fact that you have saved my life, just means that I will not kill you now." William said angrily without turning to look at Edmund. Edmund's heart stopped, he froze and stared at the backside of William. William slowly spun around to look at Edmund.

"But since you knew of Jenevy's death, and knew of my love for her and never told me of her demise only means that we are friends no more." William said with death ringing in his voice. Edmund stepped back and dropped his head in regret. William turned back to look at the Duke, he stepped over him and rushed over to Fivestar.

The guards swung out at him as he ran, but William jumped and dove over their attacks with ease. One guard was on foot, and William leg swept him, knocking him to the ground and disarmed him. He slammed the sword into the guard's exposed neck, and twisted the blade with a sickening crunch. He glared at the horizon, jumped to his feet and wielded his sword with more swiftness and more deadly types of attacks than the Duke had ever seen.

Within moments the guards were dead, and Fivestar was free. William jumped onto the stallion's back, and disappeared down the slope of the mountain.

The Duke swallowed, and stared at where William had disappeared. He had created a monster. A demon was released, and he was known as William.

Chapter Fourteen

Reunion

DARKNESS HAD FALLEN upon the forest, and Fivestar was growing tired from the rapid sprint that he had maintained well into the night. William's mind was still full of so much anger, that he was fuming. All he could think of was Jenevy. She had never filled his thoughts more than she did at that moment. He had loved her, Edmund knew of it, and yet, he had failed to tell William of her imprisonment in that foreboding tower.

William might have been able to save her, they could have escaped from that place and lived in peace. But now it was too late! He should have run off with her when he had the chance, right when he had first met her! He knew to listen to his gut, to always act upon that first instinct, and the one time that he hadn't, cost him his entire soul! William grunted in dismay, Fivestar snorted at him and flicked his tail up at him.

"It's alright boy, I'll be fine. Someday . . . . I will be fine. But until then, the Duke has to pay for what he has done!" He shouted to the woods. A roar echoed in response, and Fivestar froze. William stared up at the sky.

"What was that?!" He mused. Fivestar pranced like a pony in place as he was edging up for a battle. Flapping wings echoed through the area, and William instinctively drew his sword. He looked around the woods cautiously; something was coming and judging by the sound of the roar, it was a formidable, and most likely, a malicious creature.

William saw a dark object in the sky that was coming into view. Wings were flapping and it was getting closer. William kicked Fivestar and sent him flying into the forest. William looked behind him trying to see if the creature was in pursuit. But it was nowhere within sight.

Fivestar shrieked and skidded to a stop causing William to be thrown to the ground. William tumbled upon the dirt and pine needles, and rolled back to his feet as his training had taught him to do. He strained his eyes, trying to see in the dark.

The creature was in front of them, it was a bit smaller than William and it stood on two feet. But its silhouette looked none other than a . . . .

"Demon." William grunted. There was no mistaking it; the creature had two horns atop its head, two wings, and a pair of glowing red eyes. It seemed to be standing there, surveying him and showed no signs of aggression. William kept his sword at ready, prepared for anything.

The demon took a step forward, and William brought up his sword. The demon paused, frozen in spot.

Was it scared of him? Not likely, it was probably strategizing an attack. William knew that with him only being armed with a sword and no armor, than that would mean that the demon would use its hellish powers to defeat him instead of fight him. They were cowardly creatures, never wanting to fight anything unless it was defenseless. But then again, with powers that the demons possessed, who would blame them for wanting to use them?

"Not if I can help it!" William said aloud and he charged at the demon. He stabbed his sword out, but the demon had moved. William swung out again, but this time the demon hesitated as if it did not want to fight, or it just didn't know how to. William sneered.

'Impossible' he thought to himself. The demon stared at William as he lunged out swinging his sword again. Only this time, when the demon bypassed William's attack, William chose to swing out a fist.

His hand hit its target and the demon flew back, sliding onto the ground with a grunt. William brought his sword up again, and then yelled as he ran towards the demon.

Out of nowhere, a huge dragon landed on top of the demon and roared at William. William was taken aback and he fell onto the ground. He stared up at the dragon and went to stand, but the dragon knocked him back down. William panted, as he was quickly growing frustrated.

William brought his sword up again, and the dragon stepped forward and it roared even louder as it braced itself upon the ground. William lowered his sword hesitantly. The dragon's breath blew out, causing William's hair to ruffle back. The dragon was breathing heavily, and a muffled groaning was echoing from beneath the dragon. William looked down and the dragon growled at him.

'*Now what?*' William thought to himself. Fivestar ran out from behind him and rushed at the dragon.

"Fivestar no!" William cried in panic. The dragon snarled at the stallion, grabbed it with his talons, and then picked it up and roared so loud that Fivestar started to whimper. The dragon's mouth was wide and its sharp fangs dripped saliva as it shrieked at the stallion. Fivestar was practically inside of the dragon's mouth as the dragon roared again, sending shockwaves of air ricocheting over the horse's hair.

William jumped up and grabbed his sword; he raced over to help Fivestar. The dragon turned to look at him as William ran towards the dragon ready to fight.

"NO!" The demon yelled, stepping in front of him as William's sword stabbed the demon's flesh instead of the dragon. William stopped and stepped back, letting go of his sword. The demon looked down and grabbed the hilt of the sword and yanked it free.

William winced as he watched the demon do it, but then was shocked to see the sword had been completely bent in half. Unfaltering, the demon ordered the dragon to bring William with them. William's eyes widened.

"Oh no . . .no . . .no . . ." He went to turn and run, but the dragon was faster. William felt the dragon's talons wrap around him, and he was snatched up and yanked into the sky.

Fivestar whinnied in fear, as they both watched the ground shrinking away. The demon was flying beside William, as it kept pace with the dragon. The dragon looked over at the demon and made a hollow sound in its throat.

"I'm fine." The demon responded. William was caught off guard, they could understand one another? And they actually cared for one another? This was unthinkable! William was growing weary, where were they going? The demon remained silent alongside him, and in the moonlight William could make out certain features that he had missed before.

The demon, although hellish in form, was not a demon at all. The creature wore some kind of metal plating, almost like armor, that was shaped to make the creature resemble a demon.

But it had wings, *real* wings, and red eyes. Which made William wonder, even more so, as to what that creature really was! William looked over at Fivestar, the horse had fallen asleep. And with the metrical beating of the dragon's wings, who could blame him?

It was soothing, and no matter how hard William tried, he too was asleep. The demon glanced over at William and then up at the dragon. They nodded to one another and disappeared into the night.

When William awoke it was daylight, he looked around curiously at his surroundings.

"Where am I?" He thought aloud. He was lying on grass, and Fivestar was calmly grazing at his side. William sat up, his head throbbed but it would go away if he could get some food in his stomach. Pushing himself to his feet, he searched for his captors. They were nowhere in sight, but where was he?

There were ruins all around him, remnants of some ancient civilization all enclosed within a crater blocked by mountains. Or maybe it was a valley? William walked over to Fivestar, the horse looked up at him as he approached. William patted his neck, and then checked him over for any injuries.

"Did they hurt you boy?" he asked while checking the horse's hocks. The stallion looked back at him, snorted and then resumed its grazing.

"Guess not." William said baffled. There was a low rumble from behind him, and William spun around to see the dragon walk out from behind a disheveled building. It glared at William, and then sat down on a neighboring hill. The dragon continued its stare of disapproval and disgust, completely loathing William. William glowered back at it.

"Don't be made at me! You attacked me remember?!" He shouted. The dragon snarled warningly at him and then huffed in agitation.

"You'll have to forgive him. He's not used to strangers being here."

William twirled around and saw the 'demon' from the night before. He raised an eyebrow in surprise. She was no demon at all! The woman, whom he had assumed was a demon, was in fact a warrior just like himself. She wore armor engraved with two demonic stallions; a scarlet cape adorned her back with a silver moon glowing with blue flame, dancing upon the fabric. She had jet black hair, with bright red chunks of highlights running through it. But on her back were two large, dragon-like wings. Looking into her eyes, their green hue brought about a wave of familiarity through William, but he didn't know why. He stared at her in confusion; she looked up at him with disappointment.

"You don't recognize me do you?" She asked.

"You do look familiar, but I'm not sure as to why." William replied while shaking his head. She dropped her head in regret, William stared at her.

"Who . . . . who are you?" He asked. She looked up at him with a faint smile upon her face. She handed him a bowl of food and walked towards Fivestar. The stallion barely budged as she began to pet his sides.

"To this world, I have no name . . . not anymore. But to my enemies, I am known as the Devil's Knight." She said solemnly. Jenevy frowned. How was he supposed to remember her? After all, it had been almost five years since their last encounter, the two years within the castle and the three that she had spent training. She looked at her hands as she walked away. She *had* changed . . . a lot! Should she tell him? No, she decided against it.

'*It's not like we had anything together!*' She thought as she walked out of view. But once, she had thought that she had seen something in his eyes. But, that was only when he had kidnapped her for the greed of the Duke.

Jenevy's eyes began to fill with tears, and she quickly blinked them away. Feau looked at her with concern, as she walked past him.

"I'll be fine! I'm just going to fly to ease my mind!" She told him, and she leapt into the sky without even a glance back.

Once she was far from everyone she severed her connection with Feau and rushed as fast as she could into the sky. She let the tears build up again only this time, she cried out with every bit of rage, sadness, and despair that was built up inside of her. She yelled to the sky, and let the sorrow consume her, let the rage take control.

"Is this what you wanted?!" She screamed. "For me to use your power to free you, while I am completely forgotten?!" She screamed even louder.

"You know how it felt to die and no one remembered you! Yet you wish the same fate upon me?!" The tears were pouring out of her, and she gasped in agony.

"I will kill your Duke. I will free you as I have promised. But then I will live no more! I have died inside and there is nothing to keep me to this world!" She covered her face with her hands and wept as hard as she

HEATHER DIROCCO

could. Shaking all over, she dropped her hands to her side and let out one more remark.

"But know this . . . . killing the Duke will bring no more freedom to you than I have. An eternity alone is the same as an eternity imprisoned within that castle!!" She wailed. Jenevy dropped down out of the sky and landed upon a thick branch of a tall tree. Jenevy's eyes filled ablaze with anger and hatred. Her powers were growing stronger as the thousands of angry soul's powers inside of her reacted to her fury. She closed her eyes feeling the power growing within her.

She began to smile, as she grew hungry for vengeance, she now understood why she was the Devil's Knight. Her powers were granted from souls filled with so much anger, that their energy could be harnessed at its strongest peak, when it was used for death, despair and vengeance. Dark souls inhibited an evil power, and it was all within her just begging to be released.

Jenevy's eyes stayed ablaze with a blood red. She smiled as she felt the energy surging through her; it felt so good to be mad. She then knew how to exhibit the full extent of her powers, and she loved it. She felt needy for it, but at the same time that power of hatred made her feel disgusted.

She did not like having to feel so vile, so livid just to instill fear and death within her enemies. Madness when fighting meant that she would have to fight blind. Vengeance clouded her mind, and fogged her judgment. Jenevy's red power cooled to blue as she calmed herself. She dropped off of the branch and landed on the ground.

She ripped her cloak off of her back, and stared down at herself. Her skin was no longer the soft white that it used to be, it was bronzed and rugged. Her long black hair had streaks of fire red running thru it, but her under layers had neon blue streaks. She rubbed her hands, staring at the calluses and scars. She wondered what her face must look like, and so she ran over to a pool of water.

She jumped back in surprise at her reflection, seeing her mirrored image almost made her cry again. It was no wonder that William hadn't recognized her! Her body was bulky with its armor, and she was toned with muscles that would make any female warrior proud.

She flexed her wings, staring at their width and span. Then she saw her face and she didn't recognize herself. Her regal beauty was still there, but it was cloaked by a stern expression. The look of power rested within her, and she appeared as anything *but* a countess. What was worse, were her eyes: disguised by red power, their green hue was difficult to find.

Jenevy looked to the sky, its clouds were gathering sending small droplets of rain down upon her. The rain cooled her boiling skin, hissing upon her armor it sent clouds of steam into the air.

Her hair began to soak in the rain, darkening the red to match the ebony. Dirt washed from her skin, and as Jenevy looked into the rippling pool, her familiarity emerged.

She smiled as the rain revealed her once beautiful face. She looked to the sky and raised her arms. Closing her eyes, she listened to the rain as it hit the water of the pool. She reopened her eyes and slowly flew back into the sky, and then headed towards Feau and William. But something caught her attention, something that she had not felt in a very, very long time.

"The Duke!" She shrieked. She spun around in the air and looked through the trees. He was there, she could feel him.

Stealthily, she sank down through the trees, ducking behind them. Straining her ears, she could hear footsteps approaching and could smell the stench of the Duke. She leapt silently into the tree, and crouched up on a sturdy branch. From her perch, she could see the Duke; he was standing with twenty other guards. They were making a camp for the night, and the Duke was looking warily about. Something had him scared, and his head kept darting around more like a bird than a man of power.

Squinting her eyes, Jenevy zoomed in her vision to stare closer at the Duke. He was clutching his amulet for dear life, as he paced nervously in between his guards.

"Hurry! Hurry . . . we must hurry! I want this all up before the sun sets!" He barked rudely. The guards moved faster in reply to the Duke's orders while some went to start their nightly watch positions.

Returning her vision to normal, Jenevy leapt into the sky. She had to get back, had to get Feau so that he could help her to destroy the Duke. She stopped midflight and flapped her wings to stay upright.

"I don't need Feau!" She exclaimed. "My powers exceed his!" She said arrogantly. She turned back around and landed upon the tree branch once again. She would wait until nightfall, that way her darkest form would kill the Duke. She remained still, watching them from above like an owl seeking out its prey.

The rain continued to pour down, making the skies even darker. Jenevy unhooked her helmet from her belt, and secured it upon her head.

Her red eyes shined out in streaks upon the blackened sky. That night, was going to be perfect for her attack, she couldn't have planned it any better.

Jenevy zoomed in her vision once more to look down upon the unaware campers. Some of the guards were pacing around, standing a perimeter watch.

She would attack them first. She dove to the ground, landing softly upon the moss. She stepped towards the guards, and with a flick of her wrist, her metallic gloves protruded out claws. She grabbed the first guard and yanked him into the underbrush without even a leaf moving, the second guard she sliced her claws into and slinked him into the darkness. Then she awaited the next one.

The third one noticed her and went to sound the alarm, but she was much faster and had yanked him down to the ground and killed him before a raindrop even touched her.

At that point, the other guards had noticed their missing comrades and they had signaled the alarm.

"We are under attack!" One shouted. The Duke looked out from within his tent with fear.

"Get back inside! Don't move until we get you!" The head guard ordered to the Duke, The Duke did as he was told. Jenevy watched the flap of the tent door where the Duke disappeared to, get pulled to the inside of the tent as the Duke was hastily securing it.

The guards formed a circle around the campsite, which didn't surprise Jenevy. It was their best and only way to provide security. Jenevy laughed silently at them.

"Well, lets see how long this keeps up." She said amused. She ignited her hands with fire and watched the flame as it went from red to the black with blue-core shaded flame. She leapt up into a nearby tree and watched the soldiers as they looked blearily about.

Sending a ball of fire from her hand, she ignited the ground just yards away from the guards.

"Over there!" A guard shrieked. A few of them approached the fire to stare at it, as Jenevy used her hands to guide the flame on the ground. The fire engulfed the men, turning them to ash instantly, and the other guards cried in terror.

"Tis demonic work!" One shouted. The men's circle grew tighter as they tried to stay closer together. Jenevy closed her fist and pulled it to her, which caused the fire on the ground to dissipate altogether.

Sending another ball of fire out at the men, and just as it was about to hit the ground, she made it split into three different spheres. The balls of fire landed at the three ends of the rear of the Duke's tent. She then sent another three spheres towards the front of the tent and then spinning her hands, she made the flames coil up into a funnel. The men watched in shock as the funnels of fire stretch up into the sky only to connect together and fall back to the ground and sizzle upon impact. The men were completely encircled by Jenevy's dark black fire.

They shrieked in agony, as the panic of them being trapped sunk in. Jenevy watched as the men broke formation, and started to frantically try to escape. They looked like ants that had lost their trail.

Using the soldiers' confusion and chaos she leapt from her roost and flew towards them. She hit the ground with a crack, sending billows of dust and rocks flying in every direction. The men spun around to stare at her.

Once the dust settled, the guards screamed in terror. Jenevy stood up slowly, and stared at them, drilling a hole straight into their souls. She screeched out a scream so terrifying, that it reverberated through their minds like a banshee that was burning to death.

The men shrank back, whimpering at the sight of her. A faint whirring sound emulated from her body, as her power was rumbling to life. The guards yelped in fear as the Duke poked his head out to see what the commotion was about. But once he saw Jenevy, he yelled in alarm.

"My God! It's a demon!" The Duke wailed. The head guard rushed to his side.

"No milord. That's the Devil's Knight! It is worse than a demon. This creature comes from the very heart of hell to destroy whatever it is ordered to kill!"

The Duke's eyes filled with fear.

"Then kill it!" He barked.

"I cannot. Destroying him would bring out the devil himself. And then the world would be doomed!" The guard shouted.

"I don't care! Kill it! Kill it now!" The Duke commanded.

"Aye milord." The headguard said with a bow and he rushed up to his men.

"Shoot! Shoot it now! Destroy the Devil's Knight!"

The archer's bow strings snapped forward, sending arrows raining down upon Jenevy. But she ignited them into ash before they were even close to hitting her. She shot out her flame at the archers, and killed them as they tried to run for shelter. Their screams of pain filled the air as her fire melted them away.

Jumping into the air, Jenevy's body sizzled with sparks and bolts of lightening. A mix between thunder crashing and a low hum echoed through the campground. She landed in the middle of a group of guards, and they all spun around to face her.

With a snarl, she swung out at them. When her claws would hit flesh, she would dig them deeper down and pull the guard towards her. A sound of fabric tearing and twigs snapping would follow, and the guard would be ripped to pieces.

When she wasn't clawing, she was sending out bolts of lighting, pillars of flame, and waves of destruction in every direction. Which would send the men flying back and slamming into the ground. The guards' numbers began to dwindle down as she killed them. When only five men remained, she let her power fade to a small trickle of flame and stared at them.

"Give me the Duke . . . . And I will spare your lives!" Her voice reverberated with a metallic tone and a deep echo. The Duke stared at Jenevy with fear in his eyes. He tugged at the head guard's sleeve.

"Don't let it get me!" The Duke cried in panic. The leader of the guards patted the Duke's hand and then stepped forward.

"You will have to get through us first!" He yelled.

"So be it . . ." Her voice trailed off and her fire ignited again. She lashed out, grabbing a guard and holding him up to stare at her. He yelled and withdrew a dagger and smashed it towards her. She recoiled, and knocked the blade from his hand with the tip of her wing, and then reached up and grabbed his throat.

He stared at her with eyes wide and clenched his teeth. Jenevy growled and sent him hurdling towards a nearby guard. Feeling an arrow hit her back, she yanked it free and through it back at the archer, killing him as it went straight through his skull.

Rolling to the ground, she unarmed another soldier and stabbed him in the chest, and then wielded the blade at the lead guard. His eyes widened in astonishment at seeing the Devil's Knight knowing the skills of the blade.

His sword instantly clanked against hers, and they began to fight. Metal hit metal, sparks went flying, but the guard was of no match to Jenevy. She slid under his foiled attempt of disarming her, and retaliated with a deadening blow to the guard's midsection. The man yelped in pain and dropped to his knees.

Jenevy turned to attack the remaining guards, but they had all ran in fear, screaming like scared puppies into the night. Jenevy laughed as she listened to their pathetic cries.

The Duke was next; she dropped the sword to the ground and walked towards the tent. She stepped through the flapped door, and her black flame danced up the fabric, bursting it into flames. The Duke was inside, cowering in a corner as he shielded his face with a chair.

"Please, please! We could work together! Think of the power we would have!" He pleaded. But she ignored him. Jenevy stepped over a root on the ground and reached out to the Duke. She gripped the leg of the chair and yanked it free of his hands; it too went ablaze in her blackened flame.

She glared at the pathetic excuse of a man cowering before her. What she would give to kill him slowly, just as he did to all of the women before Jenevy's arrival. She clenched her fists, trying as hard as she could to not last out at him.

"You and I can never be fighting for the same cause." She replied slowly. The Duke gulped, as he panting heavily.

"Please . . . . I was doing you a favor! I was killing the scum of the earth!" He said matter-of-factly. Jenevy chuckled at his statement.

"Scum?! So innocent women, honorable knights, and poor townsfolk are scum?!" Her metallic voice grew louder as she screamed at him. The Duke stared in disbelief at her. He actually believed that she was a messenger from the devil, and that she had been sent to kill him.

"Yes! They are! I wouldn't expect you to understand!" The tone in his voice had changed so rapidly from scared to insulting that Jenevy could barely restrain her emotions any longer. She growled viciously at him, yanked him up by his throat and threw him to the ground. He huffed in agony.

"I know more than you think I do!" She reached a hand up and pulled the helmet from her head. The Duke, who had been shaking feebly beneath her, slowly looked up at her. He stared at her in astonishment.

"Before you . . . the only scum I had known of was my father! Now . . . I know otherwise!!!" She rose up a clawed hand to strike him.

"I send you to *your* destiny! This is for Olivia!" She screamed. The Duke closed his eyes as Jenevy slammed her hand towards his face. But something stopped her just inches from his scalp. She tried again and again, but an invisible barrier was blocking her path. She screamed as she felt a sickening stabbing pain hit her back. She released the Duke, and fell to her knees. He stood up and looked down at her.

"Aren't you forgetting something dear Jenevy?!" He asked coldly. Frantically she propped herself up on her forearm and reached to her back to find the source of her pain, but the Duke kicked her to the ground.

"With my pendant, I am invulnerable to your attacks! Whereas you, will die a very painful death by the poison that I just gave you!" He said as he laughed wickedly into the air.

"No spell, nor any power can save you now! And even if you were to make it back to anyone, they would not be able to save you either! It is a very fast acting potion. Unless you have a mage just waiting right outside that door, I doubt that you will make it!" He laughed again. Jenevy winced in pain as she felt the poison coursing through her body. She tried to reach up again, but the Duke had stepped on her arm and was leaning in towards her.

"A very wise mage made me this special poison." He said as he held up a bottle. "A mage who was great friends with the last Shempshay dragon." Jenevy could feel her blood start to heat in anger.

"And after the energy that I have seen you display tonight, I think that this poison will work rather well on you! It was designed to *kill* that dragon after all, and since you have the *same exact* powers as that beast, you too shall suffer the same fate that I will be giving it." The Duke smacked her across the cheek and stood back up. He walked towards a table and set down the bottle. Jenevy began to shake in fury, she could feel the power building up inside of her, and the unmistakable hum of energy began to reverberate from her body.

The Duke turned back around to look at her, and he held up a leather bound book.

"You see . . . . the mage wasn't the only one who knew the Beolithan language. Now, I too, know of the secrets to the demise of the last Shempshay dragon. But not only his death . . . . but his powers. And with this book . . . I will have the powers of that dragon and will rule the world!" The same smirk was on his face that Jenevy had grown to hate so much. And it was all that she needed to push her power over the edge.

Screaming, she jumped to her feet as her body ignited in a black-red flame. She lunged at the Duke and grabbed his throat. He clawed frantically at her gauntlet hand, trying to free himself. She glared at him, fuming with rage.

"But you are to be the last. And everything in this tent will die with you!" Her flames grew hotter, and spread through the tent like a flood of water, the leather book, the trunks of articles, the tent itself igniting into black-red flames.

The Duke yelped in agony, and screamed in pain. Jenevy spread her flame as far as she could, spreading it deep into the soil. She felt the Duke writhe in panic from within her grasp, as she lifted him higher off of the ground. Her strength was stronger than it had ever been.

And then her power exploded into a cloud of energy. The ground quaked beneath her, as it cracked and dissolved all around them. The Duke's squirming ended and he fell limp in her grasp. She threw him to the ground and yanked the amulet from his neck. She jumped into the air, spread her wings and floated while she pulled rocks out of the ground.

Huge chunks of earth floated around her as she wielded her power throughout the area. With a loud pop everything sank back down and then exploded, leaving only a crater of destruction. With a deafening crack, Jenevy took off into the sky and sped towards Feau. She clutched the amulet tightly to her chest, and glared at the horizon.

As her anger wore off, and her adrenaline subsided she realized how much trouble she was in. With every beat of her wings, she felt the stabbing pain of her injury. She grunted in pain, as the poison took its hold upon her extremities.

Apparently her rage had fueled its spread as well, and the poison was nearly paralyzing her. She grunted as she tried desperately to stay afloat, and she cried out to Feau from within her mind. He could save her . . . . she hoped.

❖ Embers of the fire sizzled upon the ground. Trees were turned upside down, and most were downsized to black ash. Rocks were charcoal and the ground itself had melted into a deep, steaming fissure. The Duke clambered out from beneath the layers of ash, and he sneered at the area around him.

HEATHER DIROCCO

Instinctively, he reached to his neck. The amulet was gone. But the Duke was not upset at its missing status. He grunted and pushed himself to his feet.

"Don't worry my dearest Jenevy. I *will* survive." He said with a smile as he kissed his ring.

"And you my dear . . . I fear will not live to see the rest of this day!" He added wickedly as he looked to the sky to watch the sun rise from behind the mountains.

"Give my regards to Olivia!"

❖ William walked around the area under the wary eyes of Feau. Fivestar had grown accustomed to the dragon, but William was still very mindful of the dragon's existence. William looked at the decrepit structures in amazement, as wondered as to what and where they had originated from. Feau looked at him, watching him as William brushed his hands down a wall of one of the tattered structures.

William paused for a moment, thinking that he had heard something but then shrugged in disagreement and walked back over to Fivestar. He wondered where the *Devil's Knight* had gone to, she had disappeared rather quickly the day before and had still not been heard from since. The dragon didn't seem to mind, as he sat upon his hill glaring at William.

William wondered if maybe the knight and the dragon weren't as closely linked as he had thought. As if in reply, the dragon jumped to his feet startled as both him and William heard the mysterious sound again, William looked towards it. Feau reminded William of a dog, quick to hear something and quick to react. He watched as the dragon leapt from the ground in a bound and dove towards the sky in the direction of the noise. Straining his eyes William searched for the sound's source, and focused on a black speck in the distance. It got closer and William realized that it was the Devil's Knight.

She was flying, but something was terribly wrong. She could barely fly straight, let alone stay aloft. William watched as the dragon approached her, grabbed her and then sped back towards William and Fivestar. The dragon landed on the ground with a thud and set the Devil's Knight gently atop a patch of clovers.

William rushed over to them and looked down at the knight for injuries. She was pale, too pale and a layer of sweat lay upon her as she was burning with fever. The dragon looked at her with concern.

"What happened?!" William asked in surprise. She looked over at him.

"Poisoned. I can't . . . . " She closed her eyes and took a deep breath. " . . . can't stop it from spreading." She finished slowly. William knelt down next to her, and looked her up and down.

"Poisoned? Where?" He asked skeptically. She swallowed.

"Right wing . . . on my back . . ."

William rolled her over and looked towards her right wing, embedded between flesh and metal laid a small dagger. William looked at it closely and then grabbed its handle and yanked it out of her back. Jenevy screamed in pain and Feau snarled in anger at William. William leaned back in surprise at the dragon, and the setting sun's light gleamed off of the dagger. William stared at the small blade; it was made of gold and had two distinct shaped emeralds upon its hilt.

"This dagger . . . belongs to the Duke of Greenwiche." He said in confusion. "But . . . how did you . . . ?" He looked at Jenevy with doubt.

"Because . . . I attacked him." She replied in pain as she rolled back over to face him. William lowered his eyebrows in confusion.

"Why?" he asked.

"I had to." She said coarsely. William looked back at the dagger and then back at Jenevy. He stared deeply into her eyes, and a sudden wave of realization hit him like a bolt of lightning.

"Yes William . . . it's me . . . . Jenevy." She said slowly. William's eyes filled with emotion and then instantly changed to worry.

"Jenevy . . . I'm sorry. I can't believe that I didn't recognize you!" He exclaimed bewildered. She panted in pain.

"Hold on, we've got to get this off of you." William said as he began to unhook her armor, and removed it from her body. Once all of the armor had been taken off, he loosened her clothing to allow her to breath.

"We have to get the poison out." He stated, and he went to stand up but Jenevy caught his arm.

"No. Its impossible!" She cried.

"What? Why?"

"There's no way to stop it William. Not now."

"What do you mean?"

Jenevy closed her eyes; her heart was pounding in her ears.

"The poison . . . . the Duke said that nothing could stop it." Feau roared in outrage at her statement and started to claw at the earth in protest. William glanced up at the dragon. Jenevy smiled at Feau.

"Feau I know. You might be able to . . . but it might be too late."

William was growing angry himself.

"Jenevy. I don't want to lose you when I just found you!" He said sadly.

"You will never lose me William. We will always be together." She said slowly as she reached a hand up to his face. He grabbed her hand and held it to his cheek.

"Listen Jenevy, I meant to tell you this before, but I've loved you ever since the first moment I laid eyes on you."

"I know William."

"And I'm so sorry for never taking you away from that place when I had the chance. Will you ever forgive me?" He asked sorrowfully. Jenevy smiled at him.

"I forgive you." She said as she laid her other hand up to him, he reached out his hand as he felt a cool object being dropped to his palm. He looked down in confusion and then snapped his gaze back at Jenevy in astonishment.

"The amulet!" He shrieked. "But how did . . . ?"

"Like I said . . . I attacked him and might of even killed him. But I'm not—"

She started to cough uncontrollably and then her body went into convulsions. William quickly reached down to her.

"Oh no!" He yelled. Her body went into seizures as a white foam started to seep out of her mouth.

"No . . .no . . . NO!!" William looked up at the dragon.

"Feau! That's your name right?" He shrieked. "Can't you do *something*?!"

But Feau was already running back towards one of the buildings.

"What are you doing?!" William yelled. The dragon crashed through the rocky walls of the broken building, and dug around on the ground. Within moments he returned to William's side and threw a book at William. William caught it in surprise.

"What is this?" He asked suspiciously, but the dragon continued to stare at him with hope in his eyes. William shook his head and opened the aged book.

"Spells? I'm no mage!" He cried. Feau smacked him on the back with his tail.

"Alright, alright!" William shuffled through the torn pages.

"Here's one—*for foreign poisons with no cure do the following...* "William continued to read silently to himself as Feau stared at him intently.

"Hurry!" William shouted as he hoisted Jenevy up and into his arms, placing the book snugly between her and his chest. He then stood up and raced towards a building.

"Feau! Please tell me that there is a green crystal inside one of those buildings!" He shouted in expectation. Feau grunted and rushed ahead of him. The dragon zoomed through the buildings until he reached the rear building that was carved into the mountainside.

William rushed to keep up with him and watched as the dragon disappeared through the dark entrance. Hesitantly, William walked in after him.

The hallway leading down into the depths of the mountain had been lit with torches by Feau during his descend and William could hear the dragon's grunting huffs of frustration as William got closer.

Seeing a bright light at the bottom, he rushed towards it and emerged into a brightly lit chamber. A stone table sat in the middle of a shallow pool of blue water. Feau was on the other side frantically scratching at the walls.

William approached the table and set Jenevy gently upon it as he reopened the book. The spell seemed fairly easy, and he hoped that it would work.

With a crack, the wall finally gave in and Feau dug through the rubble quickly. William stared at the dragon questioningly. The dragon jumped up in delight and rushed back to William, dropping a large, green stone at William's feet.

"Alright . . . we have the crystal!" William exclaimed. He then read the rest of the spell and looked up at Feau in disbelief. The dragon looked at him curiously.

"It says that I have to stab a shard of the crystal into the source of the infection." William said solemnly. Feau grunted and walked over to the stone table, using one talon he dragged the crystal to his side, and raised up his tail. William looked up at his tail in surprise.

"What . . . are you going to do?" Without a second's hesitation, the dragon's tail slammed to the ground on top of the crystal and shattered it to pieces.

"What did you do?!" William shrieked as he rushed towards the fragments of crystal. Feau pushed him back and dug through the pile of broken, green glass. William watched as Feau wisped away the dust and revealed a sharp pointed shard and glanced up at William expectantly. William's eyebrows raised in surprise.

"Oh!" He rushed over and grabbed the palm size splinter. He ran back over to Jenevy, and rolled her to her stomach. He gripped the shard and lifted it above his head. His fingers twitched within his grip as he fought against every fiber in his body that was urging him to not let go.

"Please let this work!" And he slammed the crystal into her back. A sound of shattering glass ensued, as it stabbed clean through her and onto the table. The blue liquid beneath began to glow in neon lights of green, blue and red and a loud whirring sound echoed throughout the cavern.

Jenevy's eyes snapped open and she screamed in terror. William pushed her down harder onto the table, as she frantically tried to escape. He grunted as he realized just how strong she was, and was slowly losing his grip. But Feau had joined his side and he too was pushing her down firmly to the stone.

"Anatsue keda wata ni shnetiue tse . . . . Anatsue keda wata ni shnetiue tse . . . . Anatsue keda wata ni shnetiue tse . . . . " William repeated over and over as the pool grew brighter and brighter. With a loud boom, William was thrown back and Feau was sent screeching to the side as his claws sent up sparks off of the stone ground.

William watched as Jenevy flipped over and arched her back. A scream unlike the world had ever heard escaped her lips, sending shivers of fear up William's spine. The flashing water soared up, twirling around the stone table. Twisting into a raging cyclone, the water shot down into Jenevy's pores, causing her veins to pulse with a blue glow. The water surged all through her, only to escape out of the crystal stabbed into her back and flow off the table and back into the pool. Jenevy collapsed onto the stone table, and the room became silent once more.

William rushed over to her and rolled her over, only to look up in shock at Feau.

"The crystal! It's gone!" He cried in surprise. Feau looked down at Jenevy and stared at her unscathed skin. The crystal had vanished, and what's more was the hole where it had been had disappeared as well.

"It . . . . worked!" William shrieked and he lifted Jenevy's chest off of the table and held her to him. "I can't believe it worked! What kind of magic was that?"

"Shempshay magic . . ."

William looked down at Jenevy, she was smiling up at him.

"And the words you spoke were Beolithan." She said as she smiled at Feau. The dragon bowed his head towards her and purred.

"Thank you dragon." William thanked Feau warmly. The dragon replied by purring loudly, which made Jenevy smile even more.

"I think he likes you." She said quietly. William looked down at her as Feau stepped up next to them. William picked her up and leaned against the dragon, he sank to his knees as the dragon curled its tail around them protectively. William would sit there, even if the world would come to an end. There was something about the dragon that made him feel safer than he had in a long, long time.

Jenevy awoke before either of the other two did. She felt hunger gnawing at her insides, and a burning thirst within her throat. She quietly wriggled out of William's grasp, and slowly stood up. Surprisingly, she didn't feel light headed at all even despite all that had happened to her. She smiled as she quickly stepped over Feau and headed towards the blue pool.

The water glistened from the firelight, as it lapped its waves upon the edge of the stone. Looking down, Jenevy stared at herself and was shocked at what she saw. Her clothes were tattered, and smelled of a murky fragrance. But her hair was what had caught her attention first. It used to be black, minus the few streaks of red on the surface and the blue underneath.

But now it the colors had switched roles, her hair was completely red, with a few streaks of black coiling around inside! Jenevy ran her fingers through her hair and pulled down a chunk to look at it.

"What the . . . ?" Her hair had also grown! It was even longer than before, and was very thick. She sighed and brushed it behind her back. She knelt down in front of the pool and stared grimly at herself.

"What is wrong child?" It was Feau. She turned to look at him.

"My hair . . . . well . . . look at it!"

Feau glanced at her and purred softly.

"I see beauty and fear all collected within your locks." Feau replied. Jenevy frowned and looked back at her reflection. Maybe he was right? But how was she to instill fear on her enemies when her hair was a flaming red?

"Your enemies will fear you whether your hair is red or black. You are the Devil's Knight." Feau always had a way of easing her mind. She smiled up at him.

"I guess you're right."

William appeared from behind the dragon and he stared at her with regal devotion.

"You would scare me if I saw you clad in armor. Wait . . . . you already have!" He said with a chuckle. Jenevy laughed in reply and William stepped towards her. He reached out a hand and Jenevy slowly placed hers within his.

"Milady."

"Sir Knight."

William smiled and gripped her hand to escort her from the cave.

"I guess I should by calling you Madam Knight now huh?" he said with a smile. Jenevy nodded and they proceeded out of the dark cavern.

"How can I ever repay you?" She asked solemnly. William looked over at her as a warm smile spread across his face. He pulled her hand to his lips and kissed it gently.

"You already have."

Chapter Fifteen

And so it begins

THE DUKE WALKED briskly up towards the castle's throne room. His clothes were blackened and charred from his encounter with Jenevy, and he wanted to inform the King of William's escape.

The King sat regally upon his throne and was shouting at his small jester in agitation.

"If you keep boring me, then I will have you killed!" The King shouted in outrage. The jester bowed in reply and tried to juggle items of fruit mixed with blades. The Duke rushed forward, making his feet echo through the chamber.

The King looked up, upon seeing Duke, he quickly waved everyone from his throne room.

"Out. OUT! All of you!" The throne room was empty within moments, and the King waited for the Duke to kneel at his feet.

"Sire, Sir William is alive."

"Then kill him." The King ordered. The Duke frowned as he tried to choose his words carefully.

"He . . . escaped Sire."

"WHAT?!!" The King shouted outraged, the Duke winced in reply.

"He defeated my guards, and the stable boy Edmund helped him!" The Duke said trying to sound helpless. The King's face relaxed and an evil grin spread upon his face.

"And this stable boy . . . did you kill him?" The King asked.

"No Sire. He is locked in the dungeon below." The Duke replied with a surprised look on his face.

"Good. And what has happened to your clothing?!" The King asked in disgust. The Duke stared down in abhorrence at his attire.

"I was attacked by a former maiden."

"*Former?*"

"Yes. I had sent her to her death, but apparently she had escaped."

"Apparently . . ." The King repeated as he looked at the Duke. "Did you kill her?" The Duke smiled evilly at the King.

"I poisoned her."

"And are you sure that she is dead?" The Duke's face dropped in fear.

"Well . . . . no."

The King jumped to his feet and rushed towards the Duke. The Duke stood in alarm as the King came within inches of his face.

"So you are telling me that not only has *one* of your slaves stood up against you, but now *three*? Do you realize the implications that could come about if the people are to learn of this? The power that I gave you, only works when the people live in fear! And the fact that *three* of your former slaves all stood up to you, and succeeded, could cause a revolt amongst the people!" The King screamed in anger. The Duke dropped his eyes.

"Know this . . . . If my people revolt and charge these castle walls, you will be the first to die." And the King rushed out of the throne room.

The Duke glowered at the King's back as he walked away. Twirling around, he too left the room and headed straight for the atrium.

As the moon rose to its peak in the sky, the Duke awaited with the King on the balcony overlooking the courtyard. The night had gone extremely quiet, and not even an insect dared to make a noise.

"You have one week before I take this into my own hands." The King stated hoarsely. The Duke nodded as they watched the men gathering within the courtyard. First came the mercenaries. They stood in a small cluster against the lower wall, and were talking amongst themselves. They had rugged attire adorned to their bodies, and casual weapons strewn over their shoulders.

On the far end, stood the bounty hunters. They were in a formation, and stood stiff as they awaited their orders. Their bodies were covered in leather and other types of body armor. They each had swords, a crossbow, and other concealed weapons hidden amidst their armor.

In the center of the courtyard, stood ordinary people who had come from the neighboring cities, who just wanted to stake a claim in the reward. Each of them had a weapon of some sort, whether it was a sword, or a staff, or a spear. But they had no source of armor and were barely clad in clothing.

The Duke looked down at crowd as they stood talking amongst themselves. The King glanced over at the Duke, and then back up at the moon.

"Your time starts now." And the King retreated back into the castle. The Duke leaned forward onto the balcony railing, and stared down at the crowd. He raised his arms to hush the people and they looked up at him in anticipation.

"There is man named William, he was last seen near the cliff behind the King's castle. He has a black stallion name Fivestar, and both are trained in the modern ways of combat. He was a Knight, and you may have seen him in some of your travels. You are to seek him out and bring him to me with his head on a pike! The one, who brings him back in a week's time, will be given the reward of your choosing. Know this, if he is not found and not brought back here, then *all* of you will be killed." The crowd raised their voices in alarm.

HEATHER DIROCCO

"If any of you choose to not complete this task, leave now." And the Duke watched as a few of the people walked away back towards the town. The Duke smiled wickedly and stared down at the men below.

"Once I dismiss you, you will have until the full moon sits at its highest point within this sky. You must return to this courtyard with William dead!"

But before he could send them away, a sudden movement caught his eye. The bushes silently moved as three cloaked men appeared from the shadows. The crowd hushed, and quickly moved out of their way as they approached the balcony. The first man appeared with an enormous wolf at his side, the second had a falcon flying above his head that screeched as he moved closer to the Duke. And the third rode atop the largest horse that the Duke had ever seen.

The men stared up at the Duke, as foreign weaponry dangled from beneath their robes. The Duke stared at them for a moment, and then stepped back in shock.

"Assassins . . . ." The Duke's voice rang in amazement. He glanced at the assassins in wonder as to why they had chosen to help in this task. He had always been fascinated at the assassin's way of life, and their choice of noble creature companionship, but they never assassinated for hire. So why did they choose William?

Even still, to see them in person was far more remarkable than the Duke had imagined, and he was ecstatic that he had finally gotten to see one in person.

"Everyone . . . . take your leave. You have one week!" The Duke commanded. The bounty hunters, robed in animal skins and adorned with remnants of their victims took off in every direction. The mercenaries ran off looking more like savages than men as they collided with one another, and killed the man that dared to cross their path as they tried to begin their hunting. And thinking that they had just embarked upon a race, the normal folk ran wildly in every direction, seeming more lost than anything else.

But the assassins waited within the courtyard until all of the hired men had left. The first assassin nodded his head at the Duke slowly and headed off to the east with his wolf walking protectively at his side.

The second, headed northwest as his falcon screeched from above. But the third and last assassin, sat upon his horse as it pranced and whinnied out a sound that both terrified and fascinated the Duke. The horse itself was more beastlike than anything that the Duke had ever witnessed. The horse reared and its eyes glowed green in the night. The Duke shuddered at the thought of what the horse was capable of. The assassin looked up at the Duke, stared for a moment, and then kicked his horse towards the South.

The Duke watched him nervously, as the assassin disappeared once more into the shadows. The King crept up quietly from behind the Duke, and whispered in his ear:

"If you do not bring me William's head in one week, than that assassin . . . . that just memorized your face . . . . will bring me yours."

LaVergne, TN USA
11 December 2010
208396LV00002B/6/P